Spoony Tooth,

the

Hairy Lummox

and the

Big Galloot

David Allen Rice

Dedication

This story is dedicated to all the girls and boys in the world like Spoony Tooth who, for one reason or another, stand out from the crowd.

Sometimes it's not that easy standing out from the crowd and being a bit different because you tend to attract attention: some people smile at you, or wave and some people even give you funny looks.

But being different and standing out from the crowd is what makes you special.

CONTENTS

Acknowledgements

This story couldn't have been told without the help of my daughter Jennifer whose thinkybrain was especially different from most people's and who saw everything in a positive light, especially chocolate buttons.

I should also mention her mummy who is odd enough to encourage me in doing at least some of the daft things that I get up to – and I encourage her in doing daft things too.

Thanks also go to Katie Mitchell and Izzy Cree for their constructive criticism.

Publishers

It's worth mentioning too that this couldn't have gone to print without the help of Amazon's Kindle Direct Publishing which has made it possible for thousands of authors to get their work out there and accessible to the public without the mind-numbing and soul-destroying business of trudging around agents and publishers, not that they don't do a fabulous job.

Let's Get Introduced...

I have been asked to tell you this story but before I begin, as tradition demands, I think it would be a good idea if you were to be seated as comfortably as you can. This is a very unusual, quite long and completely true story which will take a great deal of concentration on everybody's part. Including yours. A nice comfortable listening (or reading) position will help to cut down on the fidgeting. Fidgeting can be very distracting for all concerned.

Mind you, on the other hand, now that I come to think of it, too comfortable a position may lead to a lapse in concentration and subsequent drowsiness. Storytellers find this extremely tiresome and I am no exception. Perhaps a position somewhere between the two would be best.

Explaining Stuff

This is a true historical adventure story, not a school book. But I'd best mention that there are some strange things in this story which may be new to you so I will do my best to explain them at the bottom of the page[1] (with a small number, like that) as I go along, that is, if I feel that an explanation is necessary. Some people have accused these explanations of being either silly, unscientific, unnecessary or all three. Huh! That's just nit-picking if you ask me.

After all, not everything in life that needs to be explained gets explained, and for that matter, not everything that gets explained is worth hearing. This, as you know, is what nobody points out to you at school. A good example of the sort of useless thing that gets explained at school is sums. Like the one where a boy gets into a completely full bath where the overflow happens, as luck would have it, to be blocked by a bit of soap. Loads of water flows over the edge of the bath, gets mopped up by the boy's mummy who then squeegees the water into a bucket and she can then work out how many buckets of water the boy is equal to, not counting the water that soaked into the carpet or ran down between the floorboards. This sort of sum is only accurate under scientific conditions and it can have severe consequences if assigned as a homework exercise to a child who does not have a tiled bathroom at home. It's even worse if the family live in a flat with unfriendly neighbours below. Anyway, mums and dads always know instinctively exactly how many buckets of water their children are equal to. That's a good example of what I'm talking about: a sum that's no help whatsoever. This story takes place at a time long before sums were invented and people seemed to get along fine without them.

Anyway, where was I? Oh yes… if I am not able to provide a satisfactory explanation for something as we go along then you will have to make do with one of your own.

---

1. Strange explanations at the bottom of the page like this which, of course, you don't need to read if you don't want to.

The Dim And Distant Past...?

You will have heard or read, no doubt, that many stories begin with something like, "Once upon a time…" or "Long, long ago …". Well, I've decided that we should forget that sort of way of describing something that happened umpteen aeons[2] ago because it's too vague and we need to be a little more specific about how long a long time can be. I am going to tell you about some things that really happened but it was a ridiculously long time ago when the world was still very young and fresh and most things had yet to happen, let alone be discovered.

I could give you dates but this is all so long ago that they'd have to be carbon dates and they're not much help, I mean, try looking a carbon date up on your smart phone diary or buying a carbon date watch!

Now you will begin to understand, I think, what I would mean if I were to say "Long Long Ago", which, of course, we've already established I'm not going to do. This story took place a good bit longer ago than that. Longer ago than the longest ago that most people who are not archaeologicists[3] can think of. So you can see why it's not really all that useful to start this story with "Once upon a time…" or even, "Long, long ago.." like other stories do. By the way, most stories that begin like that are fairy stories and consequently not at all true so that's another reason for not beginning like that.

What it Was Like Long , Long, Long Ago

Very, very, *very* many long, long ages ago this land, strange as it may seem, was not very much different from how it is today. There were many more trees, and a lot fewer people, but the important things like the hills and the rivers and the sky were pretty much in the same place as they are now. If there was one noticeable difference at first glance, peering down the very-long-ages ago, then it would be that they looked a little less weary. You see the hills and the rivers and the sky were weary even then and although it was an almost unimaginably long time ago they still had very many long ages to go until they got up to even as recent as the dim and distant past which itself is a long time ago. People and trees, birdsong and monsters and suchlike tend to crop up from time to time, as time goes by, but the hills and the rivers and the sky, generally speaking, will have to stick it out to the bitter end. It can't be easy; being the landscape takes a great deal of patience.

---

2. Aeon: (pronounced "Eeon") a measure of time so long that it wouldn't fit on a diary or calendar. Aeons are quite often measured in feet or meters rather than years because archaeologicists have to dig a hole several meters deep to find anything that happened eons ago.
3. Archaeologicists: somebody who wears odd socks, glasses held together with sticky tape, has a wispy beard and appears on television with their head sticking out of a deep hole talking about eons (see 'Aeon' above). Female archaeologists look the same but usually without the beard.

The People

Around about that time, in this place, life for those people who lived here was good. Being so long ago and so early in the world, there was plenty of time to spare because not all that much of it had been used up yet, considering how much of it there is. Or is it was? Anyway, life was well ordered back then and things generally got done by and by. With a life so well ordered and easy going there was no need to get things done early. On time was fine enough. A job finished early simply left a long wait until the next job could be started so that it could finish right on time, rather than early. After all, it was early enough already, what with being so long ago. People worked just as hard as they do now, of course, maybe even harder, but rushing was a thing for which they had no need. It was a waste of time.

Now, as you can once again imagine, life for these people was pleasant. They were normal; not a bit like us. There was no out-of-the-ordinary hustle and bustle. There was no need to bounce out of bed like an electrocuted cat when the alarm goes or panicking in case you're late for school or work simply because a) there were no alarm clocks, b) there was no school to go to and c) as we've already mentioned, there was plenty of time to spare what with it being early enough as it was. So being late for work was a concept that wouldn't have made any sense. So, getting in a tizzypanic or a brainfankle[4] about timekeeping simply didn't happen. This is not to say that people back then did not have the odd trying moment, or throw the odd wobbly, hairy, bandrangenous tantrum. Everybody does that and if you don't mind me saying, you, when you were younger dear reader … Well, perhaps least said, best mended there eh? So, when they did throw a wobbly, hairy, bandrangenous tantrum, they just used to take their time over it, do it properly, and get it out of the way. Meanwhile everybody else would stand around patiently, indulgently even, with their embarrassed hands in their pockets staring into the middle distance. Just as we do today, only with less patience because we're so short of time.

The village where these people lived, not very far from where we are right now, in this very valley, had houses with walls made of timber and mud and sometimes stone, and thatched roofs of bracken and small deep windows from which warm cosy light would glow at night, and the smells of good food cooking would drift in the day.

The Creatures

All around the village there were small fields and meadows and grass parks where small nervous sheep with soft, brown and black fleeces and big horns grazed contentedly (but watchfully) alongside big woolly and slightly not so nervous goats with even bigger horns,

---

4. Brainfankle: a fankle is like a tangle only worse and unlike a tangle, can't usually be unpicked. A brainfankle is when your thoughts get so mixed up together that… ehm… eh… hmmm…

4

and where birds sang sweet new songs. All around the fields was straggly woodland of birch, oak, pussy willow and alder, fringed with juniper. As the ground rose up the hillsides, the woodland gradually thickened as the undergrowth closed in and it became deep, dark forest. Here lived strange and scary creatures like, for example, the 'extremely spiky' hedgehog, (which is now extinct and should not to be confused with the latter-day hedgehog, *jagshufflius slugmunchicus*[5] which does not have a spiky disposition unless you happen to be a slug or forget to put out its saucer of milk). There were big brown bears, giantly huge woolly mammophelumps which had the longest tusks ever seen (even back then), so long that you could hang your washing on them and giant saber-toothed tigerlions with teeth so long they used to trip over them, which is why they eventually died out. But this village was in a peaceful part of the world where fearsome creatures hardly ever came by so nobody was really bothered about them. However …

Wolves:

The most feared and hated of all creatures that roamed the hills and forests in those days were the wolves. I will tell you a little about the wolves because it will help to explain something that happens later on in this story. They were massive; bigger than any dog you have ever seen. Just to give you an idea of just how big they were, the so-

called Irish Wolfhound has that name because it is nearly as big as a proper wolf. Also, Irish Wolf Hounds are a bit on the skinny side so the comparison is a bit weak if you ask me. The wolves in our story were known (thought) to be smelly with thick, rough coats (usually dark grey with mottled bits which was usually dirt), nasty greasy, slavery jaws, long yellowish-white fangs and a fierce, glowry way of looking at you. One wolf could give you a pretty dirty look which could be quite hurtful (and worrying), but a whole pack of wolves could give you an entirely clarty[6], mawkit[7], fowl and filthy look which might ruin an otherwise merely unpleasant day.

In the long winter nights when the hunting was poor, they could be heard howling and snarling to one another as they tried to get up the gumption to raid the village where the pickings were a bit easier. Of course, people used to lock and bar the doors at the first

---

5. Jagshufflius slugmunchicus: this is the correct official name for a hedgehog in Latin, a language which is used in science books by people who think that information that they think will be difficult to understand by anybody but themselves is best expressed in language which is deliberately unclear. Sometimes school teachers do this without even resorting to Latin.

6. Clarty: very dirty indeed, but not in a nice way.

7. Mawkit: very dirty indeed and possibly maggoty. Mawks are maggots.

sign of a wolf raid, or even just the thought of a wolf raid. Wolves are not by any means stupid but they are of necessity basically sleekit[8] and totally unscrupulous and will resort to any sort of crafty tactic even when not driven by cold and hunger. This is why all the sheep and goats were herded into wolf-proof enclosures at night. This was a difficult job because there were no sheep dogs so everybody had to run around flapping their arms and yelling – at one another, not the sheep. This was only popular with the sheep and the children because it gave ample opportunity to run around like crazy and drive the grown-ups up the twist. In those days there was no real need to herd the cattle into wolf-proof pens at night because, as you probably know, all the cattle were massive, wild and hairy. They were twice the size of modern cattle, and nowadays they are called auroxen[9] but back then they were called 'wildhairies'. They had huge horns which they could use to kill anybody they took a dislike to, which was everybody except themselves. Some people think that Spanish fighting bulls are very dangerous but compared with a prehistoric wildhairy, they are actually quite tame and cuddly. Even the top predator of the day, the wolf, would have had to be completely off its chump[10] even to think about trying to attack a single wildhairy let alone a bunch of them.

When there are wolves around, if you have big horns but are small and woolly like sheep then it pays to be nervous, and if like the goats you are bigger and have even bigger big horns then you can afford to take it easy now and again but you still have to be on the lookout. If, on the other hand, you are huge and hairy, extremely bad tempered and have the biggest horns in the universe and have a lot of equally bad tempered friends who stick together then nobody bothers you much.

People had only recently decided to tame wildhairy cattle and the cattle themselves had yet to become entirely used to the concept of "being tamed" or agree with it in principle. Indeed even after much persuasion and kindness, they remained obstinately wild. Consequently they were pretty hard to handle as far as the process of being tamed was concerned. You might be interested to know that the only way to get cattle into a pen back then was to get them to attack you and then tear into the pen with them after you intent on killing you. Someone would then close the pen behind them and you would have to climb out the other side as fast as you could. Cattle penning was not a popular job and was usually given to teenage boys, for obvious reasons[11].

Anyway, we were discussing wolves: often, if efforts to repel the wolves (usually by

---

8. Sleekit: an old word which means sneaky and conniving, but in an especially selfish sort of way.
9. Auroxen: prehistoric wild cattle with an extremely dim view of humans – and everything else. At the time that this story takes place, they were known as "wildhairies" because they were, well, wild and hairy.
10. Off its chump: daft but in an enthusiastic and sometimes self-destructive sort of way, rather like a young rugby player.
11. Teenage boys: the reasons for this will be obvious to anybody who has a teenage boy at home. This method is still used today to pen dairy bulls but the cows are quite sedate nowadays.

throwing shoes at them from a window, if you were lucky enough to have a window) were unsuccessful, people would come out in the morning to find the rubbish bins up-ended and a right mess all over the place. It wasn't funny to have to walk around in the snow on a cold morning in your stocking feet tidying up bits of smelly goo from the bin until your shoes turn up. Or worse, to find that the wolves had been especially hungry and had eaten your shoes. Or *even* worse, if you forgot to bar the door one night you might get up in the morning to find the larder empty and a load of scrawny wolves curled up asleep on the fireside rug, or on the sofa, and huge muddy footprints all over the place. Who wants the job of waking up a load of dangerous wolves and throwing them out? Well, nobody, usually. After all, although through the ages people have always taken care not to risk being eaten by wolves, nobody can say for certain that it has never happened and that a hungry wolf would not enjoy an after-dinner suck at a young shin bone. Wolves, in those days were one of the commonest causes of an ailment called mid-winter flaky brain. These days, the only people who contract that ailment are farmers. Everybody else gets year-round flaky brain.

Now, as it happens, at the particular time that this story took place, the particular place in which it took had not suffered a wolf raid for many years. Indeed, it had been so long ago that only the very oldest grannies and grandpas in the village could actually remember an actual wolf raid. And since they themselves had only been very small at the time, they couldn't remember much, if anything at all, so they had gained much admiration from their children and grandchildren and great grandchildren by allowing the old stories to grow in the telling such that tales of huge wolves raiding larders and running off with whole sheep (and possibly even children) dangling from their slavering jaws eventually became true facts of history. Consequently, far from being less afraid of wolves than they should be now that they never got wolf-raided anymore, if indeed they ever had, everybody in the village went completely and utterly wobbly just at the mention of wolves. Truth to tell, not only had there not been a wolf raid on the village for generations, if indeed there ever had been, hardly anybody except the dottery old grannies and grandpas had ever actually seen a wolf and they were thought to be most easily recognised by their huge size (which was correct) and their unpleasant sheep murdering (partly true), bin raiding (probably true) and people eating (not very true) activity.

Chapter 1

The Tooths

Well, so much for wolves. We might hear from them later but this story mainly concerns a little girl called Spoony Tooth. She was an only child and was a bit odd even if for that reason alone because in those days it was quite uncommon to be only and have no brothers and sisters.

Spoony lived in a homemade house of stone at the wrong end of the village. The house was very unusual because it was made of stone, of which there was little, rather than wood of which there was a lot. It was built by Spoony's mummy and daddy and was full of some of their best ideas. They had built it bigger than usual, which in itself was very unusual and quite an innovation, most houses of the period were the same size as one another and too small for the big families. Tradition plays a big part in people's lives and nobody had thought to build a house that was big enough until the Tooths came along. Mr and Mrs Tooth were quite imaginative people but even so it hadn't occurred to them to build a house the proper way, so their house was different. It had a thatched roof , which was usual and which kept the rain out which was unusual. Usually the thatched roofs only kept most of it out. Its best feature, however, was Spoony's bedroom. Spoony's mummy and daddy had decided to make sure that she always had somewhere warm of her very own to go to when she wanted to do Spoonyish things, so they had built Spoony's bedroom in the chimney right above the fireplace. Actually, it wasn't in the part of the chimney where the smoke went; Spoony's daddy had built it so that the smoke mostly went around it. On windy days, however, it could be a tiny bit smoky and Spoony quite often had a nice, homey, log-fire sort of cosy aroma. It was a very small room, very snug and as warm as toast and she could look out of the tiny window over the village to the forest and beyond. Indeed, up until then, the chimney hadn't been invented and everybody had a hole in the roof to let the smoke out. It also let the rain in, but being traditional, everybody (except the Tooths) had a smoke hole in the roof. However, the Tooths were far from traditional (daft and eccentric) so they had invented the chimney.

But Spoony was odd for a whole load of reasons other than having no brothers and sisters and a bedroom in the chimney. For a start, her mummy and daddy were a bit "wrong-end-of-the-village-ish" as they used to say in those parts. Actually, to begin with, they (those with less sense of propriety, that is) only used to say "Toothish". However, that was considered a bit unkind since it had become the wrong end of the village at which to live because you had to put up with the Tooths, or the "Teeth", as they were affectionately, (but not always too affectionately) and grammatically incorrectly known, and their daft ways.

Spoony, of course, didn't have to go to school. She didn't have to because there were no schools to go to. Schools hadn't been invented and there was no need for them because the children learned everything they knew from helping with the things that went on about the place and Spoony had learned everything she knew from helping her mummy and daddy. This was one of the other reasons that Spoony was odd: her parents were considered to be a bit daft, so much of what she learned was also considered to be a bit daft .

Spoony's mummy and daddy were indeed as daft as brushes[12]. They kept loads of useless but old and interesting stuff in the shed instead of nice well-made, useful implements. And tame (well, not all that tame) wildhairy cattle in the garden instead of flowers. The flowers were kept in old tubs and wooden pails long past repair, an early invention by her daddy. A few other people in the village kept wildhairy cattle (mostly for show because although they were not much use for anything, they were considered to be a bit if a status symbol) but they almost all kept them in very secure pens with big high wooden fences. For reasons that we've already discussed, a teenage boy was useful for getting wildhairy cattle into a pen so cattle were usually owned by people with a teenage boy in the family. Mrs Tooth did not have a teenage boy so she just did the wildhairy

---

12. Daft as a brush: people with no manners still use this expression but nowadays polite people would say "eccentric". But they mean pretty-much the same thing.

penning herself; she was quite nimble.

Like everybody else the Tooths kept sheep which mostly provided nice soft wool for knitting clothes but the Tooths could not afford the most desirable and fashionable brown and black sheep that were considered the only thing worth having so they had to settle for white sheep with the odd brown bit. This tended to make the Tooths look different even from a distance because brown and black were considered to be the only acceptable colours for a smart outfit. The Tooths' clothes were, like their sheep, mainly white with the odd brown bit, at least when they were clean.

The Tooths also kept pets, such as cats (which were considered bad luck even by those lucky enough not to own any) and mice (for a short while each). Spoony would catch them and put them in her pockets along with a bit of bread or cheese and forget about them. Mrs Tooth would usually find them still in Spoony's pockets when she got her ready for bed and would let them go. Being in Spoony's pockets was quite popular with the mice as she never had any cats in her pockets, only bread or cheese so it usually meant a slap up feed. Several of the mice had been caught by Spoony several times and one or two were quite fat. Nobody, including the Tooths had any dogs because they were entirely unknown.

The Tooths kept open house where everybody was as welcome as they might feel they deserved to be. And on account of being odd, they got quite a lot of visitors did the Tooths. Not of the kind, however, and sorry to say, who come by just to see how you're doing or indeed to tell you how well they are doing. Mostly they came by just to see what the "Teeth" were up to next and then to go and tell the rest of the village how daft they thought the Tooths were. Often it would be to see what Tooth the Daft (as Spoony's daddy was known) had most recently invented and if it was of any use and able to be borrowed. You might be interested to know, by the way, that "daft" originally (and for that matter still does, to an extent) meant inventor. Spoony's daddy invented things.

To be fair, Tooth the Daft did occasionally invent something useful, and occasionally could be relied upon to fix something broken and useless to make it useful for something else. On the whole, however, his inventions were viewed with some suspicion as they served more to perplex than to assist. For instance, Tooth the Daft had worked for weeks in the dafting shed to improve upon the recently discovered and even more recently introduced wheel. At a special, and much heralded presentation to the whole indulgent (that is to say optimistic, but not expectant) village he had unveiled several beautifully carved and ornate wheels of impressive quality and ingenuity. Everybody was extremely appreciative and gave much encouragement but only a few were sold. Most people went off saying that they were better than expected but that they would stick to their own tried and tested round ones. A few were sold later by Spoony's mummy as occasional tables and window frames when daddy had forgotten about them and was busy dafting up something new.

Mrs Tooth was quite well liked and always drew a warm "Good morning Mrs Tooth" from the other ladies in the village. However, it was often said of Mrs Tooth (with the sincerest kindness) that perhaps that little Spoony of hers wouldn't be quite as unusual if she was fed a proper diet including goat's milk instead of that rubbish her mummy got from those awful wildhairies. If anything, Mrs Tooth was the real inventor in the family. Nobody so far had even dared think of milking cattle. They were too wild and hairy and thoroughly dangerous and the taming of them had only come about out of an instinctive need for agricultural order. And there was little or no chance of cattle milking catching on as far as anybody could see if Mrs Tooth's experiences were anything to go by. It was not uncommon, if passing by the Tooth House at milking time, which was twice a day, to hear a loud bellow and then to see Mrs Tooth come flying and yelling over the hedge with a wooden pail in her hand, or sometimes, and this was worse (you would imagine), to see the pail coming over the hedge alone. Quietly. At all events, the milking pail was usually empty.

Spoony didn't mind any of this. She didn't mind being a bit odd because it ran in the family. She was the only child in the village with her very own log. Her daddy had dafted it up in a fit of desperation to daft something somebody might want and he could always rely on Spoony. It was a log which was shaped quite like a dolly and which her daddy had tried to make look even more like a dolly. In the end he had made it look more like a log than ever, so Spoony had adopted it just to give him encouragement and because he was looking really desperate. She had a keen sense of responsibility and anyway she had more need of a pet log and an un-desperate daddy than she had of a dolly.

Mind you, Spoony had loads of friends who didn't mind her being odd because in one way or another nobody really minds if you're a bit odd. If they like you. The other children in the village would say "Hello Spoony come and play at Loupydike[13]!" and she would, sometimes. But Spoony was a bit odder than usual because she was very selective about games. She didn't play with dolls (proper dolls, that is) or throw things at cats (even if the cat deserved it) or pretend to be grown up or any of that stuff. Nor did she play much Chickmell[14] or Hingosy[15] or Puddockloupye[16] although she was always willing to join in if somebody re-explained the rules... again. Spoony wasn't usually allowed to be a Gosy when

---

13. Loupydyke: jumping a wall into somebody else's garden and then running away when they come after you. If you live in a street full of walled front gardens you can do several loupydykes in a row and get chased by several adults at one time

14. Chickmell: this is really good fun. You knock on somebody's door and run away and hide. They come to the door and nobody's there. When they go back inside you wait five minutes and do it again. And again. And again. After about an hour the person has a flaky brain episode. It's quite cruel but fun. Don't let your parents know you're doing it and if you get caught don't say I recommended it.

15. Hingosy: the word you get when you have no time to say "hide and go seek".

16. Puddockloupy: leapfrog. A puddock is an old word for a frog. If you haven't played this before, you don't actually need a frog.

the children played Hingosy as she often forgot to Gosy and everybody would have to stay Hi'n until she remembered to Gosy, which could be hours. And the rules of Hingosy even in these days are very strict: you have to stay Hi'n until you're Fu'n. Usually she was Hi'n with the other children because if she got involved in some difficult concentration and wasn't too well Hi'n then they knew she would be Fun' before very long. Spoony was well known for her non-competitive instinct, but she had a slight skill for getting well Hi'n.

Mostly she did loads of her own sort of stuff which only she knew about and which occupied her for ages. Like catching hairy oobits[17] and remembering new names for the mice in her pockets and stuff like that. And she had a lot of difficult thinking to do which took concentration but which looked as if she had drifted off into space, or at least fallen into a dwam[18] and was staring vacantly into the middle distance. Or even the far yon. (In those days remember, there *was* a far yon into which you could stare.) Spoony never said anything that hadn't had a lot of careful thought go into it. Consequently, as you can imagine, being a Tooth, she didn't have a lot to say that wasn't odd but well thought out. And as you shall learn, Spoony Tooth could fall deliberately into such a deep, most concentratey and difficult dwam that she actually did drift off.

So, generally, she was a bit misunderstood without necessarily misunderstanding. Nice ladies would stop Spoony in the village and say things like, "Good morning Spoony how are you today and how are Mrs and Mister Daft, ehm sorry Tooth?" and Spoony would stare into open space for ever such a long time trying to think of a nice reply, which usually didn't come, so instead she would give them one of her nice cheery giggly smiles and run off with her log. Then the nice ladies would say something like, "What a lovely little girl," or "Isn't young Spoony always so cheery!" or, on the other hand, "Difficult child. I blame the parents myself." and, "A bit skinny. Why is she so, sort of, smoky?" depending upon who they were. Later on, Spoony quite often would remember that she should have said something like, "Very well thank you," out loud but by then it was usually too late to go back, although sometimes she did. If the nice ladies were gone she would say, "Very well thank you," to whoever was there at the time because she had been brought up to be as polite as she could be. This, of course, only helped to confirm some people's suspicions about Spoony being an "odd child".

Ideas Can Simply Pop into your Head

One evening, in the early summer, when Spoony Tooth was tucked up in bed with her log in her nice cosy but slightly smoky (it was a bit windy outside) room in the chimney thinking some pretty difficult thoughts, it occurred to her that there was probably a lot

---

17. Oobits: the taxonomic name for caterpillars before Latin evolved and needlessly complicated everything scientific.
18. Dwam: a relaxed state of mind involving exactly no thinking whatsoever and with the same sort of expression on your face that most people have nowadays in church – and school during geography lessons.

going on outside the village (the world) that needed explaining. Perhaps it would be of use to her mum, for instance, if she could find out from the wildhairies why they were wild and hairy instead of just wild. Or hairy for that matter. Or if there were some new things about to be needed that her daddy could invent that people would want, instead of improving things that nobody really wanted anyway. Nobody seemed to want to buy Wild and Hairy Auroch milk, not that there was much to sell, or wheels that weren't round, not that they weren't beautifully made. Obviously this needed tending to so there was going to be quite a lot of thinking to be done. So Spoony decided first of all to set about getting some much needed sleep. Happily, Spoony almost always got as much much-needed sleep as she needed because, like all little girls, she really knew how to snuggle down in bed and of course, she was lucky enough to have a nice cuddly log to snuggle up with.

In the morning Spoony climbed down the wooden steps from her bedroom in the chimney and went to help her mummy with the milking. As usual she was dressed in her nice warm woolly smock which her mummy had made from the lovely soft wool she got from the small white (with brown bits) sheep. Spoony's daddy had wanted Spoony to be the same as the other children because he thought that she would fit in better if she had a nice brown and black smock instead of one simply made from the unfashionable white (with brown bits) wool which they got from their white (with brown bits) sheep. He had invented a way of dyeing wool using bits of moss and lichen that grew on the stones of the house. Unfortunately, he had not yet succeeded in making a black dye and most of his efforts had turned out all sorts of unfortunate colours. These ranged from blue-ish purple to pinkish purple with his best effort being dark purple. He had settled for dark purple because it was the nearest to black so Spoony had a few purple (with brown bits) smocks, another odd Spoonyish thing. Spoony was very easy to pick out among the brown and black smocks of the other children.

Spoony went to the goat pen and found that the goats had already been milked. She realised that her mummy must have gone to milk the wildhairies, so she went out into the road to wait, and sure enough, after a little while, there was a loud bellow and her mummy came diving over the hedge with an empty bucket on her head. She had been charged by the wildhairy cows and had thrown the bucket up onto the hedge and dived for safety, inadvertently collecting the bucket on the way. Mrs Tooth dropped down to the road and pushed the bucket to the back of her head so that it sat at a jaunty angle. She was looking altogether a bit scattered and quite unnerved and didn't see Spoony standing there on the jaunty side of the bucket. "Good morning Mum," said Spoony in her usual bright and cheery way.

"Yeeaark!" screamed Mum, getting a terrible fright, and spinning round in Spoony's direction. The bucket plopped back down over her head and she yelled "Yeeaark!" again, only this time with a nice boomy ring to it from inside the bucket. At last she grabbed the bucket and ducked out from under it. "Oh it's you Spoony," Spoony had to roll around on the grass for a bit in order to help stop a bad dose of the giggles but she got up again as it is not very nice to laugh at your mummy. "What a nice surprise you gave me," said Spoony's mummy breathlessly but not forgetting to give Spoony a kiss and have a sniff at her in her usual mummyish sort of way, "Good morning."

"Wildhairy cows' milk for breakfast Mum?" she said helpfully.

"No-oh," said Spoony's mummy thoughtfully, as if it was unusual, "But I think they're beginning to come round to the idea of being milked Spoony," she said, a little breathlessly.

"What makes you say that Mum?" asked Spoony in her best encouraging voice.

"They don't attack me straight away any more and they give me time to get out of the way. I think they're beginning to like me. They just feel they should attack me to keep up appearances... it's all done with kindness you know."

"Yes, I know," said Spoony helpfully, "I'm sure they appreciate it … Mum …? There's something I need to ask you."

"Not just now Spoony, if you don't mind, I haven't finished milking," said Mrs Tooth, sniffing Spoony again, "Was it windy last night?" she asked bending down and giving Spoony a tight hug. Mrs Tooth was always sniffing Spoony. She was worried in case people in the village would think she was a bit too smoky. It hadn't occurred to her that everybody in the village wondered why Spoony smelled smoky at all.

"Yes, but Mum ..."

"Hmm I thought so. You smell a bit smokier than usual. I must get your daddy to re-invent your bedroom."

"I like it the way it is Mummy. Mummy there's something I need to ask you."

"Well, all right," said Spoony's mummy, "But only if it'll be quick."

"Mum," asked Spoony seriously, "is there anything you need to know?"

"Anything I need to know?"

"Yes."

"No-oh-ooh," said Spoony's mummy thinking as she answered, "I don't think so. If I need to know anything I usually ask your daddy and he thinks something up. He's really imaginative you know."

Spoony couldn't help but give one of her really giggly, spluttery laughs at this but she gave her log a little cuddle so as not to hurt her daddy's feelings even if he wasn't there. It's not very nice to laugh at your daddy either. It can be a bit tricky having a daddy who has daft ideas and a mummy who thinks that they are really clever.

"There must be something you need to know. Isn't there something? Even just a winsey ickle thing?"

Mrs Tooth thought for a bit, "I wish I knew how to tame the Wildhairies so that they come when they're called."

"But they charge at you whenever they see you," said Spoony.

"Yes they do don't they," said Spoony's mummy glumly, "but I'd prefer a more sort-of relaxed amble."

"Hmm," said Spoony nodding knowledgeably, "is there anything else you need to know?"

"Well, it would be quite good if the sheep didn't all wander off and then refuse be rounded up."

"Right," said Spoony, making a mental note, "Anything else?"

"Well … er …t here's a … Why do you need to know?" Spoony stared into space for ages and gave one of her most giggly smiles. "Hmm," said her mum, knowing that there was no point in asking and no need to know as it might spoil a nice surprise or just worry her. "Should I make a list[19]?" But Spoony was already off to find her Dad, belting around the hedge, her bare feet leaving little barefoot Spoony skid marks as she turned the corner with her arm swinging her pet log around in big circles.

She found her daddy in the dafting shed[20] as usual, already covered in wood shavings. "Hello Spoony. Are you just up out of bed?"

"No, I've been down for ages, I'm trying to help sort a few things out."

"Oh, that's nice. What for instance?"

"Well, for instance, I thought I might try to find out what sort of things need to be invented."

"Oh good," said Daddy Tooth starting to chisel away at a big lump of wood, "I could do with some ideas, I haven't dafted anything really useful for ages – well not that anybody wanted to buy anyway. People don't seem to like my ideas." He sounded a bit fed up with inventing.

"I like my dolly," said Spoony, holding up her log, hoping to cheer him up.

"Really?" said her dad, "Do you want me to improve it for you?" and he held out his hand for Spoony's pet log.

"No!" replied Spoony a bit too quickly and hid it behind her back. "Thank you, it's perfect the way it is. What are you making now?"

"Well, I was hoping I would think of something to make out of this lump of wood as I went along," said Spoony's dad, "but all I've managed to do is make it smaller."

---

19. Make a List: one wonders what Spoony's mummy was going to make a list with because writing hadn't been invented and neither had paper. Well, perhaps people back in those days simply had better memories and didn't need to write things down.
20. Dafting Shed: in case you missed it, if you're daft (an inventor) then you need a place in which to do daft things.

"But you have made a lot of handy wood chips!" said Spoony already knowing, just as she splurted it out that this was not a good thing to say. Dad gave her one of his looks that said, *I'm your Daddy so please don't pick on me*, so Spoony trotted off not feeling so sorry for him that she couldn't giggle one of her trying-to-hold-it-in-but-not-succeeding, spluttery, through-the-lips giggles. She had to put her hand over her mouth and pretend she had a cough.

It was pretty obvious that there were lots of things to be found out in the world so now Spoony Tooth's mind was as made up as it could be – considering it was Spoony Tooth.

Chapter 2

An Adventure Begins

The very next morning, very early, Spoony sat up in bed and had a look out of her little chimney bedroom window at the garden. The light was still trying to get over the forest, past the village where everybody was still fast asleep and spill over the hedge onto the wildhairies who were up already and were eating the flowers in the old buckets which her daddy had forgotten to put away. Spoony had a lot to do so instead of getting up, she snuggled down back into bed to do some very heavy concentrating; if there was going to be some difficult discovering sort of stuff getting done then there had better be a bit of organisation. After a bit of heavy concentration and a lot of drifting off and falling into a dwam she had arrived at a plan (or thought she had) so she sat up in bed again and looked out of the window.

Because she was the only little girl (or person for that matter) in the whole village (or world) with an upstairs window (or an upstairs), Spoony was one of the few who could get a good view (without going to the top of the hill at the end of the village and standing one-footed on tiptoe on Farmer Stuckie's furthest away high, shoogley[21] stone gate post that is) of a very legendarily scary and mysterious mountain, the distant top of which only just stuck up above the nearest forest trees, a mountain which was usually white, except in late summer when the snow at last melted. Then it turned a stony colour with dark purple patches. Travellers who said that they had been near the mountain, and from whom all the scary stories came, were usually fibbing about how near they had got. On the whole, most folks gave it a wide berth – just in case. This mountain was called Tiptintitwisnaw.

Tiptintitwisnaw was spoken of only in hushed singsongy voices in a tone of fear and dread by all the adults in the village – mainly to frighten the children from ever going there, although since it was obviously a good two dinnertime's walk away or more, as far as the big children (those big enough to stand one-footed on tiptoe on Farmer Stuckie's furthest away high, shoogley stone gate post) could see, there was little likelihood of anybody wanting to go. Back in those days, mountains were rumoured to be magical, scarily magical.

To Spoony, Tiptintitwisnaw didn't look all that scary. She could see most of it from her chimney bedroom window, and it looked like quite a friendly sort of mountain with smooth slopes and a fringe of trees around its base. Spoony could also see that there were other, not quite so big mountains nearby and others even further away and they looked quite friendly too. Perhaps they were magical too. What's more, she alone, from the high vantage point of her bedroom window could see that Tiptintitwisnaw had another, tiny little mountain quite like it and much nearer to the village. Although it was mountain shaped, it was so much smaller than the other mountains that it hardly deserved to be called a mountain. And now that she thought of it, Spoony was the only one, as far as she knew, who knew it was there. In fact, now that she thought of it, she wasn't sure she had ever noticed it before. It wasn't scary, purple or white. It looked like a nice little mountain: it was round and cuddly and had a fringe of neat little silver birch trees and some neat little rocks and seemed to be covered mostly with grass which, at this time of year, when Tiptintitwisnaw was still tipped white with snow, looked ever so fresh and green. Spoony thought that, with its fringe of trees and its nice round top sticking out of the forest it looked just like her Uncle Rashie's baldy head. This thought made her go into one of her giggly fits so she had to lie down on the floor and flail around for a minute until it passed. Spoony usually had these giggly fits when people were watching, or, more to the point, when she was watching them and it made a change to have a good spluttery laugh with nobody standing there feeling a bit hurt and waiting patiently for her to finish.

---

21. Shoogley: a very handy word for something which is somewhere between wobbly and shaky. In other words, very shaky, but not shaky enough to be wobbly but too wobbly to be shaky.

When she had finished laughing she got back on her feet and looked out once again towards the mysterious wee mountain. If there was anything in the world to be discovered then it was just as likely to come from a mountain as anywhere else. The people that were around in those days got everything they had from the countryside around the village or from the forest so maybe you could get things from mountains.

Spoony had made up her mind: she would start to look for new things to invent for her Dad, and wildhairy and sheep taming devices for her mummy in the mountains. And since Tiptintitwisnaw was supposed to be scary she decided, just to be on the safe side to start with the cuddly wee mountain. Also, it looked close enough for Spoony to be there and back by suppertime, suppertime always being quite an important part of any of Spoony's plans.

Now, you might think that young Spoony Tooth had a real nerve even thinking of going off on an adventure without telling her mummy or her daddy and of course you'd be absolutely correct and it's not the sort of thing that boys and girls should be doing. Be doing nowadays that is, of course. Our story, as you know, takes place a very, very long time ago when there were no really bad things to be in danger of. For instance, there were no strangers so you didn't have to worry about not talking to them. There was, of course, the odd danger. There were faeries: Glaistigs, spirits whose behaviour nobody could predict; there were Banshee which could stir up a storm in the trees at a moment's notice and strike you dead with fright; there was the Kelpie, a good reason for not going near the water's edge. Also, there were wild creatures: wolves (definitely, well probably) and which were rumoured to be dangerous, and bears (it was rumoured and which definitely were dangerous, apparently) and foxes and spikies and stoatweasels and weaselstoats (even in those days nobody knew which was which) and pine martins and badgers and squirrels and eagles and buzzards and kites and hawks and wildcats and roe deer and red deer and giant elk so big that quite often their huge horns got lost in the clouds.

Things, mind you, could be just as worseley dangerous at home or in the garden where there were small brown slugs like the ones which stick to your finger when you're weeding the vegetable patch and which make you go all woozyick until you flick it over the hedge.[22]

There were house sprites with fickle and wicked ways of spoiling a nice snooze or burning the stew or making the bread rise too high so that it got a hole in the middle and you couldn't make a sandwich without the stuff falling out the bottom. Also, there was the most feared of all wild creatures: the midgey. Even nowadays people are known to run indoors screaming and tearing their hair at the first hint of a midgey attack.

But it was spring and the tiny, bitey midges weren't about yet to make you itch and

---

22. Slugs: when you think of it, evolution has dealt slugs a cruel blow because despite being flightless and having no arms and legs or wings, they seem to get airborne more often than most other creatures who are not birds.

anyway what's the point in going off on a scientific fact finding expedition adventure if you have to tell everybody before you go and spoil the nice surprise of all the new inventions and discoveries, especially if you plan to be back for supper.

The Forest

Spoony got herself a lump of her mummy's wildhairymilkcheese (a small lump, as there was never enough wildhairymilk, as you know, to make big lumps) and some of her daddy's special bread made from his latest recipe specially invented (dafted) to make the bread rise really light and fluffy, but which, being unsuccessful had resulted in Spoony's favourite bread: his usual flat and chewy. She popped her picnic in a pouch (which her daddy had made from an old woolly jumper), tucked her log in beside the picnic, slung it over her shoulder and set off across the short springy spring turf of the common grazing which stretched between the village and the river, beyond which was the raggedy edge of the forest. The grass was wet with dew and as she walked it whiffled pleasantly between her toes. Spoony looked down at her feet as she walked and noticed that they had suddenly gone a funny pink colour. Maybe this was going to be one of her discoveries. They had gone a funny pink colour once or twice before but she couldn't remember why that was. She stopped to try and rub it off but this pink stuff turned out to be difficult to shift. It took her quite a while to work out that this was because her feet, which were always dirty, had got nice and clean in the dewy wet grass. Spoony wasn't sure that she liked nice clean feet – they looked funny – so she walked along watching her feet and stepping carefully in every muddy and gooey bit she could find if they showed signs of going pink again. When she got to the river she headed straight for the big stepping-stones and hopped and bounded her way across the gently gurgling water without hardly getting her feet wet and clean.

After a bit she began to lose interest in her feet and fell into one of her walking along going nowhere in particular dwams[23]. When you walk towards the forest with your head down not thinking about anything in particular, sooner or later you are going to walk into a tree and this was exactly what she did. It sounded like this, "Blonk! Ouch!"

Spoony rubbed her forehead and gave the tree one of her bossy looks but the tree wasn't in the least bit put out. She looked around and discovered that she had gone quite a bit into the sparse trees at the edge of the forest before she had blonked into this one. *Quite lucky really,* she thought, *I might have had to blonk into at least half a dozen trees before reaching this one.* Unfortunately, now that she was in amongst the trees, she couldn't see much of where she was supposed to be going (which she wasn't sure she could remember anyway, having fallen into a dwam and acquired a mild concussion) so she decided to try to get a

---

23. Dwam: as we said before, a dwam is a frame of mind where not only are you not thinking of anything, you are quite content not to think of anything. Indeed, if you did think of anything then you wouldn't be in a dwam.

better look and a reminder by shinning up her Blonking Tree (as she decided to call it until she thought of a proper name for it).

The tree was a silver birch with lovely shiny, silver[24] bark and tiny bright green young leaves. The branches of Spoony's tree were low enough for her to reach so she climbed up and could just see the top of Tiptintitwisnaw above the tops of the big forest oak and ash trees. If she was going to get to the little cuddly mountain, which she couldn't see from there, then all she had to do was head off in that direction. Behind her she could still see the village and she was a bit disappointed to note that she had not gone very far so far because the houses at the edge of the village still looked quite big. So far as it went, it wasn't much of an adventure: all she had to show for it were pink feet and a sore forehead. However, Spoony was determined to get on with discovering so off she set once again and said goodbye to her Blonking Tree. The tree didn't seem to have minded being blonked into and climbed up so Spoony decided to let bygones go by so that there would be no hard feelings. Except, that is, for her forehead which still felt as if it had blonked a tree[25].

It was still very early in the morning and the sun slanted through the trees making long diagonal dappled shadows on the twiggy undergrowth. The forest clung on to the early morning mist and the sunbeams and shadows of the trees made the air all stripy. Within these stripes of light the air seemed to be alive with lots of tiny insects that you'd never normally see floating around, some bigger insects like the odd butterfly, woken early from a long winter's sleep and sparkling motes of dust so that it almost looked like snow in the moonlight. Spoony had never seen this before and she thought it was really beautiful. Perhaps it was going to be a discovery.

The woodland floor here was still fairly grassy with little patches of young saplings here and there in the clearings and narrow, well-trodden paths of the deer and other woodland creatures crisscrossing one another. Spoony zigzagged her way through the forest along these little paths and made good progress to begin with. But as she went deeper into the forest, the trees seemed to grow closer and closer together and became much bigger with giant spread out roots and the undergrowth got altogether more difficult to walk through. She had to bob beneath branches and leap over logs and jink around junipers and generally pay attention to what she was doing so she didn't have time to fall into any more dwams or bang into tree trunks with her forehead. There were no more birches or rowans or alders and instead the trees were giant forest ash and oak with here and there large glades of tall grey beech trees whose high canopy of young leaves all but shut out the light from

---

24. Silver: silver, like most things of little or no use, had yet to be discovered and when it was, it was called 'silver' after the silver birch tree and millions of years went by before anybody thought that 'silver' might be more valuable than a lovely silver birch tree. Which, of course, it isn't.
25. Trees: on average, most trees are made of wood and since heads, by and large, aren't (although some may appear to be), as a general rule of thumb, walking head first into them should be avoided.

the forest floor and made the sky look as if it had turned a dim glowing green. The forest floor was so dim here that almost nothing grew except green moss so Spoony made the most of the easy going and strode along as fast as she could. This also helped to keep her nice and warm because the air was distinctly chilly under the canopy of trees. She was quite pleased with herself at the progress she was making although she couldn't see how far she had come or how far she had yet to go. Her feet got nice and dirty again, all muddy and mossy green.

If you walk into a forest, you are usually the last person to know that you are there. The forest is a dangerous place to be if you're little and don't want to be picked on or eaten, so all the little creatures of the forest had already been keeping an eye on Spoony Tooth for quite some time. Most of the creatures of the forest had never seen a little girl before so they were not quite sure how close they should let her get before they ran away. And mostly it wasn't until they ran away that Spoony noticed them. Spoony could see the white tails of the roe deer and the rabbits as they boinged out of her way not quite sure if she was dangerous, and she could hear the scurrying of all the wee furry beasties as they hid behind things until she went by. Sometimes she would just see a leaf or a blade of grass move as a tiny mouse or vole nipped under cover but she hardly ever saw who it was that had moved the leaf or the blade of grass. As the morning progressed the sun rose a bit higher in the sky and it slanted downwards through the trees making the occasional clearing nice and warm to walk through and lighting up the gossamer wings of the insects in the misty air. The birds were singing away and the forest seemed quite a nice place to be. Not in the least scary. Not in the least scary, that is, unless you know you are being watched by something that isn't as scared of you as you should be of it. Which Spoony, being Spoony, didn't.

In fact, Spoony was enjoying her walk in the forest. It seemed that the forest was just like the village, only bigger. She did her best not to appear to be intruding and tried to put everybody at their ease, something she considered herself to be quite good at. All the creatures of the forest seemed to belong and were quite at peace with living there. Apart from being careful of this new forest visitor, they didn't seem to find it any scarier than she did and she wondered if they thought the village was scary. She decided to say a polite good morning to everybody that she saw and even to those that she didn't see. She said, "Good morning!" to the Roe deer and "Good morning!" to the fox, and "Good morning!" to the stoatweasel (or was it a weaselstoat). She said, "Good morning!" to the pine martin and the spudger, and the tattiecorbie and the sparrowhawk. She even said, "Good morning!" to the big brown bear. Spoony had never seen a bear before so she didn't recognise it for what it was. She thought it might be a very big mouse or something.

Good morning! is quite a nice thing to have said to you if you are a big brown bear. Most creatures of the forest give a bear a pretty wide berth (except bees) but Spoony just walked right past and said, "Good morning!" although, being a bear, he didn't understand herHowever, what she *had* said sounded very cheerful and the bear immediately felt better pleased with the morning than he had. As a result, he got back to the thankless task of stealing honey from a beetree with a much better disposition. Bees don't just give their honey away and they certainly don't wish you a good morning. Being stung to pieces is always a bit easier to take when a nice, if slightly strange and skinny creature (little girl) gives you one of her special Spoony smiles. All in all, the creatures of the forest began to relax as Spoony Tooth made her way through the trees. She seemed to be a very nice new addition to the forest, she seemed to have a cheerful disposition and looked altogether pretty harmless, harmless that is, except for her companion, of whom she was entirely unaware.

Spoony didn't say "Good morning!" to the wolf because she didn't see it. But the wolf could see Spoony. Wolf kept Spoony just in view as it sneaked its way silently through the trees behind her. You know, sometimes you should just listen to your mummy and daddy when they tell not to go too far from the house, or talk to strangers, or walk through the forest on your own where there are many, many different kinds of creatures, some nice and friendly, some nice but unfriendly and some wild and potentially fiercely dangerous. Like wolves.

After walking for quite a bit more, the forest began to thin a little and the gentle slope up which she had been travelling began to level out. Soon she found herself in the broad sunshine and once again amongst small birch trees. Through them she could see the great big (much bigger than she had expected it to be now that it was a lot closer), white-topped Tiptintitwisnaw towering over her with its usual cap of misty white cloud clinging firmly to it despite the gentle spring breeze. And just in front of her was her cuddly wee mountain with the sun blazing down all over it making the leaves of its straggly birch trees sparkle. It seemed much bigger than she had expected but altogether it seemed like a very friendly mountain, sitting out on its own in the sunshine.

Spoony was really pleased to have got there so soon and trotted happily out of the forest and up the slope of this, her very own mountain which she was sure that nobody but her knew about. Even though she had come to think of it already as her cuddly wee mountain it was still quite a long way to the top. The sides were quite steep so that she was quite out of breath when, after a while, she reached the grassy dome of the summit. The first thing that she did, even before she had a look around at the mountain itself, was to stand on her tiptoes and try to see her chimney. Sure enough, far away, she could just make out the thin grey coil of smoke rising from her chimney at the near end of the village, a tiny clump of browny little specs and she thought she could just about make out her tiny wee bedroom window in the chimney and the tree growing out of the roof of the living room. What surprised her most was how her wee mountain was actually nearer to the village than it was to the big mountain. This made it feel even more like her own special mountain than ever.

Looking around now, Spoony could see what a nice little mountain it was. It had a few rocky outcrops at the top and some bracken just beginning to uncurl, but mostly it was covered in fresh green grass. All around she could see over the tops of the forest trees. The forest stretched for miles and miles[26] in every direction and the different types of trees gave it a nice warm soft look – just like upside-down green clouds she thought. There was the bright sparkly green of the birches and beeches, the browny green of the sycamores, the feathery leaves of the ash trees not quite fully out yet and the deep dark green of the pine trees.

The Wolf

Right at the very top of the hill, a large bare, grey rock, the very rock of the little mountain itself, grew through the grass and Spoony sat down there for a rest. The rock had a nice smooth round feel to it and the spring sunshine seemed already to have warmed it a little. Its few crevices held little colonies of moss and lichen but mostly it had a nice smooth texture as if it was a place where any creature could sit at peace. She was quite puffed with her long walk through the forest and all the concentrating that she had had to do what with Good Morning!-ing everybody that she met. The rock seemed to be making her as welcome as it could so Spoony thought she'd just sit there for a while before she put any effort into seeing if there was any inspiration to be had about solving her mummy's sheep and cattle management problems and helping with her daddy's inventing endeavours. She felt really at home. It was a nice place just to sit and be and not think about anything in particular.

The wolf was still watching Spoony. His huge mangey body was concealed by the trunk of a large pine tree as he keeked[27] one eye around the side of it to try to get a better look without being seen. He sniffed the air again and caught Spoony's funny, sweet, sooty aroma. He wasn't at all sure what to make of this funny little creature which he had been following. It didn't smell like any other type of animal he might have thought about eating. He was pretty sure that it was a human but he had never seen one before. He had always thought that they would be bigger than this but by all accounts they could be dangerous which was why he had been taking his time and assessing his prey's potential for running

---

26. Miles and miles: Yes you're right, miles hadn't been invented yet but we need to get some idea of how far it was so we'll just say *miles*. I mean, saying *kilometres and kilometres* just doesn't sound right. Plus, it's not so far as miles and miles. And anyway, you'd be in France.
27. Keeking: an old word which means peering at something usually by sneakily just putting one eye round a corner and secretly watching somebody.

away or fighting back.

The wolf had not eaten for a very long time and was very, very hungry indeed and if this was a human it had to be worth a try. He was sure that they were edible as he could just remember his mother telling him that although there were no recorded cases of a human having been eaten by wolves, they had never been proved beyond doubt to be inedible. It looked edible too; it had a woolly, sheepish sort of coat. It looked as if he could catch it too – it was quite small, it only had two skinny legs and had a funny jaunty lollopy way of walking. It didn't look as if it could put up much of a fight. This would be perfect as he was pretty-well exhausted with lack of food. The more he thought of having a full belly the more he slavered and he pulled back his lips and snarled the dirtiest wicked silent sort of growl in Spoony's direction that he could.

The wolf slunk off around the hill to get another look from the other side. The human was sitting down on a rock at the very top of the hill. It was grassy, open and treeless up there with virtually no cover to sneak through so he decided that he would have to rush his quarry uphill from the bracken at the edge of the trees. He crept up the slope on his belly, through the last of the sparse birches and prepared himself for a final rush towards his prey. He hoped that he would get quite near to it before it saw him so that he would not have to chase it for long; he was very tired.

Spoony was getting nice and warm on her warm and comfy mountain and had fallen into one of her pleased-with-herself dwams. Consequently, she had no idea whatsoever that she was in mortal danger of being eaten. It was not until almost the very last moment that she turned her head and saw the huge dark form of the wolf charging up the hill towards her, its huge slavering jaws snapping and snarling and its hackles bristling. It takes a little while to come out of a nice warm dozy dwam and the wolf was almost on her when it suddenly shuddered to a halt a few inches from her with an extremely puzzled look on its face. He had expected the human to run away, terrified out of its wits so that he could run it down in traditional wolf manner.

"Poo!" said Spoony.

"Grrraaooww!" said the wolf towering over Spoony and opening his huge jaws to show his fangs – great long sparklingly white and sharp. He really was very big indeed.

"You're not supposed to give people frights like that," said Spoony although she had been in too much of a dwam to get a real fright.

"You're supposed to run away terrorfied," said the wolf huffily and a bit angry.

"Why?" said Spoony.

"So that I can chase after you and catch you and eat you. That's the way it's done.[28]

28. The way it's done: this is technically correct – wolves chase after things to catch and eat them. This used to be frowned upon by humans who thought that it was undesirable behaviour because they themselves might get chased and eaten. However, it has now dawned on humans that if you don't want to be overrun by things at the bottom of the food chain

You're not supposed to just sit there."

"I'm too tired to play chasing games. I haven't had any breakfast and I've walked for miles and miles."

"Well, that's how it's done. And it's not a game, it's deadry selious," said the wolf indignantly but a little relieved that he didn't have to chase after the human as he too was very tired and hadn't had any breakfast either.

"Well I'm not doing it," said Spoony, also indignant, although she hadn't done indignant ever before.

"Well ... do you want me to eat you here then?" asked the wolf and he gave Spoony a sniff to see if she was as appetising as he had hoped. She wasn't – she smelled sweet and sooty. She smelt of fire, something which scares all creatures, including humans.

"Poo!" said Spoony and sniffed the wolf just to get her own back. "You're stinky."

"I am not!" snapped the wolf and he gave himself a sniff to prove it, "See? I rolled in something nice this morning. A dead crow. You're pretty stinky too. Who'd want to eat you – stinky human? You're inedible – so there!"

"I am not!" said Spoony, getting the hang of being indignant, "I'm pertfreckly edible. My mummy always says I'm good enough to eat."[29]

"Yuck!" said the wolf and stared over Spoony's head in a huffy but puzzled way. He didn't know what to do. He hadn't had very many successful hunts (in fact, he hadn't had any except the ones he'd been on with his pack), and this one wasn't going particularly well either.

"What's your name?" asked Spoony after a while in her nice friendly Spoonyish sort of way. Spoony always tried to be as friendly as she could be. And since she was naturally friendly anyway, when she tried to be even friendlier, it usually put others in a friendly mood, even if she was 'an odd child'. Even people who didn't want to be friendly gave in after a bit and they were almost always friendly in return.

"My name's Ploppy," said the wolf, caught quite off his unfriendly guard and before he could stop himself. He felt himself blush under his fur.

"Ploppy?! Pfffff," spluttered Spoony, "That's a funny name." Then she got a fit of the giggles immediately and rolled off the rock onto the grass where she flailed around for a minute clutching her ribs and laughing. After a bit she got up and apologised, "I'm sorry, I didn't mean to be rude."

"Oh, that's alright, everybody's rude to me. What's your name?" asked Ploppy, still blushing wildly under his fur.

---

then you need the odd predator. As a result, wolves are gaining in popularity.

29. Good enough to eat: this is true as far as mummies, lions and crocodiles etc are concerned, Spoony *was* good enough to eat (if a bit skinny) but as far as wolves are concerned, there has never been a properly documented case of a wolf eating a human and this was no exception to the *never* rule.

"Spoony Tooth."

"Stupid name. Spoony Tooth is a stupid name," said Ploppy. Spoony nodded in agreement. "You don't even have proper teeth," continued Ploppy, "these are proper teeth," and he snarled a huge snarl right into Spoony's face, once more showing off the hugest teeth that she had ever seen.

She wasn't impressed. They were beautiful white teeth but being Spoony, and sometimes a bit slow on the uptake, they didn't seem all that dangerous. "Poo!" she said, "you must think you're a wolf or something."

"Wolf? I *am* a wolf!" he replied, almost yelling.

"But wolfses are dangerous."

"I am dainjlious!" He began to splutter and mutter and appeared to be getting quite upset. He sat down on the rock beside her and carried on muttering, "I *am* a wolf and I *am* dainjlious," as if to reassure himself.

"Poo!" said Spoony. Not really very sure whether to believe him.

"You're very rude," said Ploppy.

"I'm never polite to people who are going to eat me," said Spoony.

"I'm not going to eat you. I wouldn't eat you if you were the last dinner in the world. You're rude and stinky." They were quite in the huff and sat facing in opposite directions ignoring each other for quite a few minutes.

Eventually Spoony said, "Let's be friends. I didn't mean to be rude. I'm sorry. I never met a real wolf before, you do look very dainjlious , I mean dangerous, and you really did give me a bad fright." Spoony was stretching the truth a bit here but it sometimes helps not to be too truthfully blunt when you're negotiating a new friendship, in case you hurt some feelings.

"All right," replied Ploppy, not really sure if she was being truthful, "let's be friends, I didn't mean to frighten you. Do you really want to be friends?"

"Oh yes!" replied Spoony quite truthfully, "I'm friends with everybody."

"Me too," said Ploppy, "sort of." He gave her a funny quizzical look then said in a quiet voice, "I hope you don't mind me asking... but ehm... where did you learn to talk?"

"I've always been able to talk," said Spoony, "as long as I can remember."

"I never knew humans could talk," said Ploppy the Wolf.

"They can all talk."

"Fascinating," said Ploppy, clearly surprised, "I had always heard that they were totally stupid and just made funny cackly noises."

"That too," said Spoony, "Can all *your* friends talk too?"

"Yes." he replied glumly, "On the whole they've got quite a lot to say. In fact, they can be quite outspoken." He began to fidget a bit.

"Where are they?" asked Spoony, "I thought wolves were supposed to go round in packs."

"They do mostly ... I'm afraid I've become a lone wolf," he said rather defensively.

"Ah, a lone wolf," said Spoony, nodding her head as if she knew what a lone wolf was, "What kind of lone wolf?"

"Ehhm, the kind that goes around lone?" replied Ploppy, not really sure he understood the question.

"And why did you become a lone wolf?"

"Well...ehm... I got losted." Like all creatures, Ploppy wasn't good at thinking up fibs so he always told the truth[30], even when it wasn't something he wanted anybody to know.

"Oh, I do that all the time," Spoony said matter-of-factly, "but somebody always comes to look for me, I expect your pack will be along soon looking for you. Or your mummy, wouldn't your mummy come to look for you?"

"Hmm, I don't think so. I think they were all quite glad when I got losted. In fact, I think they snuck off and losted me deliberately."

"They wouldn't really do that would they?"

"Well they might ... To tell you the truth, I'm not a very good wolf you see. I mean, I couldn't even catch you for dinner could I? I can't catch anything that can run away. I haven't eaten anything except beetles and slugs and worms and stuff like that for days and days and days. That's why they losted me I think. I'm not a good enough wolf to be a Lummox."

"What's a Lummox?" asked Spoony.

"Oh I'm a Lummox. It's my pack," said Ploppy and he stood up straight and recited in a very serious howly sort of wolf voice:-

"We are the Great Wolf Pack of Lummox ...

"Howoooo,

"We are smart and proud and keen ...

"Woohowoo,

"We hunt the Wild Boar and the Giant Elk ... and Bunnies ...

"Howoooo!

"We are very dainjlious, I mean dangerous .... so watch it, right?

"Woohowoo, Grraowwll!"

Ploppy sat down again and said glumly, "I think that's the way it goes, but I'm not a very good wolf."

"*I* think you're a *very* good wolf," said Spoony helpfully but Ploppy just gave her one

---

30. Told the truth: this is true too: humans are the only creatures in the entire world, and for that matter, probably in the universe, that deliberately tell fibs. With the possible exception of domestic cats.

of those polite looks that say *thank you but you don't know what you're talking about.*

"I'm not a very good wolf. I forget things and I sit and think about stuff when I should be howling or hunting or whatever, or I fall into a dwam and have to hurry to catch up and I forget how to do things and have to have it re-explained to me again."

"I don't think I'd make a very good wolf either," said Spoony. All of that had a very familiar ring to it. "Poo!" she said.

"Poo!" said Ploppy. He was quiet for a little while, sort of wondering away to himself. "What are you doing here anyway? I mean you could get eaten."

"Oh I came here to look for ideas to help my daddy find new things to invent and to help my mummy look after her dangerous wildhairy cattle.

"Your mummy looks after wildhairy cattle?! She must be completely crazy! Or very brave."

"Oh yes," said Spoony, "she's completely both. And so is my daddy."

"Imagine even going near a wildhairy. That's very scary. My mummy said never to go near them because they're very dainjlious and will kill you at a moment's notice."

"Mine did too," said Spoony, "What are you doing here?"

Ploppy fidgeted a bit. He was a bit embarrassed, too embarrassed to say, *'Well I was going to eat you'* again, so he left that bit out and just said, "I come here sometimes. You can keep a look out for something to hunt and watch out for your mummy, er, I mean your pack from up here." He stuck his bottom lip out and looked pretty glum.

"That's nice," said Spoony.

"Thank you," said Ploppy.

It was nice and warm and sunny on the top of Spoony's little mountain and so they just sat together and savoured for a little while the pleasure of having a new friend. Spoony was especially pleased for although she was friends with everybody in the village (something she made a point of) she had never before had a friend who was quite as odd as she was. The wolf seemed odd, but in a nice way. It was nice to have a friend with whom you could fall into a dwam and be odd. After a while Spoony began to notice that she was hungry and she opened up her satchel. First of all she took out her log and laid it on her lap.

"Are you hungry Ploppy?" she asked."

"Not more than usual," said Ploppy, looking at Spoony's log and wondering if this was the sort of thing that humans ate. "I caught a beetle and a worm yesterday."

"Would you like some of my picnic?" asked Spoony and she offered him some of her daddy's flat-and-chewy bread. He sniffed it carefully.

"It smells nice. What is it?"

"It's bread, and this," she said, announcing the cheese as she pulled it proudly from the satchel, "is cheese! You can have some if you like." She broke the bread in half and offered a bit to him.

"Are you sure you can eat it?" he said in a hopeful sort of tone.

"Oh yes," said Spoony and immediately Ploppy took it in his huge jaws and went chomp, chomp, chomp and swallowed it in one with a big gulp. When she offered him a piece of the cheese he nearly snapped her fingers off and he swallowed that in one gulp too. Spoony ate as much of her share as she wanted and gave the wolf what was left because he was drooling all over the place and shaking like a leaf and looked as if he might faint. "I'm afraid there's none left. Was it all right? Did you like it?"

"It was wondleyful! It was wondleyful, wondleyfully wondleyful," he said, "I was so, so hungry and now I'm not!" and he got up and ran around in little circles in a very babyish sort of way with his long legs all tangled up beneath him and his straggly tail tucked in. His eyes bounced and rolled around in his head and his tongue waggled around from the side of his mouth. Spoony watched him with surprise because that sort of joyful running around in silly circles was the sort of thing that she did when she felt suddenly happy. Except that Ploppy the wolf seemed to be exceptionally good at it. After a bit he came back and sat beside Spoony again with a big stupid, happy grin on his hairy, out of breath, panting face.

"You're my best friend in the whole world Spoony Tooth," he said and gave her a great big, slobbery licky kiss on the cheek, "Thank you for my full tummy."

Spoony stood up and put her arms around his great big hairy neck and gave him a big hug even though he was pretty smelly. "You're my best wolflummox in the whole world," she said, and she gave him a big slobbery licky kiss too.

"Oh good," said Ploppy, "and your my best Spoony thingummy."

"Oooh," said Spoony bashfully because she had never been called a thingummy before, "Would you like to cuddle my logdolly?" she asked and handed the wolf her log.

"Oh thank you," said Ploppy and he took it in his great big jaws, plopped it down between his paws and gave it a jolly good slobbery lick. He sat quietly for a minute and then jumped to his feet, "I know what I'll do,' he said and suddenly darted off down the hill. Spoony was quite startled by this and after quite a bit she began to think that the wolf had just decided to go without saying goodbye. Maybe it was something that wolves did. But in a while she saw him bounding up the hill looking very pleased with himself. He was completely covered in dirt and his big front paws were very muddy indeed. "I gaw oo umhing," he said.

"Pardon?" replied Spoony.

"I gaw oo umhing – a urrung." It was plain that Ploppy had something in his mouth,

"I gaw oo a urrung," he said again and dropped a great big wriggly worm on Spoony's lap, "I got you a worm," he said proudly now that his mouth was empty.

"Oh! Oh… thank you very much indeed," said Spoony remembering her manners.

"You can eat it now if you like. It's a special thank you for giving me a full tummy."

Spoony was not all that keen on worms; she found them a bit chewy (especially the big ones like this) on the odd occasions when she had eaten them in her Daddy's garden, but so as not to offend the wolf she held up the worm, bit off the end and sucked out the juicy stuff. Then she offered the chewy skin to Ploppy who chomped it up with a big cheery chompy chewy grin.

"Where do you go to hunt that cheese and bread stuff that you gave me? It's very tasty?"

"Oh, you don't hunt it. My daddy makes it. He makes the bread in his special bread making oven that he dafted up and he makes some of the cheese from wildhairymilk that my mummy gets from the wildhairy cows. But there's not a lot of that because it's very hard to collect, so most of the cheese is made from sheep's' milk."

"Poo!" said Ploppy again. Making food didn't make much sense to him because wolves don't make food, they have to go out and hunt for it. It all sounded very strange and this business of collecting wildhairymilk, whatever that was, sounded much more dangerous than worm hunting, even if the results were very tasty indeed. His own mummy had told him not to go near wildhairy cattle because they were incredibly dangerous and not in a nice way.

"Does your mummy hunt the wildhairycattle to get their wildhairymilk?"

"Oh no," replied Spoony, "It's usually them that chase her." This just made Ploppy's head go all twirly inside so he decided not to think about it.

Making Friends

They stayed together on the top of the little mountain for quite a while. It seemed like an even more very special place to be now that they each had a new friend. They spent ages talking away about all sorts of stuff that they had in common, which was mostly to do with being different from everybody else. Spoony told Ploppy how everybody was afraid of wolfses, sorry, wolves even though it was many years since any had come near the village and Ploppy told Spoony how the wolves never came near the village because they believed that humans were very crabby and could be quite unpleasant and a bit smelly. Spoony said that in the main, this was very often true but that nobody bothered about it.

Spoony showed Ploppy how to pick flowers and make a daisy chain. This was something that Spoony could do without help and without having to be shown how to again and again. She had to concentrate though and held the daisies up to the light with one eye closed and her nose all wrinkled and her tongue sticking out, as everybody does when they're taking aim. As it turned out, Ploppy was quite useless at this even if he closed one eye, wrinkled his nose and stuck his tongue out. Although he could pick the flowers quite gently with his great big jaws, he couldn't get them to join together, even when he laid them in a row and stared hard at them. If he picked one up in his teeth, they were so small that they disappeared beneath his nose. He tried staring hard with one eye shut to see under his nose[31] but it didn't work. Next he tried picking them all up at once and chewing them into a daisy chain but this didn't work either and seemed to make them mushy and even more difficult to join. He got quite annoyed with himself so Spoony made him a very special wolf daisy chain of his very own and hung it round his scrawny big neck. Even though he was a bit smelly and grimy, he did look very nice with his daisy chain round his neck and although neither of them knew it, he was the first wolf in history to wear any kind of fashionable outfit.

Ploppy showed Spoony how to chase her tail by running faster and faster in little circles until she caught herself up and could grab her tail with her teeth, something that you can do if you have a tail. Spoony ran and ran and ran in tighter and tighter circles until she was just spinning on the spot and eventually she fell down on the grass all dizzy and breathless and laughing her dizzytwirly head off. She wasn't very bothered not to have a tail to chase and, to be fair, she had never before noticed that she didn't have one. The subject had never come up.

Presently they both fell into a nice dwam on the warm rock on top of the nice little mountain. "This is the bestest mountain in the whole widely world," said Spoony after a while when this thought popped into her head.

"Oh it's not a mountain," said Ploppy knowallishly, "it's a galloot[32], and quite a big one."

"A Galloot? What's a Galloot?" asked Spoony, who didn't know what that was, even though she was sitting on one.

"Oh they're all over the place apparently, there's another away, away, away over there and another away, away, away over there," said Ploppy, furrowing his brows in the direction of the far away yonder over there, "They're supposed to be magicly... my mummy told me that they were magicly"

"Poo," said Spoony, "A magicly Big Galloot. I bet that would help my daddy daft

---

31. The underneath of noses: no creature on earth can see underneath its nose without a mirror. If you hang upside down from a tree branch you can see under your nose but only because what was the underneath is now the overneath. This is cheating. Besides, you have to go googley-eyed even to see the overneath of your nose unless you have a particularly big one. Scientists have wasted millions of public spendymoney on research into how to see under your nose, but still haven't managed to work it out. They have now moved on to researching the answer to more pressing questions such as this: If a bit of string has two ends and you cut one of them off and throw it away, why does it still have two ends?

32. Galloot: now, we already know that this story is a true one, which means that Galloots really did exist, and for that matter, still do. In fact, they're all over the place, particularly in Scotland, a strange land where people still eat the sort of food that Spoony Tooth would have enjoyed (not counting worms). Famous historians and geologists have tried to discover which particular Galloot it was where Spoony met Ploppy but it might have looked a bit like Quothquan Law or North Berwick Law. Of course, the word *Galloot* has fallen out of use when discussing small mountains and has been replaced with 'Law'. However, it is still used to describe somebody over six feet tall who doesn't move around much except to get in the way, as in, 'He's a useless big galloot."

stuff."

"What's *daft* stuff?" asked the wolf. He had learned a lot so far and having some food in his tummy made him even more curious. His wolfcraftythinkybrain was starting to become a little bit more thinky and crafty than it usually was now that his tummy had stopped shouting at it all the time about being empty. It would take quite a bit more food before his wolf brain would become fully craftythinky. Spoony expanded a bit more on her daddy's daft inventions and Ploppy listened with interest although he hadn't a clue what most of it was about and was rather worried that most of what he didn't understand might turn out to be as highly dangerous as messing around with wildhairy cattle.

Sitting in the warm sunshine on the little mountain and talking about all sorts of Spoonyish and Ploppyish things that they had in common, they were enjoying one another's company so much that it didn't seem long before the day had quite got along without them and it was getting late. The sun had gone right across the sky and Spoony was forced to admit to herself that she had better get home before it got dark or she would miss supper.

"I better get home now or my mummy and daddy will wonder where I am and I'll miss supper," she said.

"What's supper?" asked the wolf.

"Well we usually have something nice to eat before we go to bed."

"More to eat?!!" said the wolf in disbelief.

"Oh yes, you should come to supper one time, we always have lots to eat and Mummy makes all sorts of different stuff. Sometimes we have stewed rabbit, or egg thingumies with bread and cheese and ... are you all right?"

The wolf looked as if he was going to pass out and he lay down with his huge jaws between his big floppy paws, "Poo!" he said, "more to eat ..." He was struggling to imagine how it would feel to have more to[33] eat when he had already eaten that very day.

"Would you like to come home with me for supper?" Spoony thought it would be rather nice to invite a wolf home for supper. Her mummy and daddy were always pleased when people dropped by. It never occurred to her that a huge wolf might receive an entirely different kind of welcome.

"Oh no thank you," he said glumly, "I don't know if a wolf would be very welcome where the humans live. Besides, I was planning on have a nice worm and slug supper myself." Even though Spoony had turned out to be quite nice, he wasn't sure that all

---

33. More to eat: unlike many humans, wolves rarely have too much to eat. Wolves usually don't eat every day. Occasionally they will have "too much to eat" at one dinner after a successful hunt and they will lie around with a sore tummy making rude, smelly noises and feeling very full indeed. But even then, there will be nothing left for the next day, or the next after that because like many humans, wolves usually eat it all at one sitting. Wolves can't hunt on a full tummy so they usually wait until they're very hungry before they go looking for the next meal. And if their hunt is unsuccessful then they stay hungry. This is why Ploppy was exceptionally hungry, he really wasn't very good at hunting.

humans would be as nice as she was. Not all wolves were nice so perhaps humans would be like that too.

"Yuk," said Spoony, "Worm and slug supper? Worms might be quite nice for supper but I don't think slugs would make a very nice supper."

"Well, they're not so bad," said Ploppy defensively, "not all that bad."

"I suppose so, if you say so," said Spoony, "but wouldn't you rather have another big piece of my dad's nice chewy bread? You'd be very welcome."

"No thank you Spoony, perhaps some other time," he said. It was all very new and confusing for Ploppy. He had never been invited anywhere before and certainly not for the sort of delicious sounding food that Spoony had described.

"Tomorrow then?" said Spoony springing to her feet, "You can come for supper tomorrow. I'll tell Mummy to make an extra supper for you."

"Oh... Oh," he couldn't think of an excuse, "Oh I ehm... I mean I er ..."

"Good, I'll tell Mummy to make extra," said Spoony who was quite proud of her ability to organise things, although quite often her idea of organising things was a bit odd, "and we can have a nice evening at our place." Then after a pause she said, "Well, I suppose I'd better get home now Ploppy. Will you be here tomorrow if I come back? We can look for stuff to invent and stuff like that."

Ploppy tried to look as if he was thinking whether he had anything else arranged, "Yes, if you like, I don't think I have anything in particular arranged for tomorrow ... ehm, nothing that I couldn't postpone," he said.

"Oh, goody!" said Spoony and she did one of her very pleased Spoonyish jumping-up-and-down-for-joy dances. Ploppy stood up and did one too with his big hairy tail waving backwards and forwards and his big stupid grin back on his face. He was every bit as pleased to have a new friend as Spoony was, especially a friend that might not run away and leave him like his wolf friends usually did.

"I'll meet you here tomorrow morning then," said Spoony.

"Yes," said Ploppy, "I'll be back here in the morning." Actually, poor Ploppy had nowhere else to go and had decided just to find somewhere sheltered to sleep in the woods near the Galloot, "I'll walk down to the bottom of the hill with you." So they set off down the same side of the little mountain that Spoony had first climbed up and they chatted away cheerfully about nothing in particular. When they got to the level ground back on the forest floor they walked along in silence together for a while. They were both a bit glum and neither one really wanted to say goodbye, even though it was only until tomorrow.

Eventually Spoony stopped and she reached up and wrapped her arms around his scrawny, smelly neck and gave Ploppy one of her best Spoony hugs and said, "I suppose

I'd better say goodbye now Ploppy, you don't need to come any further if you've got some worm hunting to catch up on."

Ploppy gave her a funny puzzled look. He hadn't understood a word she'd said and it had all sounded a bit cackley to him. Perhaps it was a special cackley, Spoony way of saying goodbye so he gave his new friend a special slobbery lick and said, "Woowoo wowf growf." Spoony was a bit puzzled by this but she thought that it must be wolf for goodbye so she tried to say it too. "Woowoolf wowf gowrf," she said, only not so deep and growly. Ploppy couldn't understand why she was making funny gibbering noises so he gave her another big slobbery licky kiss and tried cackling. It made him cough. Spoony made some more funny cackley noises, shrugged her shoulders gave him another hug and a kiss on his big wet nose and trotted off through the forest, back the way she had come. When she had gone quite a long way away from the Galloot, she heard a long, long, miserable, lonely wolf howl coming from where she had left Ploppy. She had never heard a wolf howl before but she hoped that they always sounded lonely and that she hadn't left a lonely, miserable young wolf behind.

Back on the Galloot poor Ploppy wandered around feeling ever so lonely now that he'd met somebody nice and made friends. Being a lone wolf was a very lonely existence but he'd almost got used to it, or at least, that's what he'd told himself, but having had, for a little while, the company of a strange little human who was nice and friendly and gave him big hugs made being a lone wolf seem very lone indeed. He wandered down to the edge of the Galloot, found a holly bush and curled up under it with his nose under his tail. Oh well, he thought, at least I've got a full tummy. But it didn't help with being lone.

Chapter 3

Oh no, the Sheep have escaped!

Spoony made her way home more or less by the same route as she had come and in between falling into the odd walking along dwam she remembered to say "Good afternoon!" to all the woodland creatures she saw on her way. She was really pleased that she had found a new friend and a nice little mountain and was pretty sure that she would soon discover lots of useful things for her daddy to invent and lots of problem-solving, wildhairy taming ideas for her Mum. The going was mainly downhillish and she had really begun to get the hang of walking through thick forest so she made much quicker progress on her way home than she had in the morning. Presently the trees began to thin out again and Spoony was once more in amongst the silver birches at the edge of the forest. She looked around for the tree that she had bumped into in the morning but they all looked very similar so she pressed on towards the village, doing her best to pay attention so that she didn't walk head first into any more trees. This took quite a bit of concentration because her tummy kept interrupting by pointing out to her that it was getting near suppertime and she had better get a move on. It wasn't long before she was crossing the grassy fields towards the village, scattering the timid, nervous sheep and lambs as she went. It did occur to her that most of these sheep looked like her own mummy and Dad's sheep because they were mostly white in colour with splotchy brown and black bits and that in the distance there were some wildhairy cattle looking extremely contented and munching away at the new spring grass. However, she didn't give it too much thought because she was very keen to get home for supper. The late afternoon sun was really nice and warm after the shade of the forest and she had a nice happy warm coming home sort of feeling. She could see her very own bedroom window in the chimney and was looking forward to being snuggled up in bed with a full tummy to make more plans for her discoveries.

When Spoony arrived back home she went straight to her dad's dafting shed to find a giant pile of wood shavings even bigger than before, but no new inventions and no Dad. Her mummy wasn't in the wildhairy cattle pen trying to tame the wildhairy cattle and indeed, there was no sign of mummy or the wildhairy cattle either and somebody had made a nice cow shaped hole in the hedge. After a bit she found her Mummy and Daddy sitting in the late afternoon sun at the side of the house.

"Hello!" said Spoony, "I'm back from discovering!"

"Oh hello Spoony," said her mummy and Dad, "Where have you been? We've been looking for you." They both looked extremely flustered and a bit depressed. Spoony noticed that her Mummy had bits of twig in her hair but this wasn't particularly unusual what with her mummy being quite out of the ordinary.

"I've been very busy. I've been and discovered a Hairy Lummox and a Big Galloot!" said Spoony, really pleased with herself and hoping for some congratulations.

"Oh that's nice," said Mummy, "We've been busy too. Unfortunately."

"Yes," said Dad. He sounded a bit hoarse, "The wildhairies charged through the hedge and got out and Mummy had to dive for cover to save herself from being completely flattene. And then they knocked over the sheep pen and all the sheep got out and we can't catch any of them up again."

"And we've tried everything," interrupted Mum, "None of the usual stuff seems to work. They just don't want to go back in the pen."

"I'm not surprised about the wildhairies, they hate being tame," said Dad, giving Mummy one of his sympathetic smiles, "But the sheep need to be penned up to prevent safety, I mean prevent danger."

"Poo!" said Spoony, "Have you tried running around yelling and flapping your arms?" This, as you know, was the usual method for shooing sheep into a pen.

"That was the first thing we tried," said Mummy, "My arms have gone quite stiff."

"Yes," croaked Dad, "and I've got a stiff voice, I mean sore throat."

"But nothing worked and they all just split up and ran around in circles. I think they were enjoying it. And the angrier we got the more they seemed to enjoy it."

"So we've decided to leave them until the morning and see if they calm down."

"Yes, but what if there's a wolf attack?" said Mummy. She sounded quite worried.

"We haven't had a wolf attack here for many years but it would be just typical Tooth luck if we got one tonight. There are wolves around even when you think there aren't."

"Oh I don't think we'll get a wolf attack tonight," said Spoony trying to sound knowledgeable without being too smartypantsish, "There are hardly any wolfses anywhere near here and there definitely isn't a whole pack."

"Well you can't be sure," said Mummy, "Your Daddy knows about these sorts of things." Which everybody knew he didn't but Mummy gave his knee a little squeeze to make him feel as if he did.

"Oh, I can *assure* you that there will *not* be a wolf attack tonight. There are *no* wolfses anywhere near here at the moment," said Spoony, with her hands on her emphatic hips. She nodded with the best knowledgeable and emphatic nod that she could muster. Mummy and Daddy Tooth smiled indulgently because they knew that Spoony knew absolutely nothing about wolves or where they might be. Spoony smiled back indulgently because for once, she knew something that her mummy and daddy didn't know.

Spoony would quite have liked to go and try to catch the sheep. This was a very popular job with most of the children in the village as it gave everybody a chance to run around and make lots of noise without being told by the grownups to shut up and behave[34]. But her Mummy and Daddy looked jolly tired and she had to admit she too was quite ready for supper and a nice sit down in front of the fire. Spoony thought that that was such a nice idea that she nearly slipped off into a nice anticipatory sort of dwam and forgot all about anything else, but just in time she caught herself and taking her mummy and daddy by the hands she hauled them to their feet and said, in her best confidence-boosting voice, "Let's all go in and have a nice supper and go to bed and when we get up in the morning we'll be able to sort out the sheepses and the wildhairy cowses and we can get some help from the neighbours.

"I suppose you're right Spoony," said her Dad. He wasn't very confident about asking the neighbours for help because they all thought he was daft and if they did offer to help to gather in the sheep (which, of course, they would do), they would probably ask Tooth the Daft to get on with inventing something that nobody needed and not get in the way. Most of the people in the village thought, in all modesty, that they knew a lot more about

---

34. Making lots of noise: sadly, nowadays there are few industrial jobs that children can do where running around making lots of noise is required, or appreciated although it is still required for rounding up (distributing) sheep belonging to smallholders.

Interestingly, people seem to lose the desire to run around and make a lot of noise when they become teenagers as they are busy trying to look either cool or enigmatic. When they become grown-ups their memories fail them and they can't remember what fun it was. Running around making a lot of noise requires you not to care what people think of you and grownups don't re-acquire the aptitude for this until they're in their eighties, which is a shame.

sheep and cattle penning than anybody else, especially the Tooths who did everything the wrong way.

"Yes," said Mummy, "We can have a bit of left-over rabbit pie and some cheese and have an early night."

"Oh good," said Spoony and dragged the two of them inside.

When they were seated round the fire munching away at bits of her Mummy's left-over magnificent rabbit pie and some left-over thick soup (which was always better the second time around anyway) Spoony's mum asked, "What was it you said you were doing all day Spoony?"

"Oh, I went off to try to discover things for Daddy to daft up and to help you with the wildhairy cattle taming."

"Oh yes I remember," said Mummy, "that was very kind of you. And did you find anything for Daddy to daft?"

"Yes," put in Daddy Tooth speaking with his mouth full, "and Mummy could really do with something to help her tame those wildhairies." Mummy gave him one of her looks. Neither of them expected Spoony to have discovered anything much because grown-ups, even Tooth grown-ups never really expect little girls (or boys for that matter) to discover anything that grown-ups didn't already know about.

"Well no," said Spoony, "I didn't discover anything like that but I made a start."

"Oh that's a help," Mummy had got to her feet and was busy tidying up while Daddy put some logs on the fire, "at least you've made a start." Spoony leaned over and grabbed her logdolly from her daddy just as he was about to put it on the fire in mistake for a proper log.

"Yes you need to make a start," said Dad, poking the fire with a bit of stick and re-arranging the logs so that the fire would burn all night. White wood ash was floating up out of the fire and several sparks cracked out of the dry half-burned wood as he plopped more logs on top, "If you don't make a start then you can't get on." Even daft but interesting and eccentric dads like Tooth the Daft could make boring remarks now and again.

"Well I did," said Spoony firmly, "I discovered a Big Galloot and a Hairy Lummox."

"A Big Galloot and a Hairy....?" said Dad. Several sparks from the fire had landed on him and smoke was rising from his woolly smock. Spoony's mummy patted them out with a wooden ladle as she went past and then came back for a big spark which had landed in his hair and begun to burn. She had to give him several whacks in the head with the ladle before she was satisfied that his hair had stopped burning. This was not in the least out of the ordinary and Spoony took no notice. Although her daddy was looking slightly dizzy and twirly-brained.

"...Lummox." finished Spoony.

"Lummox. What's a Lummox?" asked Mummy checking her husband for signs of fire.

"Oh it's a big hairy thing and it's called a Lummox, a Hairy Lummox. They're really nice." Spoony was starting to yawn because she now had a full tummy and was very tired.

"And what's a Big Galloot?" yawned daddy picking Spoony up and carrying her to her own little stepladder.

"It's like a mountain only it's a lot cuddlier,"

"Oh a cuddly mountain, that sounds pretty good," said Dad, losing interest.

"Yes," said Spoony climbing up to her cosy little bedroom in the chimney, "a nice cuddly mountain with a Hairy Lummox on it." She plopped down on her bed, gave a great big yawn and went straight off to sleep.

"What do you suppose a Hairy Lummox is?" said Spoony's Dad.

"Or a Big Galloot," said Mummy, "you can always rely on our very own Spoony to come up with something unusual."

"Yes, it's probably just a pretend sort of thing," replied Daddy Tooth.

"Probably," said Mummy Tooth, "she has a vivid imagination."

Next Morning

Spoony woke up very early the next morning to the sound of her daddy making the fire and her Mummy, as usual, getting her wildhairy cow milking buckets ready. This was the sort of optimistic thing that the Tooths were famous for because, as you know, the wildhairy cattle were going to be more than usually difficult to milk today what with having got out and being spread around all over the place.

After some breakfast all three of them stepped out into the cold spring air of a very early morning just as the sun was beginning to rise. As expected, neither the sheep nor the goats had bothered to put themselves back in their pens during the night and, of course, the wildhairy cattle were nowhere to be seen. The Tooths decided to start trying to round up their sheep and goats again so they headed off in the dim slanting morning sunlight to look for them where they had last been seen. Sure enough, over towards the edge of the forest, in the long dim mottled shadows of the trees could be seen the bright white (with the odd black and brown bit) woolly coats of the Tooth sheep and the odd brown and white goat mixed in amongst them.

Spoony's mum and dad had each brought a bucket[35] of the sheep's favourite oatmeal and hazelnut breakfast mix in the hope that they would see the error of their ways and

---

35. Buckets: in those days, buckets were quite heavy because they were made out of wood and were hardly ever used to carry water because they leaked so much that by the time you got back, you had to go and fill them again. Water was usually carried in a bag made out of something leathery and unhygienic. These leaked just as much but weren't as heavy so you could keep up the pointless business of refilling it for longer.

follow them home for breakfast. As they walked towards them they became more optimistic that the sheep would come home with them in an orderly manner because they didn't run off immediately they saw the Tooths approaching. But as Spoony and her mummy and daddy got nearer they began to see that what they had mistaken in the early morning light for dark shadows beneath the trees were actually lots and lots of dark brown and black woolly sheep.

"Oh my goodness," said Spoony's Mum, "All the sheep in the village have got out."

"Oh no-o-o," said Daddy Tooth.

"Oh poo-oo-oo," said Spoony, who had not really been bothering much about the sheep. She had rather been looking forward to running around flapping her arms because it was cold and she wanted to get warmed up. She had a look around to see if she could see the wildhairy cattle. And she *could* see them. "Da-ad," she said, tugging at his woolly smock.

"Oh no-o-o," he said again, looking in dismay at all the escaped sheep and wondering what the villagers would say to him.

"Da-ad, Da ... ad, look. Look at the wildhairies," said Spoony, pointing back towards the village. Mummy and Daddy Tooth turned round and followed Spoony's pointed finger back towards the village.

"Oh my goodness," said Spoony's mum.

"Oh no-o-o," said Spoony's dad. The Tooth wildhairy cattle were back at the village but they weren't in their own pen in the Tooth garden; they were in other people's gardens and their hairy heads and long horns could be seen above the fences and hedges munching away at the spring flowers. The Tooths ran back towards the village trying not to panic. Not, as you know, that Spoony was one for panicking. She thought that this was really very exciting.

"Oh my goodness," said Spoony's mum, panicking like anything.

"Oh no-o-o," said Spoony's dad, panicking like Mummy Tooth.

And as they got closer they began to see more disasters and an explanation for most of the sheep in the village having escaped. Not only had the wildhairy cattle got into their neighbours' gardens, they had also broken into their neighbours' sheep pens and knocked over gates and fences and flattened hedges and there was general mayhem and disaster everywhere. There were sheep and goats everywhere too.

Well it wasn't long before the whole village woke up to find that almost everybody's garden had been invaded by the Tooths' wildhairy cattle and that most of the sheep pens had been knocked over, and most of the sheep had bolted and were enjoying their freedom by being spread out and muddled up. Nobody had to ask how their sheep had got out and who owned the wildhairy cattle that were strolling through the gardens eating everything in sight. Apart from the fact that the Tooths were the main suspects on account of their ridiculous cattle handling and milking ideas, they were caught red handed trying to shoo some very cynical and relaxed (and with full tummies) cattle out of various gardens. Thankfully, the wildhairy cattle were not charging around (of which they were very capable) when the Tooths tried to move them, but were ambling along in their own time giving anybody that came near them a steady, malevolent[36] stare.

After a while, most of the people whose gardens had been invaded and whose sheep pens had been flattened, along with several people who had just turned up to be helpful (and nosey) had gathered into a small group and were surveying the Tooths' wildhairy cattle from a safe distance. Some of them were busy trying to identify their own sheep from everybody else's sheep. They were all giving the Tooths the same kind of malevolent steady stare that the Tooth cattle were giving everybody. Later there would have to be a debate about whose teenage son would have to be the one to get attacked and have the wildhairy cattle chase him into the catching pen. Most of the teenage boys had gone missing, which they did anyway.

As you know, people in those days were very much more sedate about the way in which they went about things. Nevertheless, as the morning progressed, it became plain that no matter how much running around and flapping of arms they (the whole village) did, it was not going to be easy to get all the sheep caught up and sorted out. Tempers began to get a little frayed. It was quite plain, also, that the sheep were enjoying being chased around and most of the children were enjoying chasing them. All of the adults were giving directions to one another and nobody was obeying. Everybody at one time or another managed to take time out to give the Tooths some advice and not all of it was delivered in the politest of tones. If somebody did manage to round up a few sheep and chase them into a hastily-repaired pen it wasn't long before, in an effort to sort the sheep according to who owned them, there was an escape and they had to start all over again. What made matters worse was that the Tooth sheep, being, as they were, white with brown and black bits rather than the other way around, were the easiest to identify and were consequently going to be the easiest to collect and sort out.

Spoony was having a really exciting morning. Running around shouting and flapping her arms was something she considered herself to be pretty good at because, unlike games such as hingosy or some of the other games that the children played, it had no complicated rules that needed explaining. As you may have noticed by now, she had completely forgotten that she had an appointment.

Well, eventually, much later in the day, with help from the whole village, not only the

---

36. Malevolent: very, very nasty. If somebody gives you a malevolent stare, don't stare back, just make your excuses and leave. Giving somebody a malevolent stare can give you a headache because you have to make your eyes look pointy and rude so it's usually simpler just to be nice.

easily identified Tooth sheep, but everybody else's sheep and goats were rounded up and sorted out and re-installed in their proper sheep pens from which they could be let out in orderly and easily tended small groups to graze as usual. The wildhairy cattle, much to everybody's surprise (and relief), after some charging around and refusing to get angry enough to chase anybody into the catching pen, had ambled back to the Tooth garden and were hanging around in anticipation of some more fun when Mrs Tooth tried to milk them again. Everybody was quite puffed and Spoony's mum felt obliged to invite everybody back to the Tooth house for an early supper. Not many people accepted. Although there was a general air of satisfaction at having eventually rounded up all the livestock, not everybody felt entirely well disposed to the Tooths, and those who did, did not feel entirely well disposed to the thought of being offered some of the Tooth family's funny food such as flat and chewy bread (of which there was usually too much) or that cow's milk, not that there was much on offer. So the Tooths were allowed to get on with what was left of the day without much company other than their own.

"What a terrible day!" said Daddy Tooth as they sat round the fire before getting ready for bed, "I think I'll have to daft up a system for rounding up sheep more easily."

"Yes," said Spoony's Mummy, "and I hope the wildhairies never decide to go on the rampage like that again."

"Well, then, I suppose I had better get on with my discovering," said Spoony trying to help. "Oh poo!" she said, suddenly remembering her forgotten appointment with Ploppy, "I forgot to go and see my hairy Lummox on the magic galloot. Oh poo!"

"Never mind," said Mummy Tooth, taking Spoony by the hand and heading her in the direction of her bedroom, "I expect the hairy Lummox and the magic galloot will be there tomorrow." Mummy Tooth thought that they were probably the sort of things which Spoony just made up for a pretend adventure as little girls do. When she'd been a little girl, she used to make up adventures like that too.

"Oh I think the galloot will definitely still be there but I don't know about Ploppy, he might have gone by now," said Spoony, by now very worried about her wolf.

"Ploppy? What's a Ploppy?" asked Dad, clearly puzzled was he began to stoke the fire again.

"The hairy Lummox is *called* Ploppy," said Spoony as if her daddy was daft, which, as you know, he was.

"Oh," he said sagely, "a Ploppy Lummox and a hairy galloot."

"Something like that," said Spoony.

"Why don't you invite your friends for supper," said Mummy, trying to be helpful and not thinking for a moment that there was any risk of there being any such thing as a Hairy Lummox turning up for supper. She could see that Spoony was unusually worried.

"Yes, I could do that," replied Spoony cheering up a bit at the thought, "except that I don't think that a galloot could come even if he was asked, but can you make extra supper for the hairy Lummox please? I expect he might come." Spoony climbed up to her little bedroom in the chimney and snuggled down in bed a bit worriedly hoping that Ploppy would forgive her for not turning up. She did have a good excuse what with the terrible incident of the great entire village sheep escape but, even so, it is never nice to let a friend down and even worse if you forget all about them for almost a whole day.

Meanwhile

Early that same morning, just around about the time that Spoony and her mummy and daddy discovered that all the sheep in the village had escaped, the huge hairy form of Ploppy had arrived at the top of the little mountain. He sat down on the rock to wait for his new friend, in fact, his only friend, Spoony Tooth. He was really looking forward to seeing her again. It was going to be so good to have a nice friend to talk to and play with and just generally be unusual with. He had made up his mind to be a very loyal and trusting and faithful friend.

At first he kept a look out, hoping, and almost daring to expect at any minute now to see Spoony's cheery face emerging from the trees and her skinny legs bounding up the slope. He watched and listened and sniffed the air for quite a long time. Then he began to get up every now and again and go down towards the trees and have a look around, but there was no sign of her. Occasionally he stood up on his back legs and peered out over the forest towards the village in the hope of seeing her. The wolf was very hungry again but he didn't even take the time to go and hunt for a beetle or a worm to eat just in case Spoony turned up when he was away and he missed her. He made up all sorts of excuses and explanations for her being late but eventually, as the day wore on and it began to get dark, he had to admit to himself that his new friend was not going to come. His bottom lip began to stick out and his ears went down and he began to be a very miserable and unhappy and lonely young wolf indeed. He hadn't been very happy for quite a long time but now that he'd had a little bit of happiness enjoying Spoony's company, being unhappy and lonely was worse than ever.

The two young wolves were sleek and strong and well fed. They had thick glossy grey coats and sharp eyes and even sharper teeth. They had never been to this far corner of their territory before and were being very cautious and alert. Now they had stumbled upon something quite unexpected: another wolf. They did not sneak up behind Ploppy but being lieutenants of the Great Wolf Pack of Lummox, they moved naturally with a silent grace that had them up behind Ploppy before he knew they were there. He had fallen into a very glum dwam and was staring into space, still hoping for Spoony to turn up but knowing that she really wasn't going to come today.

"Graoowwll!" barked the wolf closest to Ploppy, right in his ear. Ploppy yelped with fright and leaped in the air with his tail between his legs which already were scrabbling to run away from whatever it was that had surprised him. The two wolves were on him before he could get even a bound or two away. In an instant one of them had him pinned down by the throat and the other had him by his back foot. They were bigger and stronger and faster than him and there was no point in trying to run away so he just did the next best thing and curled up in a cringing ball on the ground hoping that they wouldn't bite him too much.

Wolves, most wolves that is, do not tolerate fools gladly and these two made a point of ensuring that this ridiculous apology for a wolf that they had stumbled upon understood that they did not intend to put up with any nonsense. Once they were sure he wouldn't try to run away they let go of him and circled him steadily, sniffing him all over and growling a very low rumbling menacing growl. Their tails were held stiffly in the air and their hackles bristled[37] like hedgehogs. Ploppy thought he was done for; he recognised both of them as two of his own pack, Willow and Hazel. They were not much older than him but they were quite a bit more grown up; they were young scouts for the pack, always on the lookout for something to hunt, or keeping watch for danger. Unlike Ploppy, Hazel and Willow were exceptionally good at being wolves and had no idea whatsoever why Ploppy should be so uncommonly bad at it. As a result, they had no sympathy for him whatsoever. He carried on doing his best cringe that he knew how to do and rolled on his back and whimpered.

"It's that idiot Ploppy," said Hazel, with an air of distaste.

"So it is," said Willow sniffing Ploppy again, "What a disgusting mess." Ploppy cringed a bit more; it seemed to be working.

"Oh for goodness sake Ploppy, get up and stop snivelling," said Hazel.

Ploppy scrambled obediently to his feet and tried to look as wolf-like as he could, "Hello Hazel. Hello Willow," he said, trying to sound as if he wasn't surprised to see them.

"Shut up!" said Willow, "And sit up straight when a scout speaks to you! You're a disgrace!" He began to sniff Ploppy all over once again. A wolf can get just about all the information it needs about somebody just by sniffing them and Willow was drawing some pretty unsavoury conclusions about this specimen. "You stink Ploppy. You smell of worms and slugs and goodness knows what else but there's something else you smell of which I can't quite place."

---

37. Hackles bristled: when a wolf wants to show you who's in charge, the fur along its back stands up on end and its tail is held high. Altogether, it's an impressive sight. Dogs do this sort of thing when they meet other dogs out for walkies but it's not quite the same thing and they just get a tug on the lead and are told not to be so silly, or rude. Nobody in their right mind would put a wolf on a lead because if it decided to take off and go hunting, you'd get dragged along whether you liked it or not.

"That's right," said Ploppy helpfully, already knowing what it was they could smell – he could still smell Spoony's sweet sooty aroma on his own fur, "worms and slugs."

"I know what it is," said Willow, "It's the smell fire and that other smell, it must be the smell of humans! The smell of their fires." All wolves, when growing up, are taught by their pack the things that are most dangerous and which must be avoided and wolves can describe smells[38] to one another very well so Willow hadn't had much trouble in identifying this smell of fire and humans even though they were entirely new to him.

"Yes," said Hazel, "That's what it is. Have you been near a human den?"

"No," said Ploppy quite truthfully, "the nearest human den must be a whole day's run from here at least."

"Then where did you get the funny smell?" asked Willow, now deeply suspicious. He didn't like Ploppy and indeed, he himself wasn't a very likeable wolf. "You definitely smell of humans; and of fire." Willow was not afraid of very many things but like all sensible creatures he was afraid of fire and he was deeply suspicious of anything that smelled even a little bit smoky.

"I must just have been somewhere where they had been before me ... or something." Ploppy tried to change the subject, "How is everybody in the pack?"

"All the better without you around. Now speak up and tell us how you came to smell of humans." Willow grabbed Ploppy's ear and bit it hard.

Ploppy squealed, "Ow... I met a human .... owwow!"

"A human!" barked Willow.

"Only it's not really an ordinary human It's a special type of human. Its, it's … Owww ... Please don't bite me."

"A special type of human?" said Hazel who had only ever heard of the unpleasant cackly type.

"What does it look like?" demanded Willow. Neither of them had ever seen a human.

"Ehm … It's quite big, in fact it's huge, giant, comparatively, and it walks around on its back legs all the time."

"Preposterous!" said Hazel, "All the time? It would get tired and fall over."

"Well it doesn't, it's quite good at it," said Ploppy, in fact it's an expert at it."

"He's mad," said Willow, "Let's give him a doing."

"No, no!" said Ploppy, not wanting a doing, "It really is a special type of human – it's called a Spoonytooth and its magicly – it can talk."

"Don't be ridiculous," said Willow losing patience, "How could a human talk?"

---

38. Describing a smell: this is pointless because it's impossible and the best that people ever manage is to say is that a smell is " nice" or "horrible". You can try saying something like, "Well, it smells like a rotting pineapple," but then if the person you're talking to says, "What does a rotting pineapple smell like?" you're stuck and just go round in circles. Wolves don't have any trouble describing smells. By the way, describing colours is equally difficult; try describing *lilac* without using the word *purple*.

"But it's a *special* type of human," insisted Ploppy, "I was going to eat it."

"That's the most ridiculous thing yet," scoffed Willow, 'I thought you said it was huge? It takes you all your time to run down a worm. And anyway, it's never been proved beyond doubt that humans are edible."

"Well, they're not," said Ploppy emphatically, "at least the Spoonytooth type aren't. They're deadny poislious, probably. Well, I wouldn't eat one… it might eat you back!" Ploppy was afraid that Willow and Hazel would quite like to try out a bit of human and he was doing his best to put them off even thinking about eating a Spoonytooth.

"They're what?" said Willow.

"Deadny poislious," repeated Ploppy.

"He means deadly poisonous," said Hazel, shaking his head. He was starting to feel a little sorry for Ploppy.

"And they're deadny dainjlious too. They could eat you," continued Ploppy now that he thought Hazel was listening, "probably." He nodded emphatically, "This one was out hunting for … something."

"So how come it never ate you, you idiot? You're making it up!"

"Well, ehm, it didn't eat me because it had brought its dinner with it."

"Brought its dinner with it? You don't go hunting and bring your dinner with you!" yelled Willow. Willow was starting to lose his temper again. His hackles were up and he was glowering a very fierce glower at Ploppy who was trembling like an aspen leaf in a gale.

Hazel, who was a lot more even-tempered than Willow got between the two of them and said, "He didn't invent that smell did he? Look Ploppy, I don't know what you've been up to but you'll never get back into the Pack if you don't pull yourself together. Look at the state of you, and you still talk incessant drivel."

"Well, I'm a lone wolf now anyway," said Ploppy, trying to sound grown up and independent, "since I got losted."

"Who needs him," said Willow, "Let's get back and report this."

"Hmm, I suppose we should, but I don't suppose The Boss will be much interested in Ploppy," said Hazel, "not until he's grown up and started acting like a proper wolf." He turned to Ploppy, "Ploppy *do* make an effort … and don't go messing around with any more humans, you could come to a very sticky end."

"Come on," said Willow, "I've had enough of this idiot. We'd better get back, The Boss will be interested in anything to do with humans coming into Lummox territory." And with that the two wolves turned and trotted off into the forest without even saying goodbye.

Ploppy lay down in the grass and curled up into a very miserable ball.

Sometimes a wolf howl can be a bloodcurdling sort of sound which can chill you to the marrow, but the wolf howls that came from Spoony's little mountain that night were just the longest loneliest wolf howls that have ever been heard. Those kinds of howls can chill you to the marrow too.

.

Chapter 4

The Magic Mountain

Mr and Mrs Tooth had a lot to catch up on the next morning. Daddy Tooth was well behind with his dafting schedule and got up very early with the intention of dafting up a sheep catching invention. Mummy Tooth also felt that she was under some pressure to make progress with wildhairy taming and decided to try and get the wildhairies to understand the need for good behaviour. She felt that everybody else in the village who owned wildhairy cattle would be interested to know more about getting along with them. As a result, Spoony was left pretty much to her own devices that morning so she decided to get back to the little mountain as early as possible to look for Ploppy the Hairy Lummox. She packed her little bag with a huge piece of her daddy's special flatandchewybread and enough wildhairymilkcheese for two, collected her logdolly and set off once again towards the stepping stones across the river and the forest beyond.

This time, Spoony knew the exact direction and roughly how long it would take her to get there. She even knew which silver birch trees to avoid blonking into and that her feet would go a funny clean pink colour now and again so that she made even better progress than she had done the other day. Even though she was keen to hurry up, Spoony still remembered to say, "Good morning" to all the nice woodland creatures that she had met before and some of them forgot to run away and stayed to say good morning to Spoony. Even the big brown bear was pleased to see Spoony. He was in a good mood this morning because the swelling from all his bee stings was beginning to go down so he said good morning in his own growly way. Spoony, who still thought that the bear was a great big mouse, said good morning back and that she hoped his sore throat would get better soon and that he would get his mouse squeak back. The bear, who didn't understand anything Spoony said simply watched her go by. Big brown bears are usually extremely dangerous and will eat anything or anybody they can get their paws on but apart from being plainly completely harmless, Spoony looked too skinny to bother with and anyway, she wasn't afraid of him, which made a nice change.

Presently the ground began to rise up and Spoony knew that she was climbing the lower slope of her little mountain. It wasn't long before she was puffing her way up the grassy dome to the top.

On the bare rock of the top of her little mountain she looked all around. There was absolutely no sign of the wolf to be seen anywhere. She walked all round the little mountain, looking down each side and peering into the trees which circled its grassy top but the wolf couldn't be seen. She felt very glum and sat down on the rock at the top of her mountain. It wasn't very nice to think that you've let somebody down and perhaps lost a new friend. She took her logdolly out of her bag and cuddled it to help her feel better.

"I wonder where Ploppy Hairylummox is," she said to her logdolly, "I wish he was here and we could play at stuff and he could come home for supper and stuff like that." But Spoony's logdolly didn't have much to say on the matter so they sat down feeling quite glum. It was a lovely sunny morning and the bees and insects buzzed and hummed all around her and the birds were singing and she would have found it just the perfect place to fall into a dwam if she'd only had a wolf to do it with. It was the sort of spring morning when the whole world had a pleasant contented hum to it. A very distinct and comforting hum seemed to have settled about the place and, apart from not being able to find her friend, Spoony was more than ever certain that this was her very special mountain. She was pretty sure that she would find her friend quite soon.

She could see over the tops of the trees to the village far away in the distance but she couldn't see inside the forest and was wondering how she was going to go about finding Ploppy in that huge forest when she heard the sound of bumbley, shambley footsteps rustling through the undergrowth down by the fringe of the forest. Shambling out of the woodland fringe, up the slope came a very dejected (and scruffy) looking wolf. His head was down and lolloped from side to side and his ears hung all down and unhappyish and his tail flopped between his legs. Spoony knew immediately who it was and she jumped to her feet and cried, "Ploppy Hairylummox!" as pleased as she had ever been to see somebody.

The wolf looked up with a start as if he hadn't been expecting to see anybody. He saw Spoony waving from the rock at the top of the little mountain. "It's my special Spoonytooth! It's my special Spoonytooth!" he yelled and came racing up the slope as fast as he could with his gangly legs all over the place trying to run faster than they were able. He was so pleased to see Spoony that when he reached the top he gave one last joyful leap and would have bounded straight into her if she hadn't seen it coming and ducked. Poor old Ploppy somersaulted over her, giving her a great big cheesy grin and a big slobbery lick on the way past and rolled down the other side of the hill with his ears and tail and legs flailing about like a big hairy egg beater until he rolled to a halt and came bounding back up the hill. "I found my special Spoonytooth, I found my special Spoonytooth!" he sang and started to run about in little circles in a very babyish sort of way with his legs all tangled up beneath him and his straggly tail waving furiously just as he had done the other day.

This looked like such a good way to celebrate that Spoony began to run all about in circles too only she waved her arms instead of her tail (which she didn't have). She sang, "I found my special Ploppy Hairylummox! I found my special Ploppy Hairylummox!"

After a bit they were both so puffed out with running around flapping that they flopped down on the rock and Spoony put her arms round the wolf's scrawny, hairy (and smelly) neck and gave the him a great big tight squeezey hug, in exchange for which she got several slobbery big licks and had to wipe her face dry with her woolly sleeve.

"I'm awfully sorry I forgot to come and visit you yesterday Ploppy," said Spoony when she had got her breath back, "My Mummy and Daddy had a terrible time with the wildhairy cattle. They got out and so did the sheep and we tried to round them up but they kept getting all mixed up again and then we had to try to catch the wildhairies and stuff and I completely forgot to come and visit you until it was too late to come. I'm awfully sorry. Did you mind?"

Ploppy was still so pleased at having his new friend back that he wouldn't even have minded if Willow and Hazel had turned up again. "Oh I thought you'd probably be busy," he said, which was sort-of true, "so I just waited for you." "Did you have anybody to talk to?" asked Spoony.

"Oh.... not really," said Ploppy, "nobody important anyway. I just took the day off from hunting and had a nice sit down in the sun."

"Poo, I wish my Mummy and Daddy and I had had time for a nice day off. We had to run around flapping until supper time."

"Supper time?" said Ploppy, still not sure what suppertime would be.

"Yes, we had leftovers."

"Leftovers," said Ploppy matter-of-factishly, as if he knew what that might mean.. Wlves never have anything left after they've eaten because they always eat it all so they don't need a word for something that never exists and Ploppy had rarely had enough to eat in his whole life , "Leftovers? What's leftovers?"

"Yes leftovers. You know, when you've got a great big dinner and you can't eat it all so you keep what's left for tomorrow." Spoony noticed that Ploppy was beginning to look quite dizzy. The idea of having more food than he could eat at one go was something that he could never have imagined and it just made his thinkybrain go all spinny. Talking about food seemed to have this effect on him so she opened up her little bag and said, "I brought you some of my daddy's nice bread and cheese Would you like some?"

Ploppy immediately began to shake all over and dribble. He was too polite to grab or anything like that, but the sight of all this food made it very difficult to remember his manners. Spoony broke off a bit of bread and offered it to him. He took it very gently and politely from her hand using his best politeness that he knew how to do and held it for a polite moment between his great long and sparklingly white fangs. Then, unable to contain himself, he suddenly chomped it up and swallowed it so fast that Spoony hardly had time to see it disappear. Next she broke off a bit of her Daddy's nice wildhairycowmilkcheese and only just got her fingers out of the way in time as the wolf's giant jaws clopped it from mid-air where Spoony had left it. She carried on breaking off pieces of bread and cheese and flicking them towards Ploppy. He just kept on chomping and chomping with his big stupid grin on his face. Spoony had to be careful not to give the wolf all her bread and cheese because she was pretty hungry too so she broke off a few pieces and chomped away in time with the wolf and in a wolfish sort of way. It was the sort of chomping with your mouth open that grown-ups don't like you to do because it is not strictly polite table manners but it seemed to be acceptable wolf manners and anyway it made the bread and cheese even more enjoyable.

By the time the bread and cheese was finished they both had full tummies and they sat down once again on the rock at the top of the mountain. Spoony took her logdolly out of the bag so that Ploppy could say hello again, which he did. He was so pleased to have new friends that he wasn't in the least bit bothered that one of them was a skinny little human and the other was a bit of stick. It almost made it even better to know that Hazel and Willow would have been disgusted at the idea of a stick for a friend. The sun was beaming down and the whole place had a nice warm cosy glow to it. It was spring and birds were singing and busy with nesting and bumblebees and insects were busy with buzzing and humming around. The breeze ruffled the leaves of the birch trees which sparkled in the sun and the whole place seemed to have a nice pleasant, happy sort of restful hum to it. Spoony decided to hum along.

"Hm hum hum dehum, Humm hum dehum, Dehum dehum, Hum dehum."

Ploppy decided to hum along too although he had never tried it before.

"Wooooooooooo-oof, Wooooooooo, Woooooooooooooo, Uff."

It was quite good humming for a first try even if it was a bit on the wooey side for a proper hum. "I like humming," said Ploppy.

"Hmm," hummed Spoony nodding her head, "It's a nice hummy place to be."

"Yes you can be and hum. You can hummybe like a bumblybee," said Ploppy being clever.

"Let's all hum together," said Spoony and she and Ploppy and the bees and insects and the mountain all hummed happily away.

After a while they had hummed themselves to a standstill so Spoony and Ploppy just sat and listened to the bees and the mountain humming. It had become quite a loud hum. It seemed as if even the rock they were sitting on was humming. They looked at each other as it suddenly dawned on them that the rock of the Galloot was indeed humming.

"Poo," said Spoony, "A magicly humming galloot[39]."

Suddenly, the hum became a low rumble right beneath them, right from deep inside the very rock upon which they sat. It got more and more noticeable and then it seemed to form itself into a voice. "You've stopped," it seemed to say in a low rumbly, hummy way.

Spoony looked at Ploppy and Ploppy looked at Spoony. "Poo!!" they both said surprisishedly jumping to their feet and looking down at the rock.

"Hmm," hummed the voice. It wasn't so much a voice as a murmur they thought. It was a murmur just like the murmur you hear on a hot summer's afternoon when the bees are busy and the birds are singing and the leaves are rustling in the breeze. Which was why they hadn't noticed it before. Except that it also seemed to be a voice. Well, not quite a voice, but when it murmured you could hear what it was saying.

"You've stopped. Why have you stopped?" it murmured.

"Poo!" said Ploppy a bit frightened, "A magicly talkhumming Galloot."

"There's somebody inside our galloot," said Spoony. Ploppy just stood there with his eyebrows raised and his ears on top of his head. He would have liked to run from it but he couldn't work out how you would run away from the ground unless you could fly.

---

39. Magic Galloot: as we've already discussed, there are many Galloots in the countryside, big and small, but people just seem not to notice them for what they are. This is a shame because all of them are magical and some of them still contain treasure that has yet to be found. I have a list of these but I'm not prepared to hand it over just yet. I also have some Galloot treasure and I'm keeping it. So there.

"Poo!" said Spoony, "I never heard the ground talking before."

"Me neither," said Ploppy.

"Not surprising. You probably didn't listen before," said the voice in the mountain.

"How did you get stuck inside a mountain?" Spoony was quite concerned that somebody was trapped inside the mountain.

"I'm not stuck," murmured the voice, "I'm me. And I'm a galloot, not a mountain."

"See," said Ploppy, still a bit nervous, "I told you it were a magicly galloot."

"Honestly," murmured the galloot, "You Lummoxes are no use whatever. Now, can we get on with our humming It was going so well. You get a bit fed up with only the bees to hum with."

"How did you know he was a Lummox?" asked Spoony.

"Easy to spot really, they're a pretty sorry bunch for a wolf pack. Mind you, in my young day, well we had proper wolves in my young day. Hm hum hum dehum...." The Galloot was off humming away to himself and Spoony and Ploppy listened carefully in case it hummed some more words. It did. "Well, let's get humming," it said and the two of them joined in. They were a bit nervous at first, never having hummed along with a Galloot before but it was such a good hum that after a bit the three of them began to really enjoy it.

"Jolly good hum that was," said the Galloot after a while. "I think the Lummox woohumming adds a special extra something, it's better than his howling." Ploppy felt very proud at this backhanded compliment and looked around to see where the special extra something might be.

"Yes," agreed Spoony thinking how pleased her Mummy and Daddy would be when she told them she had a magic humming Galloot for a friend as well as a Hairy Lummox. "Were you here the other day? We didn't hear you humming then."

"I only hum when I get to know people. By the way, I think we should get properly introduced," said the Galloot.

"Oh yes," said Spoony who had forgotten her manners, "My name is..."

"Spoony Tooth." interrupted the Galloot.

" ... and this is ...'

"Ploppy Hairylummox," interrupted the Galloot again, "I heard you talking the other day."

"It's not really polite to eavesdrop," said Spoony, who had some cheek because she did this all the time at home. Ploppy nodded in agreement even though he had never had any friends to eavesdrop on and wasn't quite sure what it entailed. Ploppy thought Spoony was very brainy, which, as you know, she wasn't and it just went to show how even more not brainy Ploppy was than even Spoony.

"It's hard not to eavesdrop people who are sitting on top of you."

"I suppose so," said Spoony, seeing that this wasn't all that unreasonable an excuse for eavesdropping, "We didn't know that gallootses could talk. Did you know that peoples and Lummoxes can talk, and to each other as well? We didn't did we Ploppy?" Spoony was still very pleased with being able to talk to a wolf and the novelty hadn't worn off one bit.

"No we didlint," said Ploppy, "I was going to eat Spoony for my dinner but now she's my bestly friend in the whole everness."

"That's nice," said the Galloot, "but actually peoples, I mean people and wolves can't usually talk to one another. It can usually only happen with the help of a magic galloot."

"Poo," said Spoony, a little bit concerned that she'd only been able to talk to Ploppy because she'd had help from part of the landscape.

"That must be why you were making cackley human noises when we were saying goodbye the other day," said Ploppy.

"Cackley noises?" said Spoony, a bit hurt. She gave him one of her looks but she was quite worried, "Mister Magic Galloot, will Ploppy not be able to speak to me if he comes home for supper? He wants to meet my mummy and daddy. Wouldn't he be able to speak to anybody, not even me?"

"Well … not usually. I don't usually bother with that. I usually only want to hear what folks might want to say if they could talk to one another," hummed the Galloot, "You seemed to get along quite well. Most don't."

"Yes we did," said Spoony, "Ploppy didn't eat me even though he is extremely dainjlious."

"Poo!" said Ploppy, quite proud to be described as dainjlious but relieved that he wasn't really because he would have hated to have eaten Spoony.

"Hmmm," hmmmed the Galloot, "well you could always come here now and again and we could all talk to one another and do a bit of humming!" Truth to tell, the Galloot was sometimes a bit lonely.

"Oh yes!" said Spoony cheerfully because she really did like coming to the Magic Galloot. She sat down on the rock again and Ploppy copied her although he was still ready to run for it, just in case. "But what if we want to make arrangements?"

"Yes, we might want to make an appointment to come here and visit you." Ploppy had been using his wolfcraftythinkybrain.

"Hmmm," hmmmed the Galloot again, "Well, I suppose if you promise to come and visit me sometimes then I could magic up some special Everywhere Talking Magic for you." The Galloot was trying to make it sound difficult but actually, Galloots can do all sorts of clever magic if they want.

"What about my Mummy and Daddy?" asked Spoony, pushing her luck, "Will your Galloot magic work for them too."

"I suppose you can already talk to your Mummy and Daddy," hummed the Magic Galloot a bit impatiently.

"No I meant Ploppy… talk to them I mean," Spoony was getting excited, "so that he can tell them everything he knows and stuff and we can daft up some ideas for them."

"I suppose it might work… a bit," hummed the Galloot, "Are you related to them?"

"Yes," replied Spoony using some brow furrowing to remember what 'related' meant, "they're my Mummy and Daddy!"

"Well it might, if they make the effort," said the Galloot, making it sound difficult but he quite liked this funny little human and her hairy friend and he decided to let them talk to whoever they pleased; it was the most magic he'd done in a long time.

"Oh goody!" cried Spoony and she leapt to her feet and danced and sang, "I've got a special talkhumming Magic Galloot and a special wootalking Ploppy Hairylummox!"

And Ploppy did the same, only he sang, "I've got a special talkhumming Magicly Galloot and a special Spoonytooth!"

And the Magic Galloot, who was quite pleased because he hadn't really had any proper friends for a couple of million years hummed, "I've got a special Spoonytooth and a special Ploppy Hairylummox," in a very cheery springtime sort of hum, "I must hum, it's jolly nice having proper humming friends again. The bees are alright but they are too busybuzzybossy and you can't get butterflies to hum no matter how hard you try." Spoony lay down on the rock and put her arms around it and gave it a cuddle and hummed for a bit, even though rocks aren't the cuddliest things in the world.

"Oooh," hummed the Galloot, "that was nice, a humcuddle." He'd never been cuddled before, he'd only ever been sat on.

Spoony and Ploppy suggested all sorts of different creatures that might be good for humming along with and the Galloot gave his opinion on all of them. It seemed that over the ages he had hummed and been friends with just about every type of creature you could mention and some that you couldn't mention. "Well, the deer are pretty useless, they just run away. The foxes are too stuck up. Moles are all right but they don't come out often enough." He went on for a bit describing all sorts of different animals' humming ability. "Best ever hummer, present company excepted of course," he said, "was the Giant Ferocious Jawclanging Terrordragon, back when I was just a recently extinct volcano and had only just cooled off." Spoony and Ploppy looked at one another, none of this made much sense, "She could hum something terrible. Excellent ferocious roarhumming and huge jawclanging…. When she got going it was something to hear."

"Ploppy can do ferocious roarhumming and jawclanging, he's very dainjlious," interrupted Spoony. She was very proud of Ploppy.

"With all due respect," hummed the Galloot emphatically, "and no offence intended, there has *never, ever* been anything in the world more dainjlious, I mean dangerous, than a Giant Ferocious Jawclanging Terrordragon. As tall as a tree (actually, as tall as a tall tree), with huge long, powerful hind legs and a massive long tail and giant jaws with teeth the size of parsnips. Trouble was, there was only ever the two of us, she ate everybody else who tried to join in."

"Poo," said Spoony, and Ploppy looked around nervously to see if there were any giant ferocious whatever-they-were-calleds coming along to hum and eat other hummers. He didn't want to be eaten.

"Oh, you needn't worry about Giant Ferocious Jawclanging Terrordragons[40] they went extinct millions of years ago. Pity really."

"Phew," phewed Spoony, quite relieved, "did they breathe fire?" Her Daddy had told her fairy stories about dragons.

"Didn't need to breathe fire, dainjlious, I mean dangerous enough as it was. They could get so dangerously angry that if they couldn't bite anybody in two and eat them then they would get even angrier and quite often got angry enough to bite off their own arms just for spite..." Spoony remembered being this angry when she was very little and threatening to bite her arm. Her Daddy had told her just to bite it as hard as she pleased. Nowadays she was much too grown up for tantrums, not that she had ever been any good at them anyway what with her notoriously short span of attention.[41] "Eventually," continued the Galloot, "they evolved tiny little short arms so that they couldn't bite them off. This made them even angrier and you should have just seen them if somebody mentioned short stubby arms. Talk about throw a complete flakeywobbler. But we used to have some lovely times humming together."

Spoony could see that the Galloot was going to get all soppy and sentimental so she asked cheerfully, "Would you like to come home for supper with us Mister Magic Galloot?"

"Can't I'm afraid, stuck here for another couple of hundred million years until I get eroded away. Then I'll get to crop up somewhere new, I expect. Might come up as flood lava next time, make a bigger show of it."

"You could crop up at Spoony's for supper tomorrow then," said Ploppy who had no idea how long a hundred million years was.

---

40. Terrordragons: nowadays these creatures go by a slightly different name but the interesting thing is that despite the passage of time since Spoony and Ploppy learned about them, even to this day they are still extinct.

41. Tantrums: tantrums take quite a lot of effort and concentration and it's quite surprising, not to mention commendable, to see somebody as young as two managing to keep one up for as long as they do. Only certain kinds of adults do tantrums. They are: supermodels, movie stars, political dictators, sales managers and parents when the car breaks down ... again.

"Maybe some other time, in a couple of hundred million years," hummed the Galloot, being a bit more practical, "but thank you very much indeed for the invitation."

It wasn't for nothing that Spoony had mentioned supper. All this humming and making new friends was hungry work and her tummy had been trying to butt into the conversation for some time now. It knew that if Ploppy and she did not set off for the village quite soon then they might be late for supper and that would never do, especially if her mummy had remembered to make extra supper for Ploppy. "I suppose we had better get going or we'll be late for supper," she said, and for once remembering her being-polite-to-grown-ups manners, "It's been very nice meeting you Mister Magic Galloot and thank you very much for helping Ploppy and me to talk to each other."

"Woowoo growff," woofed Ploppy and Spoony gave him a surprised and worried look because he was talking wolf talk again.

"Sorry. Just my little joke," hummed the Magic Galloot.

"Thank you very much indeed," repeated Ploppy not seeing the joke.

"Now, don't forget to come back and visit me as soon as you are able. We can do some more humming and Spoony, you can report back on how your parents like talking to a wolf."

"Oh yes, we'll be back as soon as we can," they both said and Spoony picked up her bag and her logdolly and skipped off down the hill humming and singing a new Galloot tune she was composing with Ploppy trotting to catch her up and adding the odd woohum to help the tune long.

"Goodbye Mister Magic Galloot," called Spoony over her shoulder.

"Goodlybye Mister Magicly Galloot," woo-oofed Ploppy.

"Hmmm hmm," hummed the Magic Galloot.

Chapter 5

Danger! Wolf Attack!

Spoony Tooth and Ploppy Hairylummox skipped and trotted along together through the forest chatting away happily. You may have forgotten already that Ploppy Hairylummox, although not a particularly big wolf and indeed although a particularly skinny and sorry example was, being a wolf, still particularly big when it came down to it and especially when compared with somebody as small and skinny as Spoony. Consequently, even Spoony's jaunty lollopy (but quite brisk) way of walking had difficulty keeping up with Ploppy's lopey, shambley way of getting along and she had to give several reminders to the wolf to slow down a bit. Ploppy really only had four speeds: very-slow-sneaking-up-on-things speed, shambling-along-aimlessly speed (which was too fast for Spoony), chasing-after-things-to-catch-them-for-supper speed (very fast and also used for crazy-mad-joyful), and running-away-afraid speed (which was his fastest by quite a bit). Ploppy wasn't very brainy and had never thought of trying new speeds for getting along. He tried slowing down to his sneaky speed but this made him too slow and he kept getting left behind so he had to trot fast to pass Spoony and then slow down and let her pass him. This made conversation difficult so Spoony tried hanging on to Ploppy's tail and being pulled along.

The trouble with this was that it forced Ploppy to try all his different ways of loping along and it was very difficult for Spoony to match his rhythm. Sometimes he loped along with his front feet going at twice the rate of his back feet and sometimes the other way around. At other times he loped with both his right feet then both his left feet. They made very good headway but eventually Spoony tripped and had to let go. Ploppy suggested carrying Spoony, so he picked her up in his teeth by her woollen smock and carried her along like a cat carries a kitten. But when Spoony started to chat to Ploppy he chatted back and, of course Spoony fell to the ground with a thud.

Eventually they managed to find a speed that suited them both. Spoony showed Ploppy how to walk along in a going nowhere in particular sort of way, which she was good at and when he had got the hang of it, it matched her alternative jaunty lollopy (but quite brisk) way of walking perfectly. The wolf was even more impressed with Spoony than before. She seemed to know just about everything in the world worth knowing and he concentrated as hard as he could on perfecting his new walking speed.

The creatures of the forest that Spoony had said good morning to earlier in the day were all a bit surprised to see a little girl walking through the trees beside a wolf. Not many of them really knew what a little girl was but they certainly knew what a wolf was so they took the precaution of diving for cover rather than staying to hear Spoony greet them. They didn't want to get eaten but then, they didn't know that Ploppy wasn't much good at hunting and probably couldn't have caught any of them to eat them anyway. Still, Spoony said, "Good morning!" to all the rustling and bounding she heard in the undergrowth. The fact that it was the afternoon didn't matter to Spoony although Ploppy didn't understand why she should be saying, "Good Morning!" in the afternoon to things that weren't there anymore. He just thought it was another brainy thing that Spoony could do, so he did it too. None of the forest creatures had ever heard a wolf say "Good Morning!", even in the morning never mind in the afternoon.

Presently the forest began to thin out and they could see the village not far away beyond the river and the fields.

"I think we'll be in plenty of time for supper," said Spoony, "I hope my Mummy has made one of her special pies."

"Yes, me too," said Ploppy, not knowing in the least what a pie might be let alone a *special* pie but if it was half as good as flatandchewybread or wildhairymilkcheese then it would be wondleyful. However, the wolf was beginning to get a bit nervous about visiting the village. It was quite scary to think that he would be visiting the sort of place which, these days, all Lummoxes thought might be very dangerous, the den of a pack of humans. Also, Ploppy wasn't sure that he really wanted to meet Spoony's Mummy. Anybody brave (or crazy) enough to go near wildhairy cattle must be completely crazy dainjlious.

Spoony didn't notice Ploppy getting nervous because she was very keen to introduce him to her mummy and daddy so she marched on as quickly as she could. She made for the stepping stones across the river and when they got there Ploppy asked if he hadn't better wait here while Spoony went off and saw if it was safe for him to visit. Ploppy didn't get where he was today without being entirely justifiably as scaredy cat[42] as can be. He wasn't very sure of stepping-stones either. Spoony reached up and gave him one of her big confidence boosting hugs and reassured him that her Mummy and Daddy had had a very trying time of it over the last day or so and a visit from a Hairylummox was just what they needed to cheer them up. She also explained that they were going to cross the river by stepping from one stone to the next and wouldn't have to get their feet wet. "It's easy," she said, demonstrating, "you just put one foot on the first stone – like this," and she stepped onto the first stone, "and your other foot on the next stone, and so on until you're across." She stopped on the middle stone and said, "Come on, it's easy, one foot at a time." The wolf was looking a bit worried. He stood nervously on the edge of the river and in no time at all Spoony was on the opposite bank.

Now you may not have taken particular notice, as Spoony hadn't, but wolves have got four legs. And when a wolf walks along, unlike humans, who have only two legs (which is easy to organise), it has to step with a back leg, then the front leg on the opposite side, then the other back leg, then the final front leg and so on. It's a lot to think about and is one of the reasons that Ploppy Hairylummox didn't have too many walking speeds. Just the thought of trying to work out which leg should go on which stepping stone made his head go all twirly inside. He would have preferred to bound across the stones from one to the other, or even wade across, but he had great faith in Spoony and if she said the correct method was one foot at a time on each stone then he would give it a go. He decided to take off from a front leg, put a back foot on the first stone, a front foot on the second, the other back foot on the next and so on…. Once he had rehearsed this in his thinkybrain he set off and immediately lost count … the front foot goes on a back leg … no, a back foot goes on the front stone and a second stone goes on the back foot … no, wait a minute … trip … scrabble … skite[43] … sploosh! He was completely upside down in the cold water and it took a lot of flailing and splashing to get his feet under him and stand up in the river with the water coming up almost to his tummy. He had got quite a surprise even though he had expected something like that to happen. However, he thought he'd give it another

---

42. Scaredy cat: when you think of it, this expression is quite silly because cats aren't scared of anything. If they get into a situation where they ought to be scared, they simply make hissy, snarly noises, spit at you and slash you to bits with their sharp claws.

43. Skite: like a slip but much more so and much more likely to end in disaster. For instance, if you slip on the kitchen floor, you'll probably regain your balance but a skite will happen so suddenly that you'll spin upside down so fast that your socks will fly off and one of them will remain lost until somebody does some dusting.

go and instead of simply wading across the rest of the river, he went back to where he'd started from. Spoony waited on the opposite bank, worried that he might not be able to get across.

Eventually, after a lot of scrabbling and splooshing and splashing as well as much falling into the water, Ploppy got fed up with trying the one foot at a time method and bounded across from stone to stone in an ordinary sort of wolf manner. Spoony was well impressed with this method and decided to try going back across using it. She bounded from the bank with the intention of landing on her front paws (hands) and then getting her feet on the stone behind her hands (paws) as Ploppy had done. It was a miserable failure and when she did get her feet under her, the water came up to her tummy too. Ploppy jumped in beside Spoony and they both splashed around until Spoony got the shivers from the cold water and they climbed out.

"Poo!" said Spoony, "My feet have gone pink again. Poo, I've gone all clean." In those days it wasn't thought necessary for children to be clean all the time and by the time spring came around most children had forgotten what clean was. In those days being too clean was considered a bit sissy and overly fastidious[44].

Ploppy was busy shaking himself and so much water flew off his shaggy coat in all directions when he shook himself that the sunshine made a rainbow all round him. Spoony thought he looked very special, a wolf with his very own rainbow.

"Poo! look at you Ploppy. You've changed colour, you've gone all clean too." Indeed, all the grimy stains and muddy and crusty smelly bits had been washed off the wolf's fur and even though he was soaking wet he looked quite handsome. His fur was a lovely silvery-flecked grey and he had dark fur around his face and his ears were almost black. His underneath was pale grey, almost white, and his feet were almost white too. Spoony thought he was quite the most beautiful thing she had ever seen.

"Gosh," said Ploppy, looking himself over, "I've gone all clean. I look like a proper Lummox."

"You're my best clean Hairylummox," sang Spoony, who was even more pleased at having a handsome (if a bit on the scrawny and skinny side) wolf for a friend.

"You're my best clean purpley SpoonyTooth," sang Ploppy who was very pleased at having a beautiful friend who was clean and skinny too.

"Purple?" puzzled Spoony and she looked down to see that her Daddy's special purple dye was running out of her smock and turning her legs all purpley pink.

All in all they made a fine colour-coordinated pair: a silvery grey wolf and a pinky purple little girl, so they made their way towards the village feeling very special even if the only

---

44. Fastidious: on old-fashioned word which means very fussy indeed but which is mainly used these days to describe motor cyclists. You might have to work that out.

62

ones so far that knew they were special were them.

As they approached the village, Spoony could see that there were no sheep out that shouldn't be out and the place looked quite peaceful in the late afternoon spring sunshine. As you know, the Tooth household was at the wrong end of the village and so, of course, it was the nearest house to the river. Spoony pointed it out to Ploppy and said she could see her mummy walking toward the wildhairies with her optimistic afternoon milking pail. "That's my house, and that's my bedroom in the chimley and that's my mummy going to milk the wildhairies," she said.

"Poo!" said Ploppy who would quite have liked at this point not to bother meeting somebody as dainjlious as a wildhairy tamer.

"Come on," cried Spoony, "let's run up and surprise her!" and she set off at a skip and a trot calling, "Cooee!" "Mummy!" and "Wait for us!" and "Come and meet Ploppy Hairylummox, Mummy, Mummy!" with Ploppy trotting along behind, trying to skip with four legs instead of two a few feet behind. It was another new way of walking; he was learning so many useful things from Spoony.

Some of the other children from the village were playing near the Tooth house and one of them heard Spoony calling to her Mummy. He looked up and what he saw gave him a terrible fright. "Aaarghh everybody, Spoony Tooth is being hunted by a giant wolf!" All the children panicked and started to shout as they ran away, "Run Spoony, run, run as fast as you can!" And Spoony, who was not quick on the uptake and always liked to show everybody how fast she could run (although nobody ever had the heart to tell her she couldn't run particularly fast and usually let her win at races when it was her turn to win) obligingly broke into a flat-out run. The wolf broke into a loping along canter to keep up. "Run Spoony run!" the children cried as they belted back to the village to raise the alarm, completely forgetting (as is entirely understandable under the circumstances) to tell Mrs Tooth that her Spoony was being attacked by a giant wolf. "Wolf attack, wolf attack!" they shouted as they ran up the village.

Dinner

"Hello Mummy," cried Spoony as she ran into the yard, "come and meet Ploppy Hairylummox." She hadn't noticed that Ploppy had not followed her into the yard. He had had a sudden dose of nerves and shyness and had stopped at the gate. Actually, *sudden dose of nerves* doesn't really describe how he felt. He was terrorfied and was shaking like a leaf and his teeth were chattering and he really wanted to run away; but he was so sure that Spoony was the cleverest person in the world that he hung around just outside the gate, keeping an eye open in case he got mown down by one of the wildhairy cattle that Spoony had told him about.

"Hello Spoony. Where have you been all day?" said Mummy Tooth, "Goodness me, you're all wet and you've gone all clean and purpley." She gave Spoony a big hug and a kiss. "And you don't smell so sooty today. "

"I went to the Magic Galloot to bring back the hairy Lummox, come and meet him," and she took her Mummy, who was not very sure what to expect, by the hand and led her to the gate in the hedge. "Mummy, I would like to introduce," (Spoony had been quite well brought up so, she knew how to be polite and formal) "Ploppy Hairylummox. Ploppy Hairylummox, this is my mummy, Mummy Tooth."

Ploppy was sitting nervously to attention with his big paws neatly together and his tail wagging and he was blushing from ear to ear under his fur. Mrs Tooth stopped in her tracks and stared at Ploppy with her mouth open. Even sitting down he was quite big and was almost eye to eye with Mummy Tooth. Being a hardened campaigner, what with wildhairy taming and all, Mrs Tooth wasn't easy to frighten so it took a minute for her to react.

"Aaargh!" she reacted, "Wolf attack, wolf attack!" Throwing her milking bucket up in the air she turned to run around in circles panicking. Fortunately, she didn't get far because the bucket, which seemed to know where it belonged, came back down on her head and she couldn't see where she was going so she just stood there panicking on the spot and making muffled booming wolf attack noises. Ploppy didn't know where to look.

"Mummy," said Spoony taking her by the hand and shouting up into the bucket on her head, "it's not a wolf attack. It's only Ploppy Hairylummox. He's not dainjlious, I mean dangerlous." At this Mummy Tooth stopped panicking and took the bucket off her head.

"H-h-h-h-how do you do Mr Hairylummox," she said politely and shakily held out her shaky hand-shaking hand to shake hands with the wolf.

"Woo woo woof," said Ploppy bashfully but in the correct polite Hairylummox wolf manner and gave Mrs Tooth's hand a sniff to check it. Having satisfied himself that it smelled quite safe, he gave it one of his slobbery licky kisses which was not strictly correct wolf behaviour because in wolf company you're supposed to sniff one another first so a licky kiss is considered a bit too familiar but he wanted to make friends fast so that he wouldn't have to have the bucket on his head.

"I must apologise," said Mrs Tooth, "I've never met a Hairylummox before but you do look ever so much like a wolf." (Not that she had ever met a wolf before.) Ploppy was so used to being told what a poor effort he was at being a wolf that he took this to be a compliment and blushed again under his fur and his ears went all floppy and bashful.

"Oh a Hairylummox *is* a wolf Mummy," said Spoony, "and Ploppy is the best and most dainjlious wolf of them all, aren't you Ploppy?" Ploppy's face was getting so red under his fur that it began to shine through.

"Dangerous wooolf!" said Mummy, her voice beginning to show signs of surprise again, "I thought you said it was a Hairylummox!"

"He *IS* a Hairylummox mummy..."

"Phew!" said Mummy.

"And he's a wolf."

"Aaaargh!" screamed Mummy Tooth, "Wolf attack! Wolf attack!"

"Oh for goodness sake!" said Spoony, quite disappointed and embarrassed by her mummy's behaviour. She picked up the bucket and handed it to her mummy who instinctively put it on her head to hide from the wolf. "Come on Ploppy, let's go and meet Daddy," said Spoony and to calm her Mummy down she took her by the hand and led the two of them towards her Daddy's dafting shed. Mrs Tooth kept lifting the bucket up a bit to see if the wolf was still there only to find that he was looking at her and giving her his big stupid happy grin with his tongue hanging out the side of his mouth. He was really impressed with the way Mrs Tooth had managed to get the bucket on her head first try and with how fetching it looked now that it was back on, and how calm and friendly she seemed in comparison to certain wolves of his acquaintance such as Hazel and Willow. Humans didn't seem to be as bad as they were made out to be, just a bit noisy.

Mrs Tooth didn't know how to respond to Ploppy as he grinned at her. She could see his huge fangs which made her a bit nervous again so she gave him one of her own big stupid friendly grins and flopped her tongue out the side of her mouth too, just to be on the safe side. Then she let the bucket down over her head again just to be on the even safer side. Spoony could see that they were getting along famously.

Daddy Tooth could be heard muttering away to himself in the dafting shed. He had been working hard all day trying to daft up a famous new sheep catching device which involved making lots of things with his special bodging machine. As a result he had produced a giant snow storm of wood shavings and sawdust. He was completely covered from head to foot and looked like a tall skinny snowman. Spoony skipped into the shed ahead of the others and was not in the least surprised at what she saw. "Look Daddy! I've brought Ploppy Hairylummox to meet you. He's staying for supper."

"Oh that's nice Spoony." Tooth the Daft always said this no matter what Spoony said or did because he thought that she was ever such a special little girl. This was nothing special as most daddies think that about their little girls. He walked up to the door and gave her a special hug and a kiss. He was quite intrigued to find out what a Hairylummox was, if indeed it wasn't just one of Spoony's made up pretend things. Then he saw Ploppy grinning with his great big teeth showing and wagging his recently washed big fluffy tail. "Aaaaargh!" yelled Daddy and jumped up in the air with fright making a big cloud of sawdust rise up around him, "Danger! Wolf attack!"

"Yike, Squeal, Whine, Yelp," went Ploppy, very loud indeed, getting a terrible fright,

"A nasty scary snow monster,"

To everybody except Spoony it sounded like "Growl, Vicious Bark-Snarl." Ploppy's legs were already scrabbling to get a grip and make a run for it.

As you might expect, when Mummy and Daddy Tooth heard this they panicked again and ran around yelling "Wolf attack! Danger, run away!" and everybody got in a right state until Spoony had to yell, "For goodness sake!" and stamped her foot, which was so unlike her that they all stopped and pulled themselves together.

Well, of course, when they pulled themselves together and Spoony re-introduced everybody and reassured them all that nobody was dangerous, it didn't take long for them to make friends and Mrs Tooth invited Ploppy into the house for some soup. Ploppy had some difficulty understanding what Mr and Mrs Tooth were saying and it tended to sound a bit jumbled and cackley. Most of the trouble stemmed from the fact that Ploppy didn't have a clue what was being said even when he could make out the words. What, for instance, was soup?

And it wasn't easy for the Tooths to make out what Ploppy was saying either. They couldn't make head nor tail of his mixture of woofs and growly noises, tail wags and ear wags and so on. The Galloot magic obviously didn't work all that well at this distance from the Galloot and when Ploppy was talking to Mummy and Daddy Tooth, Spoony had to translate some of the time. But when they all took their time and put in the required amount of effort, it wasn't so bad. Ploppy didn't mind anyway. He thought it was utterly wondleyful to meet a mummy and daddy who weren't fierce and to have friends who didn't sniff you where you'd rather not be sniffed or bite your ear or make unkind remarks.

While they were chatting and Mummy and Daddy Tooth were asking Ploppy all sorts of embarrassing questions about his family, to which he answered in as growly and difficult to understand a way as possible so that he wouldn't have to admit to having been losted deliberately by his own pack, Daddy Tooth went over to the fireplace and began to blow the embers until a few small flames began to flicker. He put on some of his curly wood shavings and a few dry twigs and presently there was enough of a fire for Mummy Tooth to heat the big pot of soup she had made earlier in the day. Ploppy, who like all wild creatures was very respectful (or in his case, more accurately, downright terrified) of fire (not that he had ever actually seen it), stood up and retreated to a corner of the room and shivered and shook, trying not to look too scared.[45] However, Spoony reassured Ploppy that it was an everyday sort of thing and eventually he came back into the centre of the

---

45. Fear of fire: You may have read elsewhere that fire was used as a way to frighten off dangerous wild creatures back in the olden days. This is an unfortunate piece of misinformation and sadly, even today, people on safari in Africa will light campfires and sit around them with their backs to the danger thinking they're safe. Well, it doesn't sound at all like good safety practice when you think of it and may account for the odd safari person disappearing inexplicably in the middle of a campfire sing-along. A campfire, even with the addition of some twit with a guitar singing John Denver songs won't scare away a hungry lion. If you really want to scare away hungry lions, you sing Kumbaya.

room although he wasn't very sure that he wanted to eat burning soup. Everybody sat cross-legged around the fire (except for Ploppy who could only manage lying down with his front paws crossed) waiting for the soup to heat up. The Tooths didn't have a dinner table. In fact, the dinner table as we now know it today was one of Tooth the Daft's better inventions and it was such a good idea that it caught on all over the village. This, as you will remember, was how Mummy Tooth had managed to get rid of some of Daddy Tooth's beautifully made wheels: being odd shapes, they made better tables, particularly the square ones. Unfortunately, Mummy Tooth had also had a very good offer for the Tooths' very own round table so she had sold it too. So the Tooth's dinner table was now performing exceptionally well as a wheel on a big wheel barrow belonging to a neighbour. Happily, Daddy Tooth was the only one who had failed to see the irony in this.

When the soup was ready Mrs Tooth gave everybody a large wooden bowl of soup and Ploppy, being a guest, got a particularly splendid helping. He had never eaten soup before, let alone from a bowl or for that matter ever used a wooden spoon before. Spoony was very good with a spoon (as you'd expect) and showed him how it was done: she picked up her spoon, scooped up some soup, blew on it and shoveled it enthusiastically into her mouth. It was jolly good soup and just right for a hungry little girl who had been out all day discovering. Sometimes it was hard to tell the difference between Mrs Tooth's thick soup and her thin stew and indeed quite often the only clue was whether it was served with a spoon or a fork[46]. Mummy and Daddy looked on as Ploppy tried to get to grips with soup eating. He copied everything that Spoony had done. He picked up the spoon (with his big wolf teeth), plunged it into the soup and managed to scoop up a few dribbles. Then he tried to blow on it through his teeth but after a few tries settled on blowing down his nose. Then came the difficult bit. How can you get soup into your mouth when you're holding the other end of the spoon with your teeth? He decided to try flicking the soup up in the air, dropping the spoon and clopping the drops of soup as they fell. Well, after several tries Ploppy was getting soup all over himself and Spoony had to fetch him an old sack as a napkin because his newly clean fur was getting completely souped up. Eventually he gave up and just plunged his great big mouth into the bowl and chomped and slurped and gulped until he had completely finished the soup and licked the bowl so clean that it wouldn't have to be washed (but Mummy Tooth washed it anyway).

Just to be friendly and to make Ploppy feel at home, Spoony licked her plate too and Mummy and Daddy Tooth watched in a bemused sort of way and Mrs Tooth wondered

---

46. Forks and spoons: forks were another of Spoony's dad's inventions. At that time, everybody ate with their fingers but he got fed up trying to fish the yummy bits of boiling hot stew out of his bowl without burning his fingers so he went and got a bit of sharp stick to poke them with. The next day he went to the dafting shed and invented the fork.
  You might wonder why he hadn't used his spoon for this purpose but he had yet to invent the spoon as we know it. The spoon had already been sort-of invented for stirring and at that time was called 'a bit of stick' but Spoony's daddy had invented a new type of 'bit of stick' that could scoop things up. Both ideas caught on fast and he sold quite a few. But nobody gave him any credit, saying things like, "Well, I could have done that."

what had happened to her daughter's nice table manners. Of course, she hadn't thought that if you no longer have a table, you could hardly be expected to have table manners. (You may have noticed this at picnics where everybody's table manners go out the window just because there is no table, or window for that matter.) Anyway, both Ploppy and Spoony had finished their soup while Mr and Mrs Tooth had hardly had time to start theirs for watching the two of them. Mrs Tooth still had some rabbit pie to serve up so they offered their soup to Ploppy who just managed to stay away from it long enough to make some polite noises before diving into both bowls and gobbling it up. Then he sat up with a funny puzzled look on his face. He had never had such a full tummy in his life before and it felt quite strange.

Visitors

Mummy Tooth was just about to offer Ploppy Hairylummox and Spoony some of her famous rabbit pie when they heard a terrible kerfuffle outside and then a loud banging at the door. Spoony got to her feet and answered it. Outside were several, if not most, of the men from the village, all looking very excited and a bit scared. They were all armed with pitchforks and sickles and spades and at first glance Spoony thought that they had come to help her daddy sort the garden out.

"Oh, hello Spoony. We came to help because we heard you was bein' attacked by a giant wolf." It was Farmer Stuckie from the far end of the village. He had obviously taken charge of the rescue.

"Oh no," said Spoony quite truthfully, "I haven't been attacked by a giant wolf,. Well, not for days anyway."

"Mr Tooth," said Farmer Stuckie, hoping that he might get more sense from a grown-up, even if the grown-up in question was Tooth the Daft, "the other children swears blind that your daughter was bein' chased by a giant vicious wolf so we've come to the rescue." He looked around and it was quite plain that there hadn't been a wolf attack as they were all sitting down to supper. They didn't recognise Ploppy for what he was because he was lying down, had a sack round his neck and was covered in soup. This is not what most people expect a vicious wolf to look like.

"Oh they pwobabwy thaw Thpoony's fwiend Pwoppy the Haiwy Wummox," said Daddy Tooth, talking with his mouth full and nodding in the direction of Ploppy. Spoony gave him one of her looks because she was always being told not to talk with her mouth full.

"Pwoppee'airwumps? What's a pwoppee'airwumps?" asked Farmer Stuckie now looking directly at the pwoppee'airwumps.

"Ploppy Hairylummox," said Spoony, proudly pronouncing his name as clearly as she could, come and meet our visitors," and she brought the nervous Farmer Stuckie over to meet him halfway. Ploppy was still wearing his big sack napkin around his neck and his face was all splattered and covered with soup. He sat up straight and wagged his tail trying to look as friendly as possible. The sack went from just beneath his chin to his toes and he looked like a sack with a hairy head that's been used to mop up spilt soup.

"He don't look much like a wolf right enough," said Farmer Stuckie, "Is 'e at all dangerous?"

To Ploppy this just sounded like a lot of gruff cackley noises because the Galloot had only fixed it for Ploppy to be able to speak to Spoony and her mummy and daddy but he heard Spoony say, "He's very dainjlious but very nice." So he wagged his tail even harder. He felt very proud. To be called dainjlious, sorry, dangerous *and* nice was something he had never been called by his fellow wolves.

"Is them ploppee'airlumps, or whatever they're called, usually covered in soup and wearing a old sack?" asked one of the other villagers, being observant.

"That's the way wolfses like their soup," said Spoony.

"Wolfses? Wolfses! He's a wolf?! I thought you said he was a ploppee'airlumps!" exclaimed Farmer Stuckie and all of the other visitors repeated it, "Wolfses? Wolfses! He's a wolf?! We thought you said he was a ploppee'airlumps!" they all chorused together in a panicky sort of way, ready to get out of the door as fast as possible.

"He *is* a ploppee'airlumps, I mean his name is Ploppy Hairylummox," said Daddy Tooth, now speaking with his mouth empty, having gulped down the last mouthful. He had noticed that there was room for a lot of misunderstanding here, and was now taking charge in a very grown up manner. "He's a very special type of non-dangerous wolf," he said, sounding almost like an expert on wolves. Mrs Tooth was very proud of him.

"Oh well, if you say so Mr Tooth. But I don't think this is going to go down well with the rest of the village. What if other wolfses, I mean wolves comes to visit and we has a full blown wolf attack from his pack?"

"Oh that won't happen," put in Mrs Tooth, "Ploppy is a lone wolf."

There was a lot of muttering from the nervous rescuers at the back, "I 'eard them lone wolfses, I mean wolveses is the worst," said one of them.

Another said, "Yes, my granddad said they were the most treacherous,"

And from Mr Biglanky, who was standing at the back looking over everybody's head, "If he's a lone wolf, what's he doin' here. Shouldn't he be out in the forest bein' lone?" This was said in quite a smarty-pants sort of way. A few of the villagers nodded in agreement because it seemed like a very logical question and Mummy and Daddy Tooth were quite stumped for an answer.

"It's his day off," said Spoony using her thinkybrain to be clever.

"Quite," said Mrs Tooth with a firm nod. She was feeling very proud of her family.

"Ploppy has come to visit and we're very pleased to have him. He's entirely not dangerous and is very clever and helpful," said Daddy Tooth firmly, "But it was very kind of you to offer to help."

"Oh it were nothing really," said Farmer Stuckie being polite even if he was confused, "I suppose you know what you're doing." This was Farmer Stuckie being especially polite because he, like the rest of the village, thought that Tooth the Daft didn't have a clue what he was doing, "Well, we'll be sayin' goodnight then," After exchanging polite goodnights all over the place including to the Ploppyairlumps soupwolf, they turned and went off home to their own suppers. As they went off into the evening they could be heard discussing yet another weird Tooth happening:

"I don't hold with wolfses, I mean wolves-es myself."

"Yon Tooth the Daft is never finished makin' trouble with his daft ideas."

"Well he made my wife a nice table."

"Huh, it was meant to be a wheel," and

"I expect he'll be tryin' to sell us all a lone wolf next."

"That young Spoony of theirs, she in't half a odd child. Imagine bringin' home a wolf."

"Lone wolf, it was."

"Well I don't hold with wolvses myself,"

"I hope they keep better control of that wolf than they do of their wildhairy cattle."

"Yes, what if it got in with my sheep?"

"Never mind *your* sheep."

"I think young Spoony's a nice little girl."

"Odd child."

"Takes after her parents, *they're* odd."

"She coulda gottenetten."

And so on, but on the whole they felt very brave and pleased with themselves for having dealt with the first wolf raid on the village for many's a long year.

"Crikey!" said Ploppy after they'd all gone, "what a lot of humans, are they all in your pack?"

"Well, in a way I suppose they are, kind of," replied Spoony, not very sure whether the rest of the people from the village counted as the Tooth's pack.

"They were very cackley," said Ploppy, still sitting there with his sack round his neck and soup all over his face. Of course the Galloot's special magic didn't work for anybody other than the Tooths and Ploppy and only when they spoke to one another so he hadn't understood a word that Farmer Stuckie had said.

"Never mind that just now," said Mummy, starting to get the hang of speaking to a wolf as if he was an ordinary visitor, just like any other, "We've got supper to finlish, I mean finish." With that, she brought out the huge rabbit pie which she had rustled up in a spare minute that afternoon, the sort of thing that mummies can do.

When the wolf saw the pie his eyes just about popped out of his head and his head went all spinny and woozy. Or was it spoony and wizzy. After a big bowl of soup, his tummy was already fuller than it had ever been and when Mrs Tooth cut off a huge slice of pie and put it down in front of him all he could do was stare at it. "Don't you want any pie?" asked Spoony, already munching at her own slice.

"Pie," said the wolf looking up at Spoony. "Pie," he said again in a sort of pie trance.

"Doesn't he like rabbit pie?" said Daddy Tooth, "I would have thought a wolf would like rabbit pie."

"He likes everything," said Spoony, "but he usually only has a worm for supper."

"Pie," said Ploppy, still staring at it in a daze. He had been hypnopiesed. He lay down and rested his chin on the plate. His big long licky tongue came out and gave the slice of pie a prod. "Pie," he said drowsily, and fell sound asleep. He was happier than he had ever been since he was a tiny little Hairylummox wolf puppy. He hadn't even had to curl up tightly to keep out the cold.

"Poo!" said Spoony, who had finished her own slice of pie and was always hungry, "Can I have his pie if he's not going to eat it?"

"Spoony!" said Mummy Tooth disapprovingly, "He can have it when he's ready," and she started to tidy everything up except for Ploppy's pie because she didn't want to wake him. He was snoring in great wafts of delicious pie smell and dreaming of great pie and worm banquets.

The Wolves

After Hazel and Willow had found Ploppy on the little mountain, they had set off immediately towards the centre of pack territory to look for the rest of their wolf pack. Their job was to scout for things for the pack to hunt and to look out for danger such as other wolf packs that might move into their territory or anything else that might present a danger to the pack. After all, as well as having to find food for the adult wolves, the pack also had to look after the pack's youngsters and keep them well fed so that they could grow up healthy and be properly schooled in everything that a grown-up wolf needs to know to get on in the world. This may have a familiar ring to it because it is yet another similarity between wolves and humans.

The wolves were aware of humans living near the edge of their territory but they paid them little heed for they never came anywhere near the pack's main range. Humans after all, were generally not fully understood by wolves but they were thought to be (a) stupid (mostly true); (b) dangerous (but considering point a., not terribly); (c) dirty (quite often true, as you already know); (d) useless (mostly true, especially from a wolf point of view) and (e) inedible (probably true, but considering point [c]. not worth bothering with anyway).

However, although humans did not figure largely in the wolves' day to day business, when Hazel and Willow eventually ran into several of the other pack members, the news caused quite a stir: that they had stumbled across Ploppy and that he had been consorting with a 'deadly dangerous' and 'deadly poisonous', as Hazel insisted, 'firehuman'. Indeed, although the whole story had seemed a bit unlikely, after the usual polite welcoming that wolves always give one another (except useless wolves like Ploppy) they decided to tell the pack Alphas[47]. When wolves meet up they can tell an awful lot about where each other have been simply by sniffing one another so the rest of the wolves had had a good sniff at the two young scouts and there was no doubt about it, as well as the wormy, grubby smell of their former pack mate Ploppy, they could definitely smell the sweet, sooty smell of Spoony which had rubbed off on them from Ploppy's fur.

"What do you think we should do?" said one of the other young wolves.

"Nothing," said Willow, "Ploppy's a complete idiot, he made up the whole story."

"But there's definitely a smell of humans and their fire."

"He probably rolled in something," said Willow, who was feeling particularly annoyed with having to deal with anything to do with Ploppy.

"We'd better inform The Boss," said Hazel

"I agree," said Rosie, who was one of the seniors and the chief tracker of the pack, "It needs to be dealt with," The three of them turned and trotted deeper into their territory towards the den.

The Boss was lying in the sun in the clearing beside the den. Nearby, half a dozen wolf puppies[48] were playing with two of their aunties, Squirrel and Spot. It was a crazymad running around game, the sort of game that, as you know, Ploppy had never grown out of and neither had Squirrel and Spot. Neither, for that matter, had Spoony Tooth. Hazel and Willow approached The Boss very respectfully. The Boss was not actually a particularly big wolf but you don't get to be boss of a wolf pack unless you're particularly clever and certainly not if you're a complete pushover. The Boss had rather a quick temper of which everybody was quite nervous, even Willow, who was very big and fancied himself quite a

---

47. Pack Alphas: This is what modern humans call the two boss wolves of a pack. Wolf bosses always include one experienced male wolf and one experienced female wolf and they get the job because (a) they're clever and capable managers; (b) big enough or strong-willed enough to deal with any trouble and (c) most of the other wolves wouldn't want the added responsibility that goes with the job. In a wolf pack, it's only ever the Alpha wolves that have puppies, everybody else helps to look after them. A wolf pack is really just a great big extended family.

48. Wolf puppies: wolves don't have cubs they have puppies. Lions and bears have cubs but wolves have puppies. This common misconception came about when junior Boy Scouts were called 'Wolf Cub'" or 'Cub Scout'". At first they were called "Wolf Puppies" but because no small boy wants to be referred to as a 'puppy', recruitment was low, so they changed the name to 'Wolf Cubs' and it stuck.

bit. The two scouts told their news and the news made The Boss sit up immediately because news about any wolf was of interest but news about a human consorting with a wolf, especially if it was Ploppy, was altogether startling.

"Ploppy's been talking to humans? Talking?" she said. Even as an experienced female Alpha of the pack, she had never even encountered a human face to face.

"Yes," replied Hazel, "at least, he smelled of human and he definitely said it could talk."

"You don't say," said The Boss. She was still a bit suspicious that this information might just be more Ploppy nonsense.

"Well, that's what he said and he definitely smelled of human."

"And of fire!" said Willow.

"Yes, I can smell it on you," said The Boss, sniffing Willow's muzzle as he stood nervously waiting for a doing. A doing from The Boss was never entirely out of the question; a wolf pack Alpha has to exert quite a bit of discipline to keep a bunch of rowdy wolves in line, especially if some of them are bigger than her but it was something that The Boss had quite a knack for. "You smell of smoke and of Ploppy," she said, "and it's mainly round your snout. Were you picking on Ploppy again? Did you bite him?" The Boss could tell just about everything she wanted to know about Willow's movements simply by sniffing him. Wolves have got a wonderfully powerful sense of smell, so powerful that it makes a human being's sense of smell look quite silly[49]. The Boss sniffed him thoroughly, "You were picking on him, weren't you?"

"Ehm… I was trying to get him to pay attention," said Willow. Hazel was doing his best not to catch The Boss's eye.

The Boss turned to Hazel, "Hazel, tell me, has Ploppy grown up at all?"

"Ploppy? Grown up?" said Hazel, "No, sadly, not a bit by the look of it, if anything he's worse if this silly story is anything to go by. I mean, a talking human for goodness sake."

"Pity," said The Boss, "I was hoping he'd have learned some wolf sense fending for himself and we could have him back. We could do with the extra help."

"Help? From Ploppy?" said Willow sarcastically, "Some hope. He needs a doing…"

"One day Willow," said The Boss, baring her impressive teeth and looking very scary, "*you* are going to get *such* a doing." Willow breathed a sigh of relief. With The Boss you usually didn't get a warning like that, you just got a doing. Wolves are pretty much the same as humans when it comes to squabbling except that they tend not to shout at one another like we do. If they don't like one another or if somebody needs to be disciplined,

---

49. Humans' silly sense of smell:- If noses were like eyes, a wolf's sense of smell can see in full glorious colour down to the smallest microscopic detail while a human's nose would only see the equivalent of fuzzy shades of dark grey in an unlit room with the blinds drawn and the curtains closed when it's dark outside. To all intents and purposes, although we humans think we have a sense of smell, compared with wolves, we don't.

they usually just get the gloves off and have a punch up – only with their teeth. The most senior wolf always wins any dispute and nobody ever really gets hurt because it's just not worth taking on an experienced Alpha wolf, so a doing usually amounts to being grabbed by the scruff of the neck and held down until you see some sense, quite like the two scouts had done to Ploppy. "Well," continued The Boss, "we had better have a meeting, we can't have a load of humans threatening the peace and quiet or invading our territory; go and get Bear and call everybody together."

But Bear, who was the other Alpha wolf of the pack, had already heard some of the news and just then wandered into the clearing. As you know, wolves are very big animals indeed and in those days, they were even bigger. But Bear was especially big even for those days, in fact he was massive, which was why his parents had called him Bear, a quite unusual name for a wolf because traditionally, wolves are simply given the name that their parents think best suits them, or whatever springs to mind at the time, quite like Native Americans do, so they aren't bothered with having male or female names. Of course, as you've probably already spotted, there wasn't much that was traditional about the Lummox pack: as wolf packs go, they were pretty unusual and some of them had quite silly names. Wolves' fur colour is usually mostly one variation or another of grey: dark grey, light grey, grey with brown mixed in or silvery grey like Ploppy. Another reason that Bear was called Bear was that his fur, much like his sister Rosie's, was a subtle mix of grey and golden brown so that when he stood in the sunlight it shone like an autumn beech tree. He was quite the handsomest of wolves.

Immediately Bear entered the clearing the wolf puppies mobbed their father, charging around trying to get him to play with them. It was something which he couldn't resist so he crouched down and pretty soon they were crawling all over him, biting his ears and pulling his fur while he swatted them with his huge paws and rolled them over with his big snout. He picked one of them up gently by the scruff of the neck with his giant but gentle mouth and dropped it on top of one of the other puppies. Then another of the puppies wanted to be picked up and dropped (wolf puppies like nothing better than a rough and tumble) so he picked it up too, this time by the head and its puppy legs wriggled and squiggled while it made muffled puppy laughing noises from inside Bear's mouth. He was about to drop it on another puppy when The Boss interrupted.

"Bear," she said impatiently, "we've got to have a meeting. Now."

Bear looked at The Boss and was about to answer but spotted that he had a puppy in his mouth. He spat it out. "Yes, I suppose so," said Bear, still with two wolf puppies hanging from his fur and one pulling his tail, "but we should never have snuck away from Ploppy you know. He's not so bad."

"He's an idiot," said Willow.

"Nobody asked you," snarled The Boss, "and when you're sent out scouting, in future, come back with something intelligent." She turned to Bear, "I'll give this human and fire and Ploppy business some thought; meanwhile, you had better get a hunt organised and we'll have a meeting afterwards – we have hungry mouths to feed." And she called the puppies around her and they followed her into the den for supper.

At that Bear turned to Willow and Hazel, "Well? Apart from finding Ploppy, did you find anything to hunt over in that direction?" he said, looking at them directly in an in-charge sort of way.

"No," said Willow, sheepishly.

"But we did find Ploppy," said Hazel hopefully, "and a human … sort of."

"Well we can't eat either of them," said Bear, "Come on, we'd better get moving, The Boss is right, we have mouths to feed." Bear lowered his head a little and a long, low, rumbling sound began deep in his chest and as he raised his head in the air it slowly rose in pitch to a high and pure song that rang through the countryside. His sister Rosie joined in in harmony. It was a beautiful, musical sound that carried in it a whole waltz of information that only wolf ears can hear and understand. Hazel and Willow joined in too. When humans simply describe it as howling, they have no idea what they're talking about. The song continued for a while as Squirrel and Spot joined in each in turn like a wonderful woodland opera until it eased off gently with a quiet four-part harmony which eventually faded to silence. It was all that was needed. Around the valley the pack members replied with beautiful songs of their own and knowing without looking that all the wolves of the pack would follow, together Bear and Rosie bounded off at an easy lope with the pack catching up in twos and threes until the whole pack was on the hunt leaving The Boss at the den with the puppies, wondering what to do about Ploppy.

Once the whole pack had formed up on the run they stretched out at a faster but easy pace with Bear and Rosie out in front. Through the forest they ran, smooth, silent and fast through the trees and bushes like shooting stars glimpsed between clouds. They had dozens of miles to cover even before the hunt could begin but for Bear and Rosie, this was just a warm-up because they were the two fastest and best hunters in the pack. Bear was the most powerful wolf in the land with such good eyesight that he could tell a spider from a daddy longlegs two valleys away and Rosie, as well as having the greatest staying power with speed almost to match her brother's, had the best nose in the land for finding signs of their prey. Side by side they ran, enjoying the freedom and the speed and the cooling wind on their fur, for wolves love nothing better than to run.

Chapter 6

More Visitors

Spoony came down very early (early for Spoony that is) in the morning from her bedroom in the chimney to find Ploppy Hairylummox already up and about. He had eaten his slice of pie and was sniffing around exploring the house with his full tummy after having declined, on the grounds of personal safety, an invitation from Mrs Tooth to help with the wildhairy cow milking.

"Good morning Ploppy," said Spoony cheerfully, "did you sleep well?"

"O-oh," said Ploppy. He had never been asked this before and thought it might be a test question so he said, "I did my best." Truth to tell, Ploppy had never had such a good night's sleep in his life because previously he had either been with a pack of quite bossy wolves who thought he was useless which made him nervous or he had been a lone wolf and shivery cold at night, which also made him nervous. For the first time since ever he could remember he had been nice and warm and had a full tummy, the perfect recipe for a good night's sleep. He hadn't even woken up when Mr and Mrs Tooth got up and they had had to step over his great big hairy floppy snorey shape lying in the middle of the floor taking up half the room. This was no mean feat because even for a not especially big wolf, he really was very big indeed. Mummy Tooth had given him a nervous shake to wake him up because he was getting in the way. You can't be too careful, she thought, when you wake up a wild and possibly dangerous wolf, even if it is a big soppy one like Ploppy. When he was fully awake Mummy Tooth got a bucket of water and washed the soup from his face and head and then combed his whiskers straight again.

"Did you sleep well too?" he asked Spoony.

"Oh yes," she said, "I always do. My daddy says I'm a real snoozybrain. He says it's one thing I'm *really* good at." Spoony seemed to be good at everything so Ploppy wagged his tail and gave her a big slobbery morning lick.

Spoony helped herself to some flatandchewybread for breakfast and Ploppy had some too. He hadn't quite got the hang of having a full tummy yet and felt he needed all the practice he could get.

After a while Spoony decided that they should go outside and meet the wildhairies and the sheep and goats and she pushed a very nervous and reluctant wolf out of the door in front of her. To their surprise, instead of seeing Mummy and Daddy Tooth busy in the yard doing Toothish things such as wildhairy milking and sheep shooing, a great big bunch of folk, in fact almost all of the children in the village, most of their parents and several other adults had gathered at the garden gate. Word had spread fast after the villagers' brave visit to deal with the giant wild wolf attack the night before. Everybody had gathered to see what was now variously being described after the (accurate, of course) reports from their dads as a 'plopairlumps' (like a wolf but bigger and more ferocious), a "soupwolf" (if it became dangerous you had to pour soup over it), a "lone wolf" because it was on its own, or not, as the case may be or by one or two sceptical smarty-pants as a "loanwolf" because if it was any use it could probably be borrowed, like all Tooth the Daft's inventions. As usual, there was the usual contingent of disapproving people who wanted the wolf "taken care of" or "done away with" – or worse. Some had even brought pitchforks and such like just to be on the safe side. On the whole, however, the children just wanted to have a look at a real wolf and had realised that it couldn't be all that dangerous if Spoony Tooth was going to keep it for a pet. Spoony was generally regarded (as you know) as being pretty likeable but odd in a harmless sort of way.

Meanwhile, Mr and Mrs Tooth had been doing their best to calm everybody down and explain that the wolf was not really dangerous and would be out in a minute with Spoony to say hello and indeed, lo and behold there was the wolf being pushed out of the door by Spoony.

Well, although everybody had expected the wolf to be big, when Ploppy emerged nervously from the door with Spoony pushing him from behind, practically nobody had expected a real wolf to be quite as big as it really was. They could barely see the top of Spoony's head over his big hairy back. Obviously, the grannies and grampas who had last seen wolves in the village many years ago had not been exaggerating. A great shout and yell of fear and surprise went up from the grownups and of thrillsurprise and scareydelight from the children. Ploppy had been nervous enough about meeting wildhairies and this noise from the villagers was much too much of a fright for him. He gave a great loud yelp, turned right around with his big lanky legs scrabbling for grip and belted back into the house. He lay trembling in a corner of the cottage under the Tooths' bed with his bushy tail between his legs.

This was not what the crowd had expected. A few people ran away just in case it was a special type of surprise attack involving and preceded by a tactical retreat, but most just stood around saying things like "Oh!", and "Goodness me!", and "Well I never!" Spoony was pretty miffed at them all for scaring Ploppy. It had taken her quite a bit of pushing to get him out of the door in the first place, so she put her hands on her hips and gave them one of her looks. Quite a few of the onlookers' eyebrows went up and their eyeballs went from side to side at this. Then she went back inside to get Ploppy. After a bit she came out and in a very uncharacteristically bossy and official voice announced, "Ploppy HairyLummox of the Galloot will be out soon. Everybody remain calm." It was so unusual for Spoony to be bossy that everybody immediately remained calm. Mr and Mrs Tooth beamed with pride.

There was a sudden hush and all that could be heard was rude whispering from the back with things like, "Odd child, bringin' home a wolf," or, "I blame the parents."

Somebody else said, "Needs a good feed."

"Who? The wolf or Spoony?" asked somebody else.

"Both!" said somebody else.

Then one of the children asked, "Will the Happy Lairy Pummox eat us Spoony?"

"Its Plumpy Lommy Hairox," said Spoony, "I mean Ploppy Hairylummox," she corrected, "No, he has had his breakfast."

This wasn't much comfort. "Is he dangerous?"

"No, not at all."

"So he's completely safe then?"

"Yes, completely safe," said Spoony missing the point, "he's hiding under the bed."

"Is … he … very … dangerous… Spoony?" asked another patiently. Everybody knew that sometimes you had to be patient when Spoony was missing the point. She had inherited this special talent from her dad.

"Yes," said Spoony, "he is very dainjlious indeed, but quite safe." There was lots of puzzled muttering and frowning at this while everybody tried to work it out without getting into a brainfankle[50]. Spoony, as you know, practically never got into a brainfankle because she never did difficult thinking unless she was ready for it. She went back inside and dragged Ploppy out again after assuring him that everybody had come to make friends.

Once outside and sitting trembling on the garden path, Ploppy could see that most of the children looked really nice and some of the grownups did too. Everybody seemed to speak in a very cackley way and Spoony had to translate all the questions which the children asked. Eventually Spoony invited her friends into the garden to meet Ploppy properly, and most of them came in followed by a chorus from the mums and dads of, "Don't get too close!" and "Be careful!" and, "Come back here at once!"

After a while almost all the children had met Ploppy and even some of their mums and dads had plucked up the courage to meet him, although, of course, there was plenty of muttering from them about it being "not natural," and there being, "no such thing as a safe wolf," and so on. Spoony was enjoying being unusual for an even more unusual reason than usual and Ploppy began to calm down and stopped trembling. He got patted and stroked and even hugged, much to the dismay of the on-looking parents and all the children who patted and hugged him remarked what a lovely soft silky coat he had and how handsome he was. Eventually, Spoony arranged for Ploppy to give the other children impromptu wolfhowling lessons and a terrible howling racket ensued. Mummy and Daddy Tooth called a halt in case the sheep bolted or the wildhairies escaped. Eventually, when everybody had either had their wolf fears allayed or confirmed the villagers went back about their own business with the children practicing wolfhowling as they went. The Tooths went indoors much relieved that everybody's mind was now at ease about the wolf. Well, almost everybody's.

Going Visiting

A few days went by quite peacefully and almost everybody seemed to be sort of getting the hang of having a wolf living in the neighbourhood. Most of the children had been banned from going anywhere near the Tooth house for fear of being eaten so, of course, went anyway and even a few of the grownups plucked up the gumption to drop by and ask Mrs Tooth (from a safe distance) how things were going. There were two general impressions gained from the gossip and rumour which ensued: (1) the wolf was harmless but not much use for anything except eating everything in sight and (2) the wolf was only just under control and could run ravenously amok at any minute eating everything in sight including innocent bystanders.

Ploppy Hairylummox was as happy as he had ever been now that he had a best friend and an adopted mummy and daddy even if they didn't have tails or fur and weren't very

---

50. Brainfankle: Forgotten already? It's like a braintangle only more intricate and harder to unpick. A good time to see a brainfankle in action is on the news when a politician has to explain themselves when they've been caught telling a fib.

good at moon-howling. Mummy Tooth had decided that Ploppy was too skinny even though she didn't know anything about what shape wolves should be. So she set about feeding him up as much as she could and of course, Ploppy, being far too polite a wolf to refuse anything he was offered, obligingly ate as much as he could, a quantity which, happily, exactly matched everything that he was offered. He was very grateful for this and one day took his turn at organising supper by going out on a special worm and slug hunt. Unfortunately the slimy-creature hunting seemed to be poor that day so Mrs Tooth made a special stew instead because there weren't enough slugs and worms to go round. Ploppy was very touched at how everybody had insisted on him having the few slugs and worms that there were to his very own self.

Spoony ate as much as she could too (in other words as much as usual) and remained as skinny as ever. Mummy Tooth had stopped worrying about Spoony being skinny long ago. But it was amazing to see the change that began to come over Ploppy. Now that his lovely thick silvery grey fur was clean and glossy (aided by regular brushing and hugging from Spoony) and he was being well fed and getting as much joyful crazymad running around with Spoony as they both could fit into a sunny day, he began to look a very handsome wolf indeed. There is no doubt that if the Great Wolf Pack of Lummox had seen him they would not have recognised him and would have invited him to join. He got fitter and healthier and it wasn't long before he could run fast enough to catch a rabbit and fetch it home for supper, something he had never been able to do before and for which he got many more grateful thanks than he had got for the worms and slugs.

One of the problems with being odd, like the Tooths, is that what seems perfectly ordinary to you doesn't necessarily seem ordinary to ordinary folk. Mummy and Daddy and (especially) Spoony Tooth soon got quite used to things like falling over a wolf who was snuffling about around their feet, or having a wolf wake them up in the middle of the night to go out because he was too warm indoors and then, just as everybody had got back to sleep, want back in again because he was lonely. Or getting knocked over by a huge high-speed wolf crazymadjoyful skedaddling around the house closely followed by Spoony. Or going outside at night to join in with the moonhowling because it's a lovely clear moonlit night. So the Tooths failed to notice that although they had become entirely at ease with having a wolf at home with them, not everybody was at home with the idea of having a wolf for a neighbour. Even the Tooths' sheep failed to understand the need for a wolf and kept themselves tightly bunched in a corner of the sheep pen whenever Ploppy was about. The wildhairy cattle on the other hand were entirely unafraid of the wolf and simply gave him their most malevolent stare whenever he was forced to sneak past them.

One early morning after Ploppy Hairylummox had been there a week or two, Spoony decided to take him for a walk around the village to visit some of her friends. Well, as you can imagine, going to visit a wild and dangerous wolf which happens to be staying at somebody else's house is one thing, after all, you can always run away as fast as you can if things turn out bad, (even if they actually didn't – when you did), but having one suddenly turn up on your doorstep when you least expect it is something different entirely – even if you couldn't claim to have been least expecting it due to the fact that there had been a wolf living in the village for a week or more. In truth, it is almost always the case that when there is something extremely scary and doubtlessly dangerous living at the wrong end of the village, it doesn't really matter how much you try to least expect it, or indeed expect it, when it turns up you are ready to panic flat out at a moment's notice. Consequently, it will be no surprise to you, even if it was to Spoony and Ploppy that the very first house they called at rang to cries of "Wolf attack! Wolf attack!" immediately the neighbour in question opened the door and found (as it seemed at the time) a massive, slavering, ravening, bloodthirsty wolf right there on the doorstep. And also, not surprisingly, the door was shut immediately in their faces. The two of them called at quite a few houses and it seemed that if one of the children answered the door then they would say something like, "Oh hello Spoony and PlumpyLommyhairox," but if a grown-up answered the door they invariably said, "Wolf attack! Wolf attack!" Even after the mums and dads in question had calmed down they had refused to let their children go out and play at crazymad running around in circles, a game that was fast becoming fashionable because Spoony and the wolf seemed to do it all the time and it made them laugh. You should try it.

On the whole it was a bit disappointing not to get the warm (or puzzled) welcome she was used to and Spoony had to apologise to Ploppy for having such rude neighbours. Ploppy didn't mind. He was beginning to realise that people are just as mixed up and cantankerous a bunch of individuals as wolves are and looking on the bright side, nobody had bitten him yet so he felt he was making good progress. Unfortunately, by the time the two of them had arrived back at the Tooth household, some folk in the village had begun to get themselves into high dudgeon[51] at having been frightened by a marauding wolf first thing in the morning.

Angry Visitors

So, not surprisingly, later that day some of the grown-ups in the village got together and decided to ask the Tooths kindly to keep their dangerous marauding wolf under control. In fact, one or two of them had got into such high dudgeon about the dangerous

51. High dudgeon: for some reason, according to the dictionary, high dudgeon describes "a feeling of deep resentment". We have to think about this because if high dudgeon is deep resentment, then low dudgeon is high resentment, which sounds like it ought to be the same as high dudgeon. Maybe it should be "shallow resentment". It's very confusing and it's no wonder that people only ever say "high dudgeon", nobody ever says "low dudgeon"..It's altogether easier on the vocabulary if you don't get resentful in the first place.

marauding wolf that they quite forgot themselves, and while they went around the village trying to persuade other people to join their anti-marauding-wolf campaign, they neglected to make sure that everything at home was left all in good order.

Spoony and Ploppy had busied themselves for the rest of the morning with helping Mummy and Daddy with the daft Toothish jobs they had to do, like making tiny amounts of wildhairymilk cheese from the tiny amounts of wildhairymilk that Mummy Tooth had managed to get from the dangerous and wildhairycows that morning.

Daddy Tooth happened to mention that he had noticed over the last few days how nervous the sheep were when Ploppy was around. Oddly enough, instead of making them more difficult to keep under control, the sheep kept themselves tightly bunched with their lambs close to them for fear of a wolf attack, and they were less reluctant than usual to get back into their nice safe wolf-proof pen at night. The wildhairy cattle on the other hand seemed to be every bit as cantankerous as ever, if not more so.

Around about lunchtime, just when the Tooths were in the house deciding what kind of leftovers to have for a mid-day snack (two things – leftovers and snacks – which Ploppy had yet to get used to) there was a knock on the door.

"Oh, hello Farmer Stuckie," said Daddy Tooth, opening the door. Then he said, in a slightly apprehensive tone, "Oh hello everybody else." Spoony could see that there was a large group of irate (but nervous) looking villagers behind Farmer Stuckie.

"We've come about the wolf," said Farmer Stuckie. He looked a bit embarrassed. Farmer Stuckie was reputed to be dead sensible (but easily persuaded) if help was needed, so he always got elected to deal with things that nobody else with any sense would dare tackle. "It appears that your Spoony has been goin' about terrorfyin' everybody in the village this morning." This was such a preposterous idea that one or two children could be heard sniggering at the very idea. "I mean with that there wolf of hers," continued Farmer Stuckie.

"Oh my goodness!" said Daddy Tooth, "Is this true Spoony? Have you and Ploppy been terrorfying people?"

"No, we haven't," said Spoony indignantly, "We've been visiting our friends."

"Well, gettin' visited by a wolf counts as bein' terrorfied," said somebody behind Farmer Stuckie.

"Not if it's a friendly visit," said Spoony.

"Good point," said Daddy Tooth.

"Yes," said Farmer Stuckie, furrowing his brows, "I suppose that's a fair point…"

Ploppy hadn't a clue what was going on but since he heard Spoony mention his name once or twice he thought everybody had very kindly decided to drop round and visit him.

"Anyway," said Farmer Stuckie getting back to the point, "Everybody thinks that the wolf should be banished."

"Oh my goodness," said Daddy Tooth. He didn't want Ploppy to be banished because, apart from anything else, Ploppy Hairylummox was having a mysterious but helpful taming effect on the Tooth sheep.

"Poo!" said Spoony, "Double poo!"

"Ploppy Hairylummox is a very nice, quiet well-mannered wolf and he really doesn't mean to terrorfy anybody," Mummy Tooth butted in at last to help a rather flummoxed Daddy Tooth.

"Well, to be fair Mrs Tooth," said Farmer Stuckie, "he's not all that quiet. After all, what about all that moonhowling we've been gettin'. It near frightens the life outa people gettin' woken up in the middle of the night by wolfhowlin'. It fair gives you the willies. And it attracts other wolves too, you can hear them joinin' in."

"Oh, that's not other wolves," said Mummy Tooth, "that's us, we all join in the moonhowling to keep him company."

"They're all mad!" said a voice at the back, "Completely mad." It was Mrs Hingmy, who could be quite bossy.

"And they talks to it," said somebody else, "as if it could talk back."

"He *can* talk back, can't you Ploppy?" said Daddy Tooth, turning round to look for the wolf. Ploppy made a gruffly noise and nodded.

"There you go! He's talking to the wolf!" said Mrs Hingmy, "as if it understood him. Mad, completely mad!"

"Well anyway Mr Tooth," said Farmer Stuckie, being a jolly good spokesman, "everybody in the village would like to politely suggest that you gets rid of it."

"Yes," said somebody at the back, "it should be banished."

"Banished," agreed a few folk nodding, "That's right, it should be banished."

"Well," said Spoony, "if Ploppy gets banished then I want to be banished too."

"Doesn't matter! It's got to be banished anyway."

"But we can't banish Ploppy if Spoony insists on being banished too," said Daddy Tooth.

"That's your problem," said bossy Mrs Hingmy with her arms folded. There was a bit of muttering at the back at this remark. Not everybody was feeling all that terrorfied by Ploppy Hairylummox, especially Spoony's friends.

"Banish the wolf," shouted somebody again.

"But where can we banish him to?" pleaded Daddy Tooth.

"I don't care where," said Mrs Hingmay bossily, "but he has to be banished somewhere."

"Hear, hear,[52]" said a voice at the back.

"Here? Here?" said a puzzled voice at the back.

"No, hear … hear!" confirmed the first voice at the back.

"What here, here? Banish him here here?" asked Daddy Tooth who didn't know anything about how to hold meetings.

"Here, here," said somebody else.

"I agree," said Farmer Stuckie, pouncing on what looked like a good compromise, "Banish him here, here."

"Right," said Daddy Tooth, "the wolf is banished here, here."

"Not good enough," said Mrs Hingmy.

Just then one of the children came running up and shouted, "Mrs Hingmy's wildhairies have got out and they knocked down all the fences and everybody's sheep and a bunch of wildhairies are out and spread all over the place."

"Oh my goodness," said Daddy Tooth looking out to see if the Tooth sheep and cattle were out. They were safely locked up in their pens. "Well you can't blame Ploppy for this, he's been inside for ages."

"Banish him," said Mrs Hingmy.

"Send him to his room," said one of the children being brainy. Even back then this was the standard solution for dealing with youngsters who were annoying their parents.

"Good idea," said Farmer Stuckie who was fed up with the whole thing, "Banish him to his room. Now let's get these sheep in before dark and there's a wolf attack!"

"There *is* a wolf attack!" said Mrs Hingmy, "That wolf's been attacking us for days!"

"You be quiet," said Farmer Stuckie who and wanted to get his sheep rounded up.

"He doesn't have a room," said Spoony, "He's a lone wolf," but nobody was listening.

"Poo!" said Spoony, who had never been banished before and was quite in the huff even though she had volunteered to be banished with Ploppy, "I think they're smelly, and we haven't done anything bad, we were just visiting."

"Never mind," said Ploppy, "You're my best banished Spoony in the whole world." He wasn't in the least put out at being banished because it seemed a lot less hurtful than being snuck away from by a load of sneaky wolves. So just remember when you get sent to your room and you're feeling glum that it's a lot better than getting home from school to find that everybody has moved house and not told you where they've gone.

---

52. *Hear, hear!:-* or sometimes, *Here, here!"* is what you say when you agree with something somebody says at a meeting. If you don't agree, for some reason you don't say the opposite which would be, "There, there." If you disagree with something somebody says at a meeting, you say something like, "Rubbish!" You only ever say, "There, there," when somebody has grazed their knee and is crying.

Banished

It took a good deal of effort to banish Ploppy to Spoony's room. As you already know, getting to Spoony's bedroom involved climbing up a ladder and it turned out that ladder climbing was not something that Ploppy Hairylummox was much good at. Eventually Spoony's mummy and daddy managed to push him up the ladder with Spoony pulling on his ears and Ploppy hanging on to the rungs with his big wolf feet. Considering that Ploppy was very big and quite heavy despite being skinny, this was no mean feat and the final push to get him through the tiny hatch at the top of the ladder took all of everybody's strength.

"Ooooh! Owww!," said Daddy Tooth, with a very anxious wail, "I think I've put my back back out again."

"What got put back out?" asked Ploppy, very concerned by the strained tones of Spoony's daddy.

"My daddy's back," said Spoony.

"I didlint know he'd gone away," said Ploppy.

"Oh, he hasn't gone away... he's put his back back out again," assured Spoony. This made Ploppy's thinkybrain fidget for a minute.

"Just a minute," said Mummy Tooth from the bottom of Spoony's ladder, "I know how to fix that!" So saying, she grabbed Daddy Tooth, wrestled him to the floor, sat down on top of Daddy Tooth with a resounding thuddywllop. There was a loud crack and a yelp[53].

"What was that noise?" asked Ploppy, quite alarmed at what was going on at the bottom of Spoony's ladder.

"I think it was Mummy putting Daddy's back back in."

"His backback went back out? And then your mummy put his backback back in?" asked Ploppy, none the wiser.

"Yes, something like that" said Spoony, "It's nothing out of the ordinary."

"Ooooh, aaaah," said Ploppy, nodding as if he had the faintest idea of what it all meant. He peered down the ladder to see Daddy Tooth struggling to his feet.

"Oh," said Daddy Tooth, "that's better, thank you Mummy Tooth."

"Well I hope it doesn't go back out," she replied.

"Oh," said Ploppy from the top of the ladder, trying to be helpful, "shall I go and get it back for you?" He really didn't know anything about backs.

"No," said Daddy Tooth, "it's very kind of you Ploppy but Mummy Tooth will deal

---

53. Dealing with bad backs:- this was another of Mummy Tooth's inventions but today the tecunique is frowned upon. People who use sudden impact to treat sore backs nowadays are called *charlatans*, sorry, *chiropractors*, but they are so afraid of legal action if they get it wrong that they rarely sit on their patients with a thuddywallop as it is considered dangerous to all concerned. Instead, they do other, marginally effective stuff, for which you get a bill which causes deep anxiety. Then they give you the name of an anxiety counsellor who charges even more.

with my back if it happens again."

Spoony and Ploppy sat up in her bedroom in the chimney and watched out of the little window at the scene below. There were sheep and goats and wildhairy cattle all over the place and irate grown-ups and children all running around waving their arms and shouting. It looked like really good fun and Spoony wished she could join in. And despite everybody's efforts, the only thing that seemed to be happening was that the sheep and the goats and the wildhairy cattle just got even more mixed up than before.

Outside – although everybody got as angry and irate as they could and the children laughed and ran around shouting as loudly as possible until the grownups were shouting at the children as well as the sheep, goats and cattle – nothing good was happening in the way of rounding up sheep, goats and cattle. And worse still, all the wildhairy cattle had now got so wound up that they had decided not just to be wild and hairy but also dangerous and hairy and very angry so that quite a few people were now up trees and even grumpy old Mrs Hingmy had had to dive over a hedge, something she had not done since she was young and grumpy. Even the usual ploy of getting them to chase a daft laddie into the big pen didn't work because there were daft laddies everywhere and the wildhairycattle didn't know which one they were supposed to attack.

And the most irritating thing for everybody was that the Tooth sheep and cattle were the only ones this time which were still in their pens. This gave Daddy Tooth the opportunity to be a smarty-pants and tell everybody that his special wolf invention was at the root of good sheep and cattle management. Everybody told him that it was his wolf that had made Mrs Hingmy forget to shut her gate (which, due to her anti-wolf high dudgeon was more than a bit true) and they also told him to shut up. So did Mummy Tooth.

After a while, Spoony and Ploppy Hairylummox got bored watching the antics of the villagers and decided to spend their first afternoon of banishment playing games. They played 'I Spy' for a while but got bored with that. The game of I Spy had, like many other things back then, only recently been invented. Unfortunately, spelling hadn't yet been invented so you couldn't give a clue at all. Spoony would say, "I spy with my little eye, something." This didn't narrow it down much and Ploppy, even using the best bits of his wolfcraftythinkybrain[54], couldn't get the answer, even after a hundred guesses. When it was his turn he wasn't much use at that either because he would say, "I spy with my little eye ... the window," or, "I spy with my little eye… the bed." Most of the time Spoony would get the answer right straight away, but not always. After, that they played easy games

---

54. Wolfcraftythinkybrain:- the wolfcraftythinkybrain is the main reason that wolves are the most intelligent animals in the world because it can deal with several things at once such as running, tracking by scent, listening and communicating. Humans, on the other hand, are only able to do two things at once: breathe and something else that they're doing whilst breathing. They can sometimes do a third thing, like bump into something but that hardly counts.

like making funny faces and seeing who could do the longest dribble but they even got bored with that until Spoony suddenly remembered one of her favourite games – "Thinking up something dead brainy". This was quite a challenge for Spoony because, as you know, she wasn't very brainy at all. She had inherited this special talent from her daddy who also wasn't very brainy and usually when he tried to think up something dead brainy, came up with something absolutely daft. For Ploppy, who had great difficulty even thinking up something daft, the thought of thinking up something dead brainy just got him in a brainfankle[55] straight away. But he decided to give it a try.

The two of them sat on Spoony's bed with their brows as furrowed as they could get them and thought as hard as they could for ages. Spoony nearly thought of something a couple of times but they turned out to be false alarms and once, Ploppy actually did think of something that seemed quite brainy to him but he got such a fright that he fell off the bed and forgot it immediately.

Some considerable time passed with both of them employing lots of strenuous brainy effort but neither Spoony nor Ploppy thought up anything dead brainy. Spoony was quite disappointed with this because she usually managed to think up something which she considered to be at least a bit brainy without very much effort at all, and could sometimes manage something very dead brainy after employing the deep brow-furrowing method. Ploppy, on the other hand, had never managed to think up anything dead brainy on purpose in his entire life so was not in the least put out. In fact, the real truth was, that being a wolf, he naturally had an extremely clever wolfcraftythinkybrain but it only ever worked properly when he didn't give what he was thinking about any thought whatsoever. Actually, this is a method which had worked for Spoony too: a dead brainy idea would sometimes suddenly and accidentally, without any effort or warning, pop into her head for no apparent reason and then she could take all the credit when really her thinkybrain had done it all on its own without any help from her.

She explained this to Ploppy who thought that was quite brainy. "Let's try not thinking up anything dead brainy at all and see if that works," he said. Spoony thought that that was a dead brainy idea in itself so she agreed. They both un-furrowed their brows and got down to the relatively easy business of falling into a dwam and not thinking anything in particular.

Loads more time passed with Spoony and Ploppy sitting in a dwam not thinking anything in the hope of thinking something up. At one point Ploppy started to snore but Spoony nudged him in the ribs to make sure he was awake and deliberately not concentrating. Being asleep and not concentrating was cheating and you might miss the chance of an idea popping into your head for no apparent reason or mistake it for a dream

---

55. Brainfankle:- look, we've been through this already. It's like a braintangle but... oh never mind.

and ignore it because most dreams are quite silly.

After a bit Ploppy, who had been looking out of the window now and again at the antics of the villagers trying to round up the sheep, goats and cattle, said, 'How long does banished last Spoony?'

"Oh, I don't know,' replied Spoony, "I've never been banished before – probably until suppertime I would think; even banished people need to stop for supper."

"Oh good," said Ploppy, "I thought we might have been banished forever." Ploppy had been worried that 'banished' might have amounted to the same as when he was "losted" by his pack and he didn't want to be losted again. "I was thinking," he said after a bit of thought.

"Y …e…s," said Spoony, who thought he was very clever.

"If we can't think of anything dead brainy..."

"Ri ...ght," said Spoony.

"... and its nearly suppertime ..."

"Ri ...ght," said Spoony again.

"Why don't we go and help everybody round up the sheep and goats and stuff and then we can have supper and come back to being banished?"

"Poo!" said Spoony, "What a deadbrainy idea, I expect they'd appreciate some help by now."

"Poo!" said Ploppy, because he hadn't really thought it was a dead brainy idea, he just thought that would be something to do until a brainy idea popped into his head.

So the two of them decided to go out and help. The only problem was that if Ploppy couldn't climb up a ladder, he certainly wasn't going to be able to climb down one. Well, he only got down one rung from the top when he slipped and fell and landed on the floor with a thud. Spoony thought she'd go back up the ladder and give the new head-first ladder descent method a try. Fortunately, Ploppy broke her fall and she bounced off his skinny ribs, did a somersault and landed flat on her bottom. Although Ploppy seemed to be quite satisfied with landing on the floor from high up she thought that in future she'd just use her ladder.

Back at the Wolf Den

Bear the Wolf lay around on his back and let the wolf puppies romp all over him. It had been an unusually successful hunt, he had an extremely full tummy and was most comfortable lying on his back. Two of the puppies were playing tug of war with his ears. This was making this head feel as if it would get pulled in two but he didn't mind because although he was the biggest wolf and could be quite scary to look at, he was really just a big puppy at heart himself.

"Yikes!" he yelped in a very un-wolf-like (or bear-like) manner and jumped to his feet.

One of the puppies had just decided to chew his tail. Now he had a puppy hanging on each ear and one hanging from his tail.

"If you're not careful," said The Boss, "those puppies will all grow up like Ploppy."

"What's wrong with Ploppy?" asked Bear, shaking himself. He shook himself again to dislodge two puppies who were still clinging onto his fur with their sharp little teeth. The two that had been playing tug of war with his ears were still hanging on for dear life. He gave another huge shake and they went flying off into the undergrowth in opposite directions. One of them landed on their Aunt Rose's tummy. She was also lying on her back digesting a very large supper. Rosie couldn't be bothered with puppies so she growled at it. This had no effect because the puppy grabbed her ear and started pulling it. She stood up and swatted it away with her paw.

"For one thing, Ploppy never grew up," said Rosie, "He didn't get enough discipline, like his father." She gave her brother one of her looks.

"Aw, what good's discipline," said Bear, "I never had any when I was a puppy and it didn't do me any harm, I mean, I've made it all the way up the chain of command."

The Boss gave him one of *her* looks. "Hmm...," was all she said.

"It's about *self*-discipline," said Rosie, who could be a proper madam sometimes and was quite unlike her brother in most things other than hunting skills and being big: Rosie wasn't quite as big as some of the other wolves, particularly Bear, but she made up for it by having a "big" outlook.

"Indeed," said The Boss, "we need to do something about Ploppy before he has too much to do with those humans."

"Oh, he's not silly enough to get too involved with them is he? Anyway, I mean, he's not likely to get eaten or anything like that," said Bear, "Everybody knows that humans are supposed to be more, sort of, stupid than dangerous. I mean, there's never been a proven case of a wolf having been eaten by a human."

"That's probably just old wolflore," put in Rosie, "We don't know for certain what humans are really like."

"Well, he shouldn't have had anything to do with them anyway," insisted The Boss.

"I would *never* do that," said Rosie, being a bit of a madam again, "It's not natural." Bear sighed to himself. Although he was Alpha Male, and a particularly good one, he sometimes felt outnumbered with so many Alpha-type females around.

"If what Willow and Hazel say is true, he might be in danger," said The Boss, "let's get him back into the pack. He should have learned how to look after himself by now and be ready to become a proper Lummox."

"Oh, I agree, totally," said Bear, "Totally. I'll organise a search party when everybody's slept off their dinner." Wolves, as you probably know, can often be quite lazy, and only hunt when they really need to. The pack had just had a very successful hunt so everybody was lying around digesting a huge venison supper with no intention of getting involved in anything that involved effort – just like some humans do when they've just had a big Sunday lunch, except that wolves don't read the Sunday papers[56].

The Round-up

Outside, things were every bit as confused and exciting as they had appeared from the window. Everybody was running around waving their arms and shouting at the sheep and goats (and each other) and trying to shoo them back towards the sheep pens. Nobody was attempting to round up anybody's wildhairy cattle who were now so crabby that if anybody went anywhere near them then it was the wildhairies who did the shooing so they decided to sort the sheep out first and then work on the wildhairies. Meanwhile the cattle were wandering off, browsing on low-hanging leaves of trees and fresh clover.

Spoony and Ploppy (who still hadn't given their deadbrainy idea much thought) trotted happily into the melee expecting to be welcomed as an extra pair of helpers. "Hello everybody," said Spoony at the top of her voice, "We've come to help!"

"Yes," said Ploppy, at the top of his voice too, "We've come to help." And Spoony and Ploppy ran happily into the fray to help, Spoony flapping her skinny arms and Ploppy waving his flaggy tail and galumphing his boundy big legs.

Everybody stopped dead in their tracks and looked round. Of course, as you know, what they had heard was Spoony saying, "Hello everybody. We've come to help!" ... and a giant dangerous wolf saying. "Howoooo... Howooooo.. wowf! woooo.. woooo. wooooooooooooooooooooooo!"

There was a short pause, which included doing things like standing open-mouthed in astonishment, being completely aghast and also totally petrified. And then suddenly…

"WOLF ATTACK! WOLF ATTACK!" shouted those most likely to dread a wolf attack, such as Mrs Hingmy.

"Don't PANIC!" shouted those most likely to panic, which was most of the grown-ups.

"Head for the hills!" said Mr Biglanky on his way up a tree and not taking his own advice.

"Yippee!" said some of the children whose arm flailing was failing to round up the livestock and who had become a bit bored.

---

56. Sunday papers: in point of fact, back then, even the humans didn't read the Sunday papers, because (a) Sunday hadn't been invented yet, or weeks*; (b) neither had the newspapers and more to the point, (c) neither had reading or writing. Even so, lying around doing nothing whenever they got the chance was just one of the things that humans had in common with wolves although neither of them knew anything about one another and that they actually had quite a lot in common. * Months and years *had* been invented: a new month simply started when a new moon showed up in the night sky (if it wasn't too cloudy to see it) and years started around about the winter solstice (if it wasn't too cloudy to spot it happening, which it usually was and is in winter anyway).

"Oh No!" said Mummy and Daddy Tooth, "Oh No!

Spoony didn't take any notice because she had assumed that everybody had just stopped to watch what a help she and Ploppy were going to be so she kept on running. And Ploppy, who had become quite good at chasing things since he had come to live with the Tooths put on a burst of speed and ran towards the sheep and goats.

There was a lot more shouting of "WOLF ATTACK!" and "Don't PANIC!" as well as plenty of standing staring not knowing what to do next while a giant mad dangerous wolf seemed to be attacking their livestock aided and abetted by a completely potty little girl.

Ploppy had put on a burst of speed and had completely overshot the sheep and goats, even though they were widely spread and some were far away. This was most of the sheep's first sight of the wolf (or any wolf for that matter) and they had been about to get back to grazing contentedly while the humans got on with their usual commotion. They had been paying little attention to the shouting of the humans because sheep and goats find it extraordinarily difficult to tell the difference between an angry human who is running around trying to round them up, and a panicky human running around trying to find a safe place to panic because of a ravenous wolf. So, up until then they had been ignoring the humans and getting their breath back ready for the next bout of capture evasion. Suddenly, however, they caught sight of a madly dangerous sheep-attacking wolf and that certainly made them take notice and it was only going to be a bit more than a moment or two before they too began to panic.

The wildhairy cattle, on the other hand, weren't in the least bit bothered about a wolf attack because (as you know) they considered themselves (quite rightly) to be far more dangerous than a measly wolf, especially one as measly as Ploppy.

As Spoony ran towards them, Ploppy sped past them in a blur of gallolloping legs, and the sheep and lambs and goats began to panic as much as they could and came running in towards the middle of the meadow bleating and baa-ing for all they were worth. By now, Ploppy had shot into the trees and bushes at the edge of the forest and after a bit of crashing and twig snapping he reappeared with leaves and twigs flying from his fur and ran round the far side of the panicking sheep, zooming up to and buzzing past the stragglers.

Almost before the terrified onlookers knew what to be terrified of, Spoony and Ploppy had all the sheep, lambs and goats rounded up into a tight circle. Of course, Spoony was as surprised as anyone at this strange behaviour on the part of the sheep and goats because everybody expected them to do what they usually did which was to scatter themselves all over the place. Ploppy had not known what to expect because he knew nothing about rounding up sheep but he thought that if you were supposed to round them up, then running round them might be part of it so he ran circles around them a few more times for good measure until they were quite dizzy and his own head was a bit woozyick. Then he went and lay down in the long grass on the far side of them. Spoony was skipping around the circle of sheep and goats singing, "We rounded up the sheepses and goatses, we rounded up the sheepses and goatses."

"And lambses too," woo-wooed Ploppy.

One thing you might have noticed about watching from a safe distance, which is what all the villagers, including Mummy and Daddy Tooth, were doing, is that you don't exactly get a good view of what is going on. In fact, if you're short sighted (which most of the older villagers were) then it's absolutely impossible to watch from a safe distance because if you're close enough to see then you're too close for comfort and if you get far enough away to be at what might be a safe distance, the danger is almost out of sight. And if the danger is out of sight then you don't know where it is, which is, in itself, quite scary, all of which will keep you running for some considerable distance.

Most of the villagers had decided that the wolf was going to kill all of the sheep and goats so there was no point in doing anything other than panic, which they all continued to do as best they could. However, it wasn't long before people began to notice that the wolf hadn't actually attacked and murdered any of the sheep yet. Every time one or two of the sheep thought about making an attempt to break free of the tight bunch they were in and escape from the wolf, Ploppy would simply sit up and give them a good stare and they would scuttle back into the flock.

"Look everybody, look! Ploppy the Hairylummox and me have rounded up all the sheep and goats!" shouted Spoony.

"I think you mean Ploppy the Hairylummox and *I* have rounded up the sheep," said Mrs Hingmy, who was quite bossy about everything.

"Mrs Hingmy, you didn't round up nothin' at all," said one of the grown-ups.

"I think you mean, *I didn't round up* anything *at all,*" said Mrs Hingmy.

"Oh for goodness sake!" said Farmer Stuckie, who couldn't be bothered with a grammar lesson right now.

"Correct! You 'ad nuffin' to do with it Mrs Hingmy," said Spoony indignantly. Spoony wasn't especially good at grammar but she didn't see why Mrs Hingmy should get any credit at all. "Anyway, it was definitely Ploppy Hairylummox and me what rounded up the sheep! And that's a true fact!"

"I think you mean, *It was Ploppy Hairylummox and* I who *rounded up the sheep,*" insisted Mrs Hingmy.

"Oh do shut up you stupi…," said Farmer Stuckie who wasn't usually impolite and stopped himself before he gave Mrs Hingmy an excuse to get wound up about anything else, "Look, we do need to get on with getting on with things."

"We agree!" came a voice from behind something safe, and peering out of the branches of trees and from behind bushes, quite a lot of people could see that the sheep had indeed been rounded up.

"What do you think Farmer Stuckie?" asked one of the sheep owners who obviously still considered him to be an in-charge sort of person.

"Well," said Farmer Stuckie, "I don't know what the 'Airylumps' and Spoony thought they was doin but at least the sheep and goats are all back together again in one bunch."

"Yes," said Mr Biglanky, getting down out of his tree, "if we can just get rid of the wolf now we might be able to get them back to the pens and sort them out.

"We'll all be killed!" shouted Mrs Hingmy from her seat up in the branches of a tree.

"You be quiet!" said Farmer Stuckie, and then, "Let's see what we can do now that they've been rounded up. If the Airylumps was going to kill anybody he could have done it to start with."

"Yes," said Daddy Tooth, "and he could have killed the sheep if he wanted."

"He still could!" shouted Mrs Hingmy who had gone up a branch or two, "he'll kill them all. And us. He'll kill all of us!"

"But he didn't," said Daddy Tooth.

"Problem is," said Mr Biglanky, "how do we get the sheep out of the clutches of yon wolf and back in the pens without them runnin' around all over the place again?"

"Oh, that's easy," said Spoony, "Ploppy and me will chase them in."

"Ploppy and *I* will chase them in!" yelled bossy Mrs Hingmy, still doing grammar from the safety of her tree.

"Just you stay in that tree!" said Farmer Stuckie to Mrs Hingmy, "You'll be a lot safer up there I can tell you!" And then to Spoony, "Do you think you and that Lumpyhairox can do it Spoony?"

"Just you wait and see!" said Spoony and she turned on her heel and trotted back towards the flock of sheep. When they saw her coming, a few of the sheep decided to bolt for it, but Ploppy immediately stood up and moved a few inches towards them and the break-aways immediately panicked and ran back to join the bunch.

Spoony trotted round the sheep and said to Ploppy, "That was a very brainy idea you had, Ploppy, because we've rounded up the sheep just like we said we would."

Ploppy immediately jumped to his feet and ran around singing, "We rounded up the sheep, we rounded up the sheep!" and Spoony, because she couldn't resist a chance to run around crazymad, immediately joined in, her short span of attention taking over once again from the business at hand. Of course, the sheep thought this was their chance to escape while the wolf was busy so they immediately bolted in all sorts of directions.

"I knew it!" said Mrs Hingmy in the distance.

"Oh no," said Spoony.

"Oops," said Ploppy and immediately took off and ran out wide around them all at full speed as he had done the first time, scaring them back into a bunch. He noticed that if he went on one side of the flock and got too close, they would all run in the opposite direction and if he then ran round the other side and sat down they would stop and stand around looking confused.

When he had the sheep tightly bunched up and too confused and puffed out to think of trying a break-out, Spoony strolled up and said, "You're my best Ploppy Hairylummox in the whole world!" and gave him a great big hug.

"And you're my best Spoonytooth in the whole world," said Ploppy and they both jumped around doing crazy-mad-joyful for a minute. This time, none of the sheep thought they'd try a break-away and they all just stood there wishing, like Mrs Hingmy, that the nasty wolf would go away.

At last, Mummy and Daddy Tooth, came over from where they'd been hiding with everybody else, taking care to give the sheep a wide berth in case they bolted and spoilt all Ploppy's good work.

"We rounded up the sheep," said Spoony, "We invented wolfysheepgatheringup." Ploppy just grinned and panted because he was now quite hot from his sheep rounding-up exercise.

"You certainly did," said Daddy Tooth.

"Yes," said Mummy Tooth, "I wish you could do that with my wildhairycattle."

"We could give it a try," said Spoony, being a bit too overcome with their success with the sheep. Ploppy didn't like that idea at all and he shook his head so hard that his ears flopped around. "Well, maybe we'll leave that for now," said Spoony.

"Spoony," said Daddy Tooth in the sort of way he had of saying things that usually had Spoony and her mummy waiting for something daft.

"Ye…s," said Spoony.

"Do you really think Ploppy Hairylummox could keep the sheep rounded up and chase them into the big pen?"

Ploppy, who was getting the hang of Tooth the Daft's way of approaching things, simply jumped to his feet and walked towards the sheep at quite a leisurely pace. As he got closer to them, the sheep started to move away from him, now not in the least inclined to make a break for it in case they got wolf-circled and nervous and dizzy again. If they moved off in the wrong direction, Ploppy just dodged to that side and they realised they were going to get rounded up again and that made them dizzy and scared so they didn't bother. To everybody's amazement, watching from the safety of their safe distance in the trees and bushes, they saw the sheep moving toward the big sheep pens in a tight bunch.

"Blimey!" said Farmer Stuckie, "look at that, the Ploppyairlumps is driving the sheep towards the pens."

"I've never seen the like," said somebody else.

"It's stalking them to kill them all!" cried Mrs Hingmy from her tree.

"Look, they're nearly at the pens," said Mr Biglanky."

As you probably know, as a general rule, sheep hate being made to go into pens but they were so dizzy from wolf-circling and quite panicky that for once the sheep pens looked like a nice safe place to be. Once they got within a few yards of the gate they suddenly all bolted into the pen, and Mummy Tooth rushed up and closed the gate behind them. Then she gave Ploppy a great big hug which was followed by a hug from Spoony and one from Dad.

Farmer Stuckie and a few others now approached nervously and Daddy Tooth said, "What do you think of that Farmer Stuckie? The dangerous wolf just rounded up our sheep for us and put them in their pens."

"I've never seen the like," he replied.

"It were unbelievable," said Mr Biglanky.

"It's all a fiendish trick!" said Mrs Hingmy from even further up her tree but nobody was bothering with her – they were all so impressed with Ploppy and Spoony's sheep-rounding-up endeavours.

"I didn't know wolves could do that," said somebody else, "Can you get me one of them Lommypairyhummoxes Spoony?"

"Wouldn't think so," said Mr Biglanky who was being a smartypants again, "it's one o' them lone Humpylorxylaipies."

"That's right," said Spoony, "PloppyHairyLummox is the only sheepwolf in the whole wide world."

"He's one o' them unique thingummies," said Mr Biglanky, nodding in agreement with himself.

"Oh no, he isn't one of those uniqueses," said Spoony, who didn't know what unique meant, "he's the only one in the whole wide world."

"Wrong!" said Mrs Hingmy from further up her tree, "There can only be one unique thing."

"Rubbish!" said somebody else, "I can think of several unique things."

"Anyway," continued Mrs Hingmy, "it's supposed to be banished – along with that child."

"Oh. Good point," said Spoony, who had forgotten that, "We'd better be getting back to being banisheded."

"Well… ehm," said Farmer Stuckie, "ehm… is there any chance that the Airylumps could help us all get our sheep back home to their own pens once we've sorted them all out? It looks like he could do it in half the time."

"I'll ask him," said Spoony, and she bent down and whispered in Ploppy's ear, "They want to know if you'd chase everybody's sheep and goats back home once they're sorted out."

"Oh yes," said Ploppy, making what sounded to everybody like growly snuffling in her ear "it's great fun!"

Spoony used her craftythinkybrain for a minute, "He said he wants to know what's in it for him."

"No he didn't," said Spoony's mummy, although everybody had got the point. "Come on everybody, let's get started or we won't get any supper." That was enough for Ploppy so he stood up and wagged his tail enthusiastically.

"I blame the parents," shouted Mrs Hingmay from her tree, "And what about my wildhairy cattle?"

"Oh, Ploppy and I will round them up too," cried Spoony, who was feeling very pleased with herself. Ploppy didn't fancy rounding up the wildhairies one bit, so he shook his head until his ears flappe. But Spoony soon persuaded him, "It'll be easy Ploppy, you just go and annoy them and they attack you and then you run into the big cattle pen and they run in after you and we shut the gate." Ploppy stuck his bottom lip out and furrowed his wolfcraftythinkybrain as he wondered what came after that; surely he'd be stuck in the pen with a horde of dangerous cattle. It didn't sound like a very safe plan. "Oh, forgot to mention," added Spoony, "you have to jump out of the cattle pen before you get killed." This wasn't very effective in allaying his misgivings about the plan, but he had loads of faith in Spoony because she had such good ideas so he nervously agreed to give it a try. He loped off in the direction of the cattle who by now were quite a long way away and had enjoyed their freedom so much eating everything in sight that they were ready to lie down and chew the cud and have a nap. What they didn't need was a wolf turning up. Ploppy ran straight past them as he had done with the sheep and then ran a few rings around them so fast that they couldn't make up their minds in which direction to launch an attack. They were all tossing their horns and bellowing angrily so that when Ploppy eventually peeled off from circling them they were all as angry as they had ever been and charged after him.

Well, as you know, just about nothing can run faster than a wolf and it soon became plain to Ploppy that they couldn't catch him if he didn't want to be caught, which he didn't, on account of not wanting to be killed, dead. So every now and then he would slow down to let them catch up so that they thought they had him and then he would speed up again.

This made the wildhairies even angrier, so that by the time they were nearing the cattle pen they had lost all notion of where they were. With only a little way to go before they reached the cattle pen, Ploppy slowed down again to let them get nearer whereupon they all put their heads down in full-on attack mode with their tously hair over their eyes and then he ran into the cattle pen with the whole herd tearing after him bellowing and being almost as angry as Mrs Hingmy. Round and round the pen ran Ploppy until the cattle were quite exhausted (charging at something is quite tiring work and being very angry is even more exhausting) so all Ploppy had to do was a few circuits of the cattle pen and then jump over the high fence to leave the cattle doing a few more angry circuits wondering where the hated wolf had gone.

"Crikey!" said almost everybody except Mrs Hingmy.

"Did you see that?" said Mr Biglanky.

"Yes!" said almost everybody.

Farmer Stuckie added, "Blimey! That's the easiest cattle penning exercise there's ever been, and all done without the use of a single teenage boy."

"Perhaps there's no need for teenage boys if you have a Plompylairyhummox," said somebody.

"Huh! I wouldn't go that far," said the indignant parent of a teenage boy.[57]

"Yes, but you know what I mean," said the first.

"Hmmm…" said the parent, "I suppose so."

However, everybody else stood around being extremely impressed while Spoony sang Ploppy's praises.

"I hope my cattle haven't found the experience too upsetting!" cried Mrs Hingmy, "That dangerous wolf has got them all upset."

"Which ones are yours?" asked somebody, knowing very well that since all wildhairy cattle look pretty much the same, especially when they're thundering around in a pen being wild and hairy, Mrs Hingmy couldn't possibly tell, especially because, sitting where she was in a tree, her view was partially obscured by branches and leaves. And anyway, it would take a fair bit of forensic work to sort them out – after they'd calmed down.

"Exactly!" said Mrs Hingmy, "That wolf has got them all mixed up together with everybody else's."

"Oh good grief," said almost everybody in exasperation at Mrs Hingmy and they all put their hands over their faces[58] and shook their heads.

With all the sheep penned up and the wildhairy cattle penned up and extremely

---

57. Indignant parent: the parents of teenage boys often appear to be indignant in the face of criticism but it's just them trying to compensate for the embarrassing problem of having a teenage boy.
58. Hands over their faces: bossy people like Mrs Hingmy are rarely sensitive to just how patient and tolerant other people are about their impatience and intolerance and most probably it wouldn't bother them even if they were.

breathless and still very angry, all that remained to do was sort out which cattle and sheep belonged to whom. They decided to leave the cattle until they had stopped bellowing and peering over the top of the pen promising to kill anything that came near them, and to concentrate on sorting out the sheep into whose was whose. By the time they had got all the sheep sorted out and sheepwolfed back to their own pens, everybody was ready for supper, so Mummy Tooth headed home to get supper ready for Spoony, Daddy Tooth and Ploppy Hairylummox the Sheepwolf.

As they sat down to supper Ploppy, whose sense of hearing was as good as any wolf's and a million times better than a human's, could hear a thin and angry voice shouting from quite far away, "Has it gone yet? Is it safe to come down?" then less angry but more panicky, "Help! I'm stuck up a tree! Somebody will pay for this!" But to him it just sounded like the usual human cackle noises so he ignored it and ate his supper of seedy soup with lumpy bits, flatandchewybread and left-over rabbit pie.

Later on Daddy Tooth went to the dafting shed and invented the rescuing-somebody-from-a-tree device and he and Ploppy went off to help Mrs Hingmy down from her tree. "What took you so long?" she said, and "Get that vicious animal away from me! What's that ridiculous thing? One of your daft inventions I suppose? I'm not going near it!" But she was more fed up with sitting in the tree than she was afraid of the wolf. Truth to tell, Mrs Hingmy loved being grumpy and the wolf had been the best thing to happen to her grumpiness for a long time so she climbed down the newly invented ladder and stormed off without a word of thanks, giving the wolf a wide berth and a dirty look. Ploppy just gave her one of his happy, tail wagging looks in return, which made her even angrier.

Chapter 7

The Tooths Go Visiting

"Oh dear!" said Spoony after breakfast early the next morning, "What about our mountain Ploppy? We've been so busy helping with things that we forgot all about our friend the mountain!" She was quite alarmed at forgetting about a new friend, the second time she'd done this in as many days. "We'll have to go and visit the Galloot!"

"Ohh … poo!" said Ploppy with his bottom lip out. He did want to visit the magic mountain again; he was very well aware that if it hadn't been for the Galloot he might never have met Spoony, but he was also a bit afraid that he might meet Hazel and Willow again.

"Exactly! Poo!" exclaimed Spoony, "We'd better get a move on." Then she had one of her Spoonyish ideas, "Wait a minute. We should *all* go to visit the Magic Galloot." She had suddenly thought that it was a bit selfish not to include her mummy and daddy in their plans so she turned to them and said, "Yes! Mummy and Daddy should come too, Mummy, you've never met a Magic Galloot before have you?"

Ploppy thought this was a splendid idea and nodded so fast that his ears whacked about on his head like a pigeon taking off. He thought that Mummy Tooth was ever so brave and possibly fierce and dangerous when need be what with her fearless wildhairy taming endeavours, and Daddy Tooth might be able to bring along a load of scary wood shavings or one of his daft inventions. With this kind of awesome show of force at their disposal, if they did meet Hazel and Willow the two of them would be totally terrorfied and would run away.

Mummy answered, "No, I think I'd remember a Magic Galloot if I'd ever met one," although she had no clear idea of what it might be, "and I don't think Daddy has either." She looked at Daddy Tooth whose brows were all furrowed trying to remember if he had met a Galloot before, "No," she said with confidence, "I think we can safely say that he hasn't." Mummy Tooth had known Daddy Tooth for a very long time and it was just as well because he didn't have a good memory; in fact, he had one of the best developed forgetories in the village. "I think that's a lovely idea Spoony, we've had such a busy few days that we deserve a day off and it looks like it's going to be lovely weather too. You can help me get a picnic ready and Ploppy can help Daddy invent something to take with us."

Ploppy stuck with his bottom lip out because he had never invented anything in his life before – except rounding up sheep. He was a bit unsure if he'd be able to help invent useful wonderful things like not-very-round wheels. Daddy Tooth stuck his bottom lip out too because he was so impressed with Ploppy's sheep-rounding-up invention that he was feeling a little bit out-done in the dafting-things-up department. However, both of them felt that they had better come up with something as useful as a picnic so he got up and Ploppy trotted off behind him to the dafting shed.

While Mummy and Spoony were getting a picnic ready, Daddy Tooth was rummaging around in the dafting shed looking for ideas, lifting up bits of wood to see if they would inspire him to invent something with it. Ploppy watched intently because he wanted to learn everything he could about the fine art of making daft things. After Daddy Tooth had lifted just about every bit of wood in the place and inspected it for its daft potential he picked up a long piece of hazel wood from a bunch of wooden rods standing in the corner. He looked at it but it didn't give him any ideas so he stood there with it in his hand, leant his chin on the end of it and furrowed his brows and stood there for a while longer. Ploppy thought that this was a finished invention so he got one of the hazel rods and tried to do the same, standing on his hind legs with it under his chin but he couldn't work out how to do that so he lay down with his stick across his paws and wagged his tail. They both remained there for a while doing their best to think something up until Daddy Tooth took his chin off the end of the stick and said, "That's it!" The stick clattered to the floor, "We've invented the Standing There Thinking Stick!" Ploppy was delighted that a stick would help him with his thinking, something he was only starting to learn how to do, but anything somebody as clever as a Tooth said was good enough for him so he stood up with his stick and let it clatter to the floor like Daddy Tooth had done. *When you're in the company of an inspired thinker,* he thought, *you're best to go along with whatever creative wonder was being dafted up.*

Daddy Tooth did a little bit more work on the Standing There Thinking Stick prototype. Meanwhile Ploppy gathered up another three sticks and Daddy Tooth dafted them so that they'd be the right length: one medium one for Mummy Tooth, one shorter one for Spoony and one long one each for Daddy Tooth and Ploppy. Daddy picked up Mummy's and Spoony's as well as his own and Ploppy picked his up by the middle, and they both headed out the door to tell Mummy and Spoony how clever they'd been. After a minute Daddy noticed that Ploppy was still inside the dafting shed so he went back and together they worked out why he couldn't get out of the door with a long stick in his mouth.

"Look what we've invented!" said Daddy, "We've invented the Standing There Thinking Stick!" and he handed them out and showed them how to use them.

"Oooh! They're ever so clever," said Spoony and to test hers out she stood with her chin on her stick and did some thinking. This made her fall into a Spoonydwam straight away and Ploppy had to give her a nudge.

"Yes," said Mummy, giving her stick a try, "Mmmm, nnng…"She took her chin off her stick, "And they work – you can't even talk or move around when you use your Standing There Thinking Stick, you can only think. Let's take them with us and we can stop and do some thinking on the way." Everybody thought that that was a splendid idea, especially Spoony and Ploppy, both of whom, as you know, could easily forget to do any thinking at all.[59]

In no time at all they had everything ready for their expedition, so with Spoony in front leading the way with the picnic in her picnic bag slung over her shoulder and her Standing Their Thinking Stick in one hand and logdolly in the other, they headed off. It wasn't often that Spoony got the chance to be in charge, but she sort-of knew the way by now so she forged ahead with Mummy and Daddy following in line and Ploppy at the back all carrying their Standing There Thinking Sticks.

As they headed off, one or two of the villagers watched them go.

"There's them Tooths going' off somewhere," said Mister Biglanky, always intrigued as to what the Tooth's would get up to next.

"Yes, and they're getting chased by that dangerous wolf," said Mrs Hingmy.

---

59. Standing There Thinking Sticks: you may have noticed that even to this day Standing There Thinking Sticks are still in regular use. If you go to an auction market you'll see that almost all of the farmers around the ring are standing with their chins on a Standing There Thinking Stick. Of course, modern Standing There Thinking Sticks are a bit more technologically advanced than Daddy Tooth's prototype because they have ornately carved crooks at the top end, but the basic invention dates back thousands of years to the Tooth dafting shed.

"If they was gettin' chased, they'd be running as fast as they could, it's just followin' them."

"If they *were* getting chased," corrected Mrs Hingmy, "but it's stalking them, that's what it's doing. Those wolves are sneaky and stealthy."

"Those wolves?" said one of the children, "But there's only one of them … it."

"Why have the Tooths got long sticks with them?" asked one of the other children.

"It'll be one of Tooth's daft inventions," said another of the grown-ups. And indeed it was.

"Maybe they're gettin' rid of the wolf."

"I hope so," said Mrs Hingmy, "It's dangerous."

"Well, I think it was quite useful, we could do with a couple more of them sheepwolfses around here for sheep work."

"I think you mean, *We could do with a couple more of those sheep*wolves around here," said Mrs Hingmy, correcting grammar as usual, and immediately spotting her mistake, "I mean…"

"Gosh," said Mister Biglanky, "there's a surprise! Hey everybody, Mrs Hingmy wants more wolves around here!"

"No I do not!"

"For goodness sake, make up your mind!"

Very soon the Tooths and Ploppy Hairylummox reached the river and the stepping stones that Ploppy had had trouble with when he followed Spoony back to the village the first time. "Now," said Spoony, still feeling like an in-charge sort of person, "does everybody remember how to do stepping stones?" There were some troubled looks from her mummy and daddy because they hadn't been across the stepping stones for quite some considerable time. "Right, it's time to do some thinking and remember how to do stepping stones," said Spoony. Always keen to indulge her daddy and she propped her chin on her stick. Everybody did the same except Ploppy, who decided to chew his.

They all stood there thinking for a bit and Spoony said, "Well, does anybody remember anything? Daddy?"

"I can remember once when I was a little boy I went on a picnic with my mummy and daddy and we went to …" and he went off on a tangent remembering picnics when he was Spoony's age.

Spoony shook her head in embarrassment and turned to her mummy. "Mummy? Remember anything?"

"Yes, I think I've left the stew cooking over the fire…"

"No you haven't Mummy," said Spoony, "I meant: Do you remember anything about stepping stones." She was a bit disappointed because her parents were being a bit dim so while they were leaning on their Standing There Thinking Sticks she gave their sticks a kick and they both nearly fell over. "Come on, Ploppy, let's show them how to do it." With that she took her Standing There Thinking Stick and used it to steady herself as she jumped from stepping stone to stepping stone. Of course, she made it look so easy that all mummy and daddy had to do was copy her and they were over in a jiffy. They all turned to watch Ploppy cross with his Standing There Thinking Stick. He stood on the opposite side for quite a while with his brows furrowed trying to think of how he could cross like Spoony. Eventually he just picked up the stick and bounded across the stones wolf-style.

When they were all assembled Daddy Tooth said, "Goodness Spoony, I think you've just invented another use for a Standing There Thinking Stick! It can be used for helping to get across stepping stones."

"Yes," said Mummy, "they're now called Standing There Thinking and Crossing Stepping Stones Sticks."

"Poo!" said Ploppy, who didn't think he'd ever remember all that.

"My goodness," said Mummy, "Another invention from the dafting shed – what a wonderfully daft family we are!" And nobody in the village would have argued with her.

They set off through the birch trees with Spoony trying to find the silver birch that she had bumped into to show everybody how to do it but they found that they had left Ploppy behind. He was stuck at two trees that were close together and was trying to get between them with his Standing There Thinking Stick in his mouth. Unfortunately, the ends of his stick were catching on the trees and he couldn't get through. Spoony went to help. "Try going through backwards," she suggested, and Ploppy tried this but he still got stuck. He had a vague recollection that this had happened before but couldn't remember when. In fact, he'd done the same thing at the dafting shed door. Spoony decided that the best thing was for her to carry his stick for him so she put her logdolly in her bag and they all set off again, this time using their sticks to help them over the rough ground and up the hills and down the hills. With a stick in each hand, Spoony could walk exactly as if she had four legs, just like Ploppy. Her parents made do with one stick, and Ploppy, who had four legs to deal with and was quite pleased to be able to go between trees again.

"Oooh, Spoony!" said Daddy, "we've invented another use for Standing There Thinking and Crossing Stepping Stones Sticks! They're now called Standing There Thinking and Crossing Stepping Stones and Helping With Walking Along Sticks!"

Ploppy tried to remember this but it made his brain go all fuzzy, so he just sat down to see what other marvelous invention that Tooth the Daft would come up with.

"Oooh," said Mummy Tooth who thought that Daddy Tooth was ever so clever, "But it's a very long name. We'll never remember all that." Ploppy shook his head in agreement.

"I know," said Spoony, "let's just call them Walking Sticks for short."

"Blimey," exclaimed Tooth the Daft, "That's clever! Walking Sticks! A multi-purpose piece of wood. I bet I can sell dozens of these to the whole village." And he did and even to this day you can see people out walking with a walking stick. It was proclaimed by the whole village to be a great aid to transport and much more efficient at covering distance than any of his oddly shaped wheels.

After a fair bit of walking and getting deeper into the forest Mummy and Daddy began to feel a little nervous, "Is this really where you came all on your ownsome?" asked Mummy. She thought that Spoony had been a bit naughty going into the deep dark parts of the forest without a grown-up so she said so.

"Oh, I'd have brought a grown-up with me but there were none available at the time," replied Spoony. That didn't seem unreasonable to either Mummy or Daddy, who were easily persuaded, but Daddy still thought it worth pointing out that there were dangerous animals in the forest. "You mean like Ploppy the HairyLummox?"

"What about bears?" said Mummy, who was looking around her nervously.

"Didn't see any bears," said Spoony, "but I did see the world's biggest, giantest mouse. In fact, there it is over there." She pointed in the opposite direction from where Mummy was looking. Mummy and Daddy were looking at the forest floor for signs of a large mouse, "No, not down there, over there!"

They both looked up and there, several yards away, was a huge brown bear, sitting with his back to a tree with his face all covered in honey and a load of angry bees buzzing around him. "Blimey! It is a very big mouse," said Daddy Tooth.

"Mouse? It's not a mouse, it's a bear!" said Mummy Tooth.

"Bear? A bear?! Really?" shouted Daddy, and they both panicked as best they could and Ploppy joined in too because he was easily panicked and he knew a little bit about bears because his own wolf mummy had taught him who you could hunt and who you ought not to hunt. Bears were on the list of things that you ought not to hunt, along with humans.

"Danger! Bear! Run away!" shouted Daddy and they ran around in circles with their hands in the air in traditional panic mode, trying to agree on a direction in which to run away. Meanwhile Ploppy ran around in a fastpanic because he was good at it and it meant that he had a bit of speed up if the bear decided to attack.

"Oh for goodness sake!" said Spoony, "Look, even if it *is* a bear, it's completely harmless, I mean look at it. It's all covered in honey. Ploppy gets all covered in soup and *he's* harmless!" Ploppy looked a bit hurt because he really wanted to be a proper wolf and not harmless. "Oh, sorry," said Spoony, "Ploppy is very dainjlious. But the bear isn't."

Meanwhile the bear was a bit puzzled at all this commotion because he had only ever seen one human and that was Spoony and here she was with two big humans, who were running about like daft things, and a daft looking wolf in tow. It was something he had never seen before and he wasn't sure if he should interfere. Bears really like peace and quiet. They prefer to bumble around snuffling for berries and honey and stuff that they can eat without putting in too much effort, so he decided to ignore them and get on with eating honey and getting stung. Luckily for him, some of the bees decided that the Tooths might be a threat to their honey, too, so they buzzed over to them. One of them landed on Daddy's nose and he stopped panicking to see what it was. "Yowch!" he yelled when the bee stung him on the nose, and he resumed panicking. If there's one thing that nobody except bears can put up with it's getting stung, so the Tooths decided that they had better beat a sensible not-panicking-too-much retreat and continued on their way.

"Come on everybody," said Spoony, "all of this bear and bee panicking is giving the forest a headache. Let's get going again."

"Well," said Mummy Tooth, "this forest is a very dangerous place and no mistake Spoony. Are you sure it's really worth looking for a magic mountain?"

"Indeed," said Daddy, "you could have been eaten by a bear or a wolf or …"

"Well, I met both and I didn't get eaten by either. Nobody's going to eat you if you're polite." This was sort of in keeping with what Spoony's mummy and maddy had always taught her, that if *you're* nice and polite, everybody will be nice and polite *to you* so they really couldn't argue even if they themselves had always been taught that bears and wolves are dangerous, sorry, dainjlious.

They carried on through the forest until at last the gradient began to steepen and they could see the light of the clearing at the top of the Galloot through the trees. "Nearly there!" shouted Spoony. "Come on everybody, let's go!" And off she ran with Ploppy trotting after her not terribly enthusiastically. He was still quite worried that they'd meet Hazel and Willow, who would be their usual bossy selves and give him another doing. More especially, he didn't want Spoony to get a doing from them. But Spoony's infectious enthusiasm soon had him cheered up and when they at last trotted up onto the sunny top of the Galloot there was no sign of any wolves apart from himself. Soon Mummy and Daddy Tooth puffed their way up to the top and all four of them sat down for a rest. "Well," said Spoony to her rather breathless parents, "what do you think of our Magic Galloot?"

"Oh…" said Mummy Tooth looking around, "it's very nice indeed."

"Yes," said Daddy Tooth, "and it's very quite high up, too. You can almost see all the way to over there."

"Oh, no," said Spoony, who had better eyesight than her daddy, "you can see a lot further than that, you can see away, away, away over there," and she pointed away over there, "and away, away, away over there," and she pointed in the other direction, "and you can see my bedroom window in the chimley over there... sort of."

"My goodness," said her mummy, "so you can. Is that what makes it a Magic Galloot?" She had never seen as far as that in her whole life.

"Oh no," replied Spoony, "it's a Magicly Galloot because it talks, doesn't it Ploppy?" Ploppy nodded enthusiastically but he was still a bit nervous, nervous in case wolves turned up and nervous because a talking mountain made him nervous and nervous because, well, he was usually nervous anyway.

"What sort of thing does it say?" asked Daddy Tooth.

"Oh, quite ordinary things really," said Spoony, "small talk and stuff like that."

This was fine with Daddy Tooth; a talking mountain with a lot of weighty opinions would have been quite disconcerting, "Oh, that's nice, perhaps you should introduce us."

"Oh," said Spoony, who had been forgetting her manners, "I'd better." She cupped her hands round her mouth and knelt down on the grass and said in her best politeness that she knew how to do, "Good morning Mr Galloot! I'd like to introduce my mummy and daddy, Mummy and Daddy Tooth." She sat up and everybody listened, Spoony and Ploppy expectantly and Mummy and Daddy Tooth indulgently. But apart from the buzzing of the bees and the singing of the birds, there was complete silence at the top of the Galloot. She tried again, this time burying her face in the grass, "Good morning Mr Galloot! I'd like to introduce my mummy and daddy, Mummy and Daddy Tooth." But there was no reply.

"Perhaps he's not at home," suggested Daddy Tooth.

"I don't think so. I don't think a mountain can do not at home. I think he's sort-of ... stuck here," said Spoony, "I'll give it another go." And quite loudly she said, "Good morning Mr Galloot! I'd like to introduce my mummy and daddy, Mummy and Daddy Tooth."

Mummy and Daddy Tooth put their hands behind their ears to listen as intently as they could, not really expecting anything but not wanting to seem as if they didn't believe Spoony. Then just as they were thinking of saying something like, "Oh well, perhaps we..." there was a rumbling beneath their bottoms where they sat and a mysterious voice said, "There ... is ... abso-lut-ly ... no ... need ... to ... shout... Spoony Tooth," in a very grown-up-talking-to-a-child sort of voice.

"Hooray!" said Spoony, "Good Morning Mister Galloot!" And she jumped up and ran around with her hands in the air followed by Ploppy who bounded around too with his gangly legs and wavy tail.

"Aaarggh!" screamed Mummy and Daddy, and they jumped up and ran around with their hands in the air panicking in a fully terrorfied manner. "A dangerous talking mountain. Run away!"

"Oh for goodness sake!" said the Galloot, "you lot are worse than those wolves, and that is saying something!" At this they all stopped running around like daft things, and paid attention. "Good morning Spoony's Mummy and Daddy. Please, have a seat … relax."

"Aaarggh!" screamed Mummy and Daddy once again and they resumed panicking and ran around with their hands in the air, "A dangerous talking mountain. Run away." Unfortunately, they had forgotten which way they had arrived from, and couldn't decide which direction to run away in. After a few seconds, they had circumnavigated the top of the little mountain several times.

"Mummy! Daddy!" shouted Spoony, and she stamped her foot.

"Woohowoo!" wooed Ploppy and he flopped a paw on the ground. Wolves, as you probably know, aren't very good at stamping. They're good at very many things but stamping isn't one of them. Even so, it had the desired effect because it was so out of character that Mummy and Daddy Tooth slowed down and came to a halt where they'd started from. Anyway, to be perfectly truthful, neither of them was truly fit enough for proper panicking and they were quite puffed out.

"Are you quite finished?" asked the Galloot.

"Y, yes, I think so," said Mummy Tooth.

"Hmm. Well, I suppose I should apologise. I don't suppose you're all that familiar with a talking mountain."

"No," said the Tooth grown-ups.

"Never met one before eh?"

"Ehhh … no," replied Daddy Tooth furrowing his brows to see if he could get a talking mountain memory up to the front of his thinkybrain, "…No, I don't think so."

"And your daughter didn't tell you I'd be here?"

"Oh I did," protested Spoony, "but…"

"…But nobody believed you," interrupted the Galloot.

"No," said Spoony.

"Story of my life," said the Galloot. Ploppy nodded; he could relate to that. "Well, if it's any consolation, you're my first humans – at least, Spoony was. Up until now, it's been dinosaurs and giant cave bears and woolly rhinoceroses and mammoths and lately wolves, but no humans. Half-a-billion years of one species after another going extinct – you'll be next in all likelihood. The dinosaurs were the best company, had them for about a hundred million years, but they vanished virtually overnight. Stop me if I've already told you this." Nobody stopped him. They hadn't heard it and not even Mummy and Daddy Tooth had the faintest notion what a dinosaur, or even a million was, considering that counting up to twenty was all they could manage or they ran out of fingers and toes after that[60]. "Since then," continued the Galloot, "it's been one ice age after another interspersed with the odd brainless megafauna for the last ten or twenty million years and lately it's just been wolves, deer, wolves chasing deer, elk, wolves chasing elk, wildhairy cattle, wildhairy cattle chasing wolves, plus the occasional pine marten and squirrel. Honestly, you might as well talk to yourself. Why, back in my young day when the dinosaurs were around …"

"Mr Galloot," interrupted Spoony, who had a keen ear for a grown-up embarking on self-indulgent melancholic sentimental drivel, "would you like to hear about how Ploppy and me helped to round up the sheepses and wildhairy cattle?"

"Oh yes please!" said the Galloot. Spoony and Ploppy proceeded to tell the Galloot about their sheep and wildhairy rounding-up successes. "You rounded up some wildhairy cattle?" said the Galloot, "Well I never. They're worse than terrordragons. Did I ever tell you about my terrordragon friend?"

"Yes," said Spoony, and she carried on with her story. Mummy and Daddy were ever so proud that they had a daughter who had a talking mountain for a friend and they were even prouder when Spoony and Ploppy boasted about Mummy's wildhairy taming project and Daddy's daft inventions.

The Galloot listened intently and seemed to know that it's hard for anybody to know when a mountain is actually listening so every now and then he said, "Blimey!" or, "Good heavens!" or, "Well I never!" at the correct intervals. He had some difficulty with understanding what Tooth life was like, particularly when it came to descriptions of Daddy Tooths inventions. When Spoony and Ploppy had finished their story, he said, "Goodness! I never knew what I was missing all these aeons, it turns out that humans are quite useful. Oh, and the very occasional Hairylummox." Ploppy felt very proud to be included as a human.

"Have you never met any humans before?" asked Mummy Tooth, "I mean, we've been around these parts for a very long time. Surely somebody must have wandered past."

"My dear Mrs Tooth, with the sincerestness of respect, you have absolutely no idea of what a very long time is. Why, I didn't even know you'd evolved until I heard some of the other creatures talking about you."

"Other creatures? Talking? Talking about us?" exclaimed Daddy Tooth. But then it dawned on him that he already knew a wolf that could talk. "What sort of thing were they saying."

"Oh… not much," said the Galloot, "Just the usual sort of thing."

---

60. Counting on fingers & toes: some of the men in Spoony's village could only count up to eighteen or nineteen, having carelessly lost the odd finger doing difficult jobs about the place. It's a sad fact that although most folk start out with more, the average human has only 9.738 fingers and 1.967 legs.

"Like what?"

"Well … promise you won't be offended." They promised. "If you must know, all the other creatures think that humans are stupid, smelly, make cackley noises, are argumentative and leave a mess everywhere they go. So I wasn't all that bothered that none of you had ever happened by." All of this had an unfortunate ring of truth to it so nobody said anything, although Ploppy still thought that humans were ever so clever, especially Spoony.

"But then one day Spoony turned up and she seemed quite nice. Useless but nice and I thought I'd let her and the nice but useless wolf talk to one another." Spoony and Ploppy stuck their bottom lips out because they weren't sure whether to be offended or flattered. "However, it's all worked out rather well don't you think?"

"Oh yes!" said Spoony, "it's all been a greatly successful."

"Yes," said Ploppy, "It's been wondleyful, tolatty wondleyful. We've had all sorts of adventures and done all sorts of cleverly stuff. I've never been so happy. Thank you Mister Galloot."

"Aw … that is nice. It was nothing really, I was just bored … and I thought it would be interesting to see what would happen if a wolf and a human could talk to each other. I tell you what though, those Lummoxes have been back here again Ploppy – looking for you."

"Ohhh!," said Ploppy. The thought of his pack turning up and finding him with Spoony and Mummy and Daddy Tooth gave him the willies. He didn't want another doing from Willow and he especially didn't want his new pack, the Tooth's to get a doing either.

"Lummoxes?" enquired Daddy Tooth.

"You know Daddy," said Spoony, "Ploppy is a Lummox."

"But I thought he was a lone wolf," exclaimed Daddy.

Spoony sighed.

"Yes, they're the local wolf *pack*," said the Galloot, "The Great Pack of Lummox as they call themselves."

"A wolf pack! A wolf pack!" cried Mummy and Daddy jumping to their feet and getting ready to panic.

"Yes, 'fraid so," said the Galloot, "but I wouldn't worry, they're miles away, I wouldn't think they'll be back today. And anyway, they're not all that dangerous. I mean, look at Ploppy, he couldn't even catch and eat Spoony."

"Eat Spoony?! Eat Spoony!?" cried Mummy Tooth.

"Oh Mummy!" said Spoony, "if Ploppy was going to eat me he'd have done it long before now. I'm sure he'd rather have a plate of your special soup any day."

"What if we run out of soup?" said Daddy Tooth who was doing too much thinking.

"Or perhaps, if we don't have enough?" His voice rose to a panicky squeak, "What do wolves eat *then*?"

"Oh dear! We ran out of soup yesterday," said Mummy, joining in with Daddy in the not-being-very-bright stakes, "Run for it Spoony!"

"Good grief! You're *cackling*!" said the Galloot. This seemed to calm things down. "That was a cacklepanic if ever I heard one. No offence but I can see what all the other animals are on about."

"What?" said Daddy.

"You humans, how you're supposed always to be cackling and talking drivel. Do you all do that?"

"I'm afraid that about sums it up," said Spoony and Ploppy nodded sympathetically. He was thinking about bossy, cackley Mrs Hingmy, which made him think of bossy wolves like Willow. Being either a wolf or a human was a complicated business.

"Oh well," said the Galloot, "it can't be helped, I suppose, it must just be the way you're made. Why, quite a few species that I've known over the millennia talk incessant drivel, have you ever listened to squirrels?: Spoony said that she had but that she couldn't make out what they were on about. "Nuts," said the Galloot, "Nuts. Nuts, nuts, nuts, nuts, nuts. It's all they ever talk about. Then there's hedgehogs. They just talk to themselves: mutter, mutter, mutter, all day long about slugs and worms. Moles, they're just as bad and I wish they would burrow somewhere else – it doesn't half tickle! Give me a Giant Jawclanging Terrordragon any day if you want some common-sense conversation."

At this, Ploppy and Mummy and Daddy Tooth all looked around nervously to see if there was any sign of the fearsome creatures around but Spoony could see that the Galloot was going off on another wistful, melancholic ramble. It seemed that talking drivel was common to every creature on the whole widely world, including galloots, so she changed the subject. "But don't you think, Mr Galloot, that it's been awfully good fun being able to talk to one another?"

"Yes, it has. it's been delightful having you and Ploppy visit, and to meet your Mummy and Daddy and learn all about your adventures."

"Well, we wouldn't have been able to have adventures together if you hadn't fixed it for us to talk to one another," replied Spoony. She was now so used to talking to the Galloot that it put Mummy and Daddy Tooth quite at ease, and they all sat around in the sunshine on the top of the Galloot and chatted about all sorts of stuff from terrordragons to leftover pie, which reminded Spoony that they'd brought a picnic so she offered everybody a share of the flatandchewybread and the wildhairymilkcheese. The Galloot politely declined his share on the grounds that he rarely ate anything, as mountains, even small mountains don't but he simply sat there being sat on and listening to the happy chomping, chewy sounds of his new friends enjoying their lunch.

If you're enjoying yourself and the company you're in, it isn't long before the day quite gets along without you and it took Mummy Tooth to remind everybody, as parents usually do, that it was time to stop having fun and go home and do the chores that had to be done. Everybody, including Daddy Tooth, said, 'Poo!' at this but, of course, she was right and after listing a few of the things that had to be don (including having supper, which had Ploppy and Spoony on their feet in an instant), they made their goodbyes to the Galloot, thanked him for his hospitality and promised to come back and visit as soon as possible. Then the Tooth family, including its newest member, a very large wolf, headed off back towards the village.

"Poo!" said the Galloot after they'd gone. He'd been really enjoying the company, "I must do more of this sort of magic," he said to himself, "Definitely helps to pass the time."

Wolves to the Rescue

"So this is where you last saw Ploppy?" Bear asked Hazel and Willow as they approached the hill where Spoony and Ploppy had first met and first talked to the Magic Galloot.

"Yes," said Willow, "he was just hanging around being useless and scruffy, but he smelt of humans, and fire."

"Well, let's go and have a look," said Rosie. "We need to get this business sorted out." She began to scout round the hillside looking for signs of whoever might have been there.

They climbed to the top of the hill, sniffing the ground and the air as they went. "Yes, Ploppy and a human have definitely been here," said Bear, "and very recently. I'd say late yesterday, or even this morning."

"More than one human," said Rosie, "Three humans, all from the same pack." A wolf's nose is so clever that it can tell not only who you are, but who you're related to, where you live, what you had for dinner and, probably, what you were thinking. "This morning certainly," she said, "between mid-morning and mid-afternoon. They sat here, at the top for quite a while then …" and she followed their scent again, "then they went back down here, probably back to the human den. They didn't do anything other than arrive, stay for a while, then leave again."

"Oh yeh?" said Willow sarcastically, "Listen to the expert."

"And one of them is the same human, too, by the smell of it," said Hazel, "The one that Ploppy spoke of when we found him, all sweet and smelling of fire."

"It stinks. So it proves he's in cahoots with humans," said Willow, "He's hanging round with this pack of humans the whole time now. He's a traitor to the Lummox pack."

"Maybe he's tamed them and is training them to help with hunting," speculated Hazel.

"Huh! That'll be the day," sneered Willow, "and it wouldn't be the other way round either, now would it? You couldn't train Ploppy to hunt anything other than worms."

"Willow?" said Bear, quietly.

"Yes, Bear?" said Willow.

"Do be quiet."

"Indeed," said Rosie, "just shut up Willow before you get a doing." Then she turned to Bear, "There's some other scent here but I don't recognise it."

"Yes, I smell it now," said Bear trotting up to the bare rock at the top where Rosie had arrived, "It's quite a nice smell. Do you think it's human food?"

"Yes, look, here are some crumbs on the rock," said Rosie sniffing them carefully, "I've never come across this smell before."

"Mmm. Quite nice," said Hazel, sniffing it for the first time.

"Disgusting filth," said Willow, "Goodness knows what sort of rubbish they eat."

"Why do you go on like that all the time?" asked Hazel, but Willow, who was bigger than Hazel, simply rumbled a low growl at his fellow scout.

Bear just shook his head, *Young wolves*, he thought, *have no respect these days*. "We'd better pick up their scent trail and see where they went." The wolves put their noses to the ground and scouted the area around the top of the Galoot.

"Here it is, for certain," said Rosie who was by far the best tracker, "This is the same way they came and went. Let's go!" Soon they were bounding at an easy canter along the path that Spoony and Ploppy and Mummy and Daddy had taken, following the scent with ease, even at a run.

"This is heading towards the human den again," said Hazel.

"Oh really?" said Willow sarcastically. He was quite put out at having to look for Ploppy, a wolf he had no time for at all. Rosie slowed down and let Willow get ahead of her, then bit him on the backside. "Ow!" he yelped.

"Your turn to lead if you're so clever," snarled Rosie, "and if you miss the trail, you get another bite." Rosie did not suffer fools gladly.

They ran fast through the trees and then suddenly in the middle of the path they came across the brown bear that Ploppy and Spoony and Mummy and Daddy Tooth had met eating the honey. He had a full tummy and sticky paws and face and he had lumps all over where he'd been stung. With eating so much honey he was on a bit of a sugar high but he had a very sore face from being stung so he didn't know whether to be happy or grumpy. Rosie, who was taking the lead once again, Willow having taken a few wrong turns, skidded to a halt. Usually bears and wolves are a bit suspicious of one another because they sometimes try to steal one another's food but this bear didn't seem to have any food left and neither did the wolves. "Hail, oh Great Brown One," said Rosie in the proper bear-greeting manner, although, it being Rosie, not really meaning it because she thought that this really was Lummox country but nevertheless keeping her distance in case the bear was in a bad mood. The bear merely lowered his head in a kind of bear nod. Bears are not very talkative at the best of times, they don't even talk to one another very much and since they don't get a lot of company, they find it easy to persuade themselves that they're the only ones in the vicinity who really matter. After a few seconds of polite silence while the wolves stood ready to dart out of the way if the bear took a swipe at them, Rosie decided to continue to open up a conversation. The bear was blocking their path and simply to have run around him without saying hello would be needlessly rude. "Oh Great Brown One," continued Rosie, trying not to sound impatient, "if it pleases you, we are hunting some humans who might be accompanied by a young wolf." Most of the animals in the forest can communicate very well with one another. Sometimes it's by speaking to one another in their different ways and sometimes it's all done with body signals and the like but unlike humans who can usually only speak to other humans, and sometimes not all that well, most of the animals could communicate with one another and all of the predators like wolves and bears pretty well had to in order to avoid any conflict. Birds can speak to other birds, insects to other insects and so on. It's only humans that are so poor at speaking to other animals.

The bear was silent for quite a while. It was hard to tell if he was thinking or had fallen into a dwam or was completely asleep. After a while, he shook himself and began to mutter something under his breath about bees and their bad temper and being needlessly stingy with their tails and stingey with their produce. Then he looked up at Rosie and, shaking his head said, "I've never seen anything like that in my life."

"Well, that's no help," said Willow from behind Rosie, "Let's get going."

Bear quietly walked up beside Willow and took his ear in his mouth and squeezed it between his huge long canines. Willow got the message: he should shut up.

"So you haven't seen such a thing?" said Rosie.

"Oh yes," said the bear, "Never seen the like in my life."

"He needs to make up his mind," said Willow under his breath, "Has he seen them or not?" He couldn't help himself. "Ow!" he said, as Bear gave his ear another none-too-gentle squeeze with his big long wolfbitey teeth.

"So you haven't seen a young wolf with some humans?" asked Rosie tentatively.

"No," replied the bear, "I have … never seen anything like it in my life."

"Oh," said Rosie, seeing where some confusion might be coming from, "so you *have* seen a wolf and some humans but you've never seen the like before?"

"Nope," said the bear, "Never seen such a thing."

"He's an idiot!" said Willow, "Ow! Ow!…sorry Bear."

"Would it be impolite oh Great Brown One," continued Rosie after giving Bear and

Willow one of her dirty looks over her shoulder, "to ask, nay humbly enquire whether you can remember where and when you saw this group of humans …with the wolf?"

The bear thought for a while then said, "No …o."

This wasn't the answer she'd been hoping for so Rosie thought she'd give it one more go. Then the bear said, "It wouldn't … be impolite"

She waited for a while, expecting an answer but no answer came. Then she spotted her mistake. He meant *No, it wouldn't be impolite to ask, so you can ask.* "Oh Great Brown One, when and where did you see them?"

"It was here, this morning … or was it yesterday," he said, furrowing his brows into a headache. Bears tend to live a quiet life when they're not getting stung to bits by bees so their memories are quite often switched off for long periods. Because they lead such a quiet life, even when their memories are switched on, they don't have a lot to remember. And of course, if you spend half the year hibernating, which bears do, then you've got twice as much of nothing to remember as anybody else has. "Yes it was here … this morning … three humans and a wolf. Never seen the like."

"Did you eat any of them?" asked Rosie, hoping that the bear might have thinned the marauding humans out a bit

"Oh no," said the bear, "I'm not sure they're edible. Besides, I was busy getting stung, I mean, harvesting honey. Hmm … Oh yes, they got stung too so they went away for quite a while. Then they came back and got stung a bit more, then they went back where they came from in the first place. I've seen the little skinny one before. Never seen such a thing."

"He's an idi…." Willow nearly said it but he stopped himself before Bear bit his ear again.

"Skinny little runt of a thing," continued the bear, "Even if they were edible, you wouldn't bother with it. Nothing much to eat anyway. Too skinny. But it seemed like quite a nice little thing."

"Well, thank you for your help oh Great Brown One," said Rosie.

"Think nothing of it," said the bear.

"I don't think anything of it, " said Willow, unable to stop himself from being difficult and unpleasant, "Ow!" Bear the wolf bit his ear.

"Well, we'd better be going," said Rosie, and she looked over her shoulder and said to her brother, "Come on Bear, let's get after them."

"I'll do nothing of the kind!" said the huge brown bear indignantly. As everybody knows, you simply do not address a bear as Bear.

"Oh," said Rosie, "I beg your pardon oh Great Brown One. I was talking to my brother."

"Your brother's a bear? Ridiculous! Are you toying with me young lady?" The bear's tone changed to one of rage, and he stood up on his hind legs and waved his giant claws around and roared. Ten huge claws the size of coat hangers and huge white teeth albeit surrounded by very honeysticky bear lips – it was a pretty impressive sight even for a bunch of able-bodied wolves. He was so tall and massive that the wolves stepped back a few paces, ready to run for it.

But Bear, who was really quite brave and not easily startled or frightened stepped forward. "My *name* is *Bear* oh Great Brown One. I was named after the great masters of the forest such as yourself. It is a great honour."

"Honour for whom?" said the bear and he dropped back down onto all fours having satisfied himself and the wolves who it was that was in charge. "But I suppose you meant no harm. Look, if you find these humans that you're hunting …"

"Yes?" said Bear.

"… and if they turn out to be edible, bring me back a chunk, I always like to try new things, if they're nicely edible, in a nice way. What's the word? Nice to eat."

"Palatable," suggested Bear.

"Yes, that's it. Palatable, bring me a chunk if they're palatable."

"We certainly will," said Bear, "Well, we must be off oh Great Brown One. Thank you for your help." And the wolves ran around the bear who was sitting down now wondering about all of these new experiences, a human with a wolf, humans and a wolf getting stung to bits by honey bees, humans again, then wolves hunting humans then a wolf who was a Bear, but wasn't a bear. It was all very perplexing, but quite interesting. It made his brain itchy to think so much so he simply lay down and had a snooze until it was dinner time and he could go and get stung again while he tore open the bees' nest in the bee tree again.

As the four wolves approached the forest edge nearest the village they slowed and walked very stealthily towards the open birch trees where the forest thinned out onto a grassy slope.

Wolves are usually impossible to see unless they want you to see them, in which case, they're still almost impossible to see. Bear and Rosie stood just inside the edge of the wood, looking towards the village. They stood perfectly still, knowing that very few creatures will see you if you're in the shade with your back to a tree or you're amongst the undergrowth while remaining absolutely motionless[61].

As they approached the edge of the forest the wolves had also been careful not to get

---

61. Remaining motionless: you can try this yourself: just stand absolutely still in a quiet and dim corner. It's a very good way to give your mummy or daddy a fright. Just wait until they walk past you then jump out and scream at them like an angry monster. Going "Boo!" is not much use if you really want to scare the willies out of somebody and see them jump clean out of their slippers. Very loud angry monster noises work best. Do not do this to your grandparents.

upwind of the village in case they gave themselves away by scent but fortunately, there was hardly any breeze that day so it wasn't as big a problem as it usually was when they were hunting.

Being virtually invisible gave each of the wolves time to survey the village, and their keen eyes could pick out every detail and every movement even at the distance they were from the village. They saw Mrs Hingmy going about her business in her usual high dudgeon and Farmer Stuckie hoeing his crops. "Why is that human poking the ground with a long stick?" asked Hazel.

"I would never do that," said Rosie emphatically.

"I know," said Bear. There were many things that his sister thought were not in her job description, even if she didn't know what it was intended to achieve. "Who knows why anybody would poke the ground with a long stick. My father told me that his grandad told him that humans are all silly and useless and can't do anything that wolves can do."

"That'll be why Ploppy gets along with them then," said Willow, "He's silly and useless."

Bear simply sighed in exasperation at the young wolf.

Just then they saw movement at the bottom end of the village. A strange shape came flying over some green bushes and landed on the ground. It was Spoony's mummy being tossed over the hedge by one of her wildhairy cows.

"Did you see that?" said Bear.

"Yes I did," said Rosie, "I didn't know humans could fly."

"Maybe it only jumped," said Hazel.

"Maybe they can jump," said Rosie, "They don't look as if they could jump but maybe they can."

"Fat chance," said Willow, who was always being disparaging about everything, "Everybody knows that humans are useless. It's only got two legs – how could it jump?"

"One day Willow," said Rosie, "you are going to get *such* a doing."

"Oh really?" said Willow sarcastically to Rosie. He was no respecter of rank and quite fancied himself. Rosie, was no respecter of size and her hackles went up. She was on the verge of giving the young upstart a doing there and then. As you may know, wolf society is usually quite well balanced and everybody gets along with one another most of the time. However, every now and then some young upstart who doesn't know his place needs to be assisted in the business of getting to know his place and a "good doing" was how it was done. A doing usually amounted to being grabbed by the scruff of the neck and pushed to the ground and given a proper growling with much baring of teeth. It was quite scary but not generally harmful. When done in front of the whole pack, it was more embarrassing than harmful. Failing to learn good manners or good sense or respect for your elders could result in a series of doings of increasing severity. Rosie was walking towards Willow on the tips of her toes with her hackles up and her tail held high, about to skip a few stages in Willow's series of doings and go straight in at the harmful kind.

"With any luck Willow," said Bear, getting between Rosie and the youngster before she did give him a doing, "you'll get a doing from a human. I would think a small skinny one could show you a thing or two. Now shut up and pay attention." They were, after all, supposed to be being stealthy and invisible so that they could spy on the humans undetected. A snarly wolf squabble was the last thing that Bear needed.

Just then there was a huge kerfuffle at the same part of the village where the human had flown over the hedge. A young half-grown wildhairy came thundering out of the Tooth's gate which had been inadvertently left ajar by Mummy Tooth. The youngster had decided to make a bolt for it while Mummy Tooth wasn't looking. However, she jumped to her feet, grabbed it by its horns on the way past and wrestled it to the ground. Then she helped it to its feet. Thinking better of its escape plan, the young wildhairy bolted back into the pen and Mrs Tooth shut the gate behind it. Its mother, now ferocious at seeing her daughter wrestled to the ground, stuck her head over the gate and bellowed a loud and dangerously ferocious bellow. Mrs Tooth hit it on the head with her bucket then climbed in over the gate to have another go at milking it.

"Did you see that?" said Bear, "That flying human thing just attacked two wildhairy cattle on its very own with no help."

"Incredible. I knew humans were crazy but that's incredible. It just attacked a wildhairy," agreed Hazel.

"I would never do that," said Rosie.

After that it quietened down around the Tooth household until Spoony's dad, as usual, covered in wood shavings and sawdust, came into view looking for Mrs Tooth.

"Good grief," said Rosie. "What's that?"

"I have no idea," said Bear, "Another kind of human, I suppose, the snowy dusty kind."

Just then Mrs Tooth came flying over the hedge again and landed on Mr Tooth. They both crashed to the ground in a cloud of white sawdust.

"The flying one just attacked the big dusty one."

"Looks like they're every bit as vicious as they're rumoured to be," said Bear, "I wonder what's become of Ploppy. It's a bit worrying really, if they're that vicious with each other."

"They probably ate him," said Willow hopefully, and Bear and the others had to wait a couple of minutes while Rosie gave the young idiot a quiet doing using her well perfected stealthy doing technique. They didn't get another squeak out of him for quite some time.

The wolves stood and surveyed the village for a good while longer but there was no sign of Ploppy. Then suddenly, just as they were about to turn for home, Hazel saw some movement in the distance. "Look, over there, a wolf, in the distance! Behind those bushes."

"Is it Ploppy?"

"No, I don't think so," said Hazel, "he's much too big."

"And too clean," said Willow sarcastically. He obviously hadn't had enough of a doing and couldn't help himself.

"Yes," said Bear, "it doesn't look like Ploppy but it does kind-of shamble a little bit like Ploppy." Just then, Ploppy came fully into view, shambling along in his usual Ploppyish manner with Spoony hanging onto his fur to keep up with him.

"Good grief," said Rosie, "He's being hunted by that skinny little human."

"I don't think so," said Bear, "I think they're together, or he's being held prisoner."

"I told you," said Willow, getting angry and disliking Ploppy even more than ever, "Only Ploppy could get held prisoner by a skinny little thing less than half his size. Either that or he's in cahoots with them, he's a traitor. We were right to banish him."

This sort of negative talk was too much even for Bear so he turned to the young wolf, "Willow, I wonder if you'd be kind enough to come with me for a minute please, I need to discuss something with you in private."

"Oh, OK." said Willow, thinking that Bear might need some of his advice.

When Bear came back he was on his own.

"Did you give him a doing?" said Rosie.

"No," said Bear, "I just asked him to sit down. Then I gave him one of my looks." It was all Bear ever had to do.

"Was that all?" asked his sister.

"Well, I did ask him to explain 'banished' to me and to suggest who he thought might be next to get banished." Bear was supremely good at politics. But it helped to be very big.

"I think that wolf definitely is Ploppy," said Rosie.

"Yes, it could well be," said Hazel, "and if so, he seems to have cleaned himself up. What do you think we should do, Bear?"

"Rescue him, it's our fault, my fault, I should never have agreed to teaching Ploppy a lesson. We need to get him back."

"What, just the four of us?" said Hazel, quite afraid of any creature that would dare attack wildhairy cattle.

"No, we'll need to watch and make a plan then come back with reinforcements." They stood just inside the edge of the wood for a while watching silently and invisibly to see what would happen next but nothing much happened at all. The two big humans got up on their feet and spent a few minutes with the skinny little human and Ploppy. The little human had its arm around Ploppy's neck.

"Yes," said Rosie, "it looks like he's being kept prisoner. The little skinny one has hold of him."

From the shadows of the forest they watched for a while longer. The humans just seemed to be standing around doing nothing, something that wolves do too.

"Do you think they're talking?" said Hazel, "they look as if they're talking to each other."

"Wouldn't think so," said Rosie, "I mean, they're not really very intelligent are they?"

"According to what I was told by my parents, not at all intelligent. Well, we might as well get back to the den," said Bear, "Hazel, go and get that idiot Willow." Bear wouldn't normally have referred to another wolf in that manner in company because he didn't consider that sort of thing to be good management practice but he was a little tired of Willow. Rosie, on the other hand, had no such reservations.

"Yes Hazel," said Rosie, "go and get him and take him as far away as you can." Then she turned to Bear and said, "Yes, we've got other things to worry about apart from Ploppy and humans. There are wolf puppies to feed and a territory to patrol. He doesn't seem to be in any immediate danger from what I can see but he belongs with us."

"Yes," said Bear, "it was a mistake sneaking off without him, I never really liked the idea in the first place but who'd have thought that he'd end up getting mixed up with a bunch of cackly humans? Whose idea was it in the first place?"

"I think it was Willow's idea," said Hazel, showing up with Willow, "it was your idea wasn't it Willow?"

Willow gave Hazel a dirty look, "Hmmm … ehrrr … Might have been," said Willow. This was the nearest a wolf can get to telling a fib. Wolves, as you know can be sneaky and sleekit[62] and occasionally nasty (to one another) but they never tell lies. This is because if you tell a lie you have to remember it but the truth doesn't take any memory capacity at all so it's much easier to do. If you want to tell lies and get away with it by not forgetting them, and consequently not get found out then you need to write them down at the time and it's rather obvious what you're doing, especially when it comes to looking for your notebook to check which fib went where. Besides, wolves don't read and write so they just tell the truth because it saves a lot of bother. In those days humans couldn't read and write either but they weren't always smart enough to know that they weren't smart enough for telling fibs so sometimes they did.

"Would you like time to think about that Willow?" asked Bear patiently.

"Yes please," said Willow.

"Fine," said Rosie, "if that's your attitude and there's any trouble freeing Ploppy from

---

62. Sleekit: as you will recall, sleekit means sneaky and two-faced and conniving, and not in a very nice way.

the humans, I know who's going to be the first to fight with the humans. Any questions?"

"Happy to oblige," said Willow, launching into one of his smarty-pants diatribes, "They don't look dangerous at all. Only Ploppy could get held priso…." Both Rosie and Bear gave him a dirty look and he shut up. Just then the big humans and Ploppy, with the skinny human holding onto his neck went into the dark doorway of the Tooth cottage.

"Look, they've gone into that silly looking cave thing," said Hazel.

"Yes, they seem to have some kind of control over him," said Bear, "I wonder what it could be."

"Shut up Willow," said Rosie, who had just seen Willow's hackles start to rise and thought she'd be nice and stop him from saying something else disparaging that would lead to another doing. "Let's go back and speak to The Boss and make a plan of attack."

"Yes," said Bear. From where he stood, Bear could have called the whole pack to him even if they were some twenty miles away from the den, for a wolf howl from a wolf the size of Bear can carry not only for many miles but can echo for many hours. But to howl from there would have alerted the humans so he simply turned and began to canter into the forest with his sister Rosie at his side. Soon their canter became a run and in moments they were speeding through the forest faster than the wind with Hazel and Willow struggling to catch up.

It wasn't too long before they were back at the den, trotting into the clearing and panting with their tongues hanging out. Wolves don't pant because they're out of breath – they don't really ever get out of breath because they're so fit and strong that even running flat out doesn't bother them. But they do get hot from the exercise so they pant to keep cool. All four of them headed for the stream that ran past the den and had a long drink to help cool off. The two young wolves got into the shallow water and lay down in it. Meanwhile The Boss had come to greet them and Bear looked up at her with a big mouthful of water which he quickly gulped down. "Well, Bear," asked The Boss after the usual affectionate greeting that Alpha wolves always give one another (a tail wag, a sniff and rubbing their faces together). "What did you find out about Ploppy?"

"It's all a bit strange," replied Bear. We found Ploppy, or at least, we're pretty sure it's Ploppy, it looks like Ploppy, mostly, sort of …"

"Is it or isn't it Ploppy?" said The Boss, who was getting pretty anxious and a bit tetchy.

"Oh it's definitely him!" interrupted Willow.

"Willow," said The Boss, "go and stand away over there please … no, a bit further … and a bit more. Thank you."

"Yes, I think it is Ploppy, who else can it be," said Bear.

"Not much doubt about it," said Rosie. "The wolf we saw doesn't look like the Ploppy we're used to seeing. He's all smartened up like a proper wolf with a beautiful silver coat, like he had when he was a puppy. And this wolf sort of shambles a bit like Ploppy used to, but in a more, sort of, wolf-like manner."

"So why didn't you bring him back?" said The Boss.

"Well, it's not that simple. He seems to be being held prisoner by the humans."

"How many of them?"

"Three of them at least," said Rosie.

"Two-and-a-half!" said Willow sarcastically, from away over there.

"When we've dealt with Ploppy," said Bear quietly, "we'll need to deal with Willow."

"Yes Bear," said The Boss, "He'll challenge you for leader of the pack one day."

"I wish he would," said Rosie, under her breath, but Bear just shrugged. He knew that to be an Alpha in a wolf pack you didn't only need to be big, you had to be clever, a good hunter and a good politician. Willow was a bit short in all four departments.

"Come, we'd better have a council of war," said The Boss, "Hazel, get the pack together."

"Oh, oh, right-oh" said Hazel jumping to attention, delighted to have been given quite a responsible job. He trotted into the centre of the pack's forest clearing and called the pack with a long, authoritative howl, the best he could muster.

"As some of you will know," said The Boss, "Ploppy has been off being a lone wolf for some time." This wasn't wholly accurate but perhaps it wasn't the time to say to the younger pack members that some of the senior wolves had snuck away from him in the hope that he'd grow up. "But it transpires that he's been kidnapped by a dangerous pack of humans." There was a lot of muttering amongst the younger wolves, who had only heard stories of humans and weren't very sure that they really existed. The Boss continued, "We need to go and rescue him. Now, does anybody here know anything about humans?"

At this Spot, who was one of the most mature wolves in the pack and considered to be extremely knowledgeable and wise, stood up. "Well, as it happens, I know a bit about humans."

This was a bit of a surprise because she'd never mentioned it before except in telling nursery stories to the wolf puppies to which not much credence was given. Everybody pricked up their ears, which was rather unnecessary because as you know, a wolf's ears are always pricked up,

"My grandma," said Spot, "told me that her grandpa had told her that his grandma had told him that the Lummox pack used to raid the human dens every winter." This caused considerable consternation. "It's true, they used to go to the humans' dens and rummage around for food and stuff … when times were hard."

"And didn't they get attacked?"

"I don't think they got attacked all that viciously. I think, if I remember rightly from what I was told, that the humans just hid behind things and threw their feet at them." This caused even more considerable consternation, but, if you remember from before, the humans were actually throwing their shoes at them.

"They threw their feet?" said several wolves.

"Yes, by all accounts. Apparently they were very noisy and smelly, but not all that dangerous."

"What, their feet?"

"No, the humans."

"What about their feet?" asked somebody.

"Probably smelly, I would think."

"Did the pack eat any of them?" asked Willow, trying to sound tough. "If it was winter and they were edible then they'd have eaten them surely."

"What, eat their feet?"

"No," said Willow impatiently, "the whole human."

"More to the point," said one of the other wolves, "did any Lummoxes get eaten?"

"Oh," said Spot, "the story never told if any wolves or humans got eaten and I'm sure that it would have if they did. I mean wolves aren't edible so maybe humans aren't edible. And nobody's ever actually been able to say for certain that a wolf has ever been eaten by a human. "

"So what did they raid the human pack for?"

"Oh, I think they just stole food."

"I would never let anybody steal *my* dinner," said Rosie, keen to emphasise one difference between wolves and humans. And nobody in the pack could argue with that. If there was one thing that none of the wolves in the pack would do it was try and steal Rosie's dinner, even if she left it lying around.

"I think they must be quite dangerous," offered Hazel. "After all, we saw one of them, not even the biggest of them, attack a wildhairy and wrestle it to the ground."

This caused considerably more considerable consternation: nobody in the pack would even consider going within a day's run of wildhairy cattle because they were known to be completely mentally crazy and could cause totally fatal death if you tried to hunt them.

"Yes that's true," said Bear, "They don't look dangerous, in fact quite the opposite but anything that's prepared to attack wildhairies is something to be reckoned with. So it's no wonder really that Ploppy is held prisoner. He's probably afraid to try and escape for fear of being attacked."

"Ploppy's afraid of everything!" said Willow. "You wouldn't need wildhairy cattle tamers to scare him."

"This is hardly helpful talk, Willow," said The Boss.

"It's helpful talk if you want another doing," said Rosie.

"Look, dangerous or not, those humans have got Ploppy held prisoner and we need to rescue him," said Bear, who couldn't be bothered with long meetings. He always wanted to get on with stuff and meetings just slowed things down, much as they do in the human world. You would have noticed this if you ever went to work with your mummy or daddy: At meetings these days whenever somebody produces a white board or a computer slide presentation, those who don't fall instantly into a coma start thinking about how to get out of the meeting without causing offence or being sacked. "I think the whole pack except the puppies and the two aunties, Squirrel and Spot, should go down there, rush in as fierce and fast as possible, grab Ploppy and beat a hasty retreat before they set their wildharies on us ."

"Not a terribly sophisticated plan," said The Boss.

"Works for me," said Rosie.

"And me," said Hazel.

"And me," said several others until everybody had volunteered … except Willow.

"Willow?" said Bear.

"Waste of time and effort," said Willow, "but I suppose we'll have to."

"You're scared," said Rosie.

"No I am not!" said Willow.

"Good," said The Boss, "You can take the lead if we have to attack … or get attacked. Tomorrow morning before first light we'll head for the human den."

Chapter 8

The Wolves Attack

As usual, The Boss was up and about before everybody else. As we've discussed before, wolves are basically lazy and won't lift a paw as long as there's plenty to eat. There's nothing they like better, when there's no hunting to be done than a long sleep followed by a long lie (including much snoozing) which can last well into the afternoon – of the following day. However, on this particular morning there was unusual work to be done and although most of the pack had volunteered, it was still a struggle to get everybody out of bed so The Boss and Bear and Rosie had to go around nipping ears and tails to wake everybody up. There was a lot of stretching and yawning with young wolves saying *Eh?* and *Wha...?* and *Awww!* just like a bunch of modern-day teenagers. At last the pack was fully mustered, apart from the two aunties, Squirrel and Spot who were looking after the puppies. The Boss and Bear set off, first of all at a trot until all the complaining that the young wolves were doing was over with and they were all quite warmed up. The pace increased to a canter and gradually got faster until the pack began to stretch out at what they do best: their long, easy, loping strides that cruise over the ground at a terrific speed. In fact, if wolves were to do that in a modern-day town, they'd be booked for speeding and would get a big fine. In fact, if they actually ran flat out at their very fastest through town, the police wouldn't be able to catch them to book them.

So although it was many, many miles from the wolves' den to Spoony's village, the wolves, running like the wind through the forest, covered most of the distance in no time at all. The pack slowed down as it approached the Galloot because The Boss wanted to check out where Ploppy had last been seen. They stopped at the top of the Galloot for a sniff around.

"So this is where you found Ploppy the first time?" said The Boss to Willow and Hazel.

"Yes," replied Hazel, "and he's been back."

"Indeed," said The Boss, and by the scent only the day before yesterday as you reported … and he's been here with some of the human pack too … I can smell two, no, three of them."

"Yes," said Rosie, "they stayed for quite a while and then left the same way they arrived."

"Come on, let's go!" said Willow, trying to sound brave, "Time to attack the humans!" And he headed off down the other side of the Galloot, trying to look brave as well as sound it – but he was looking over his shoulder to see if the others had followed.

"Watch out for the bear!" said Rosie, "If you run into that bear Willow, you'll be in big trouble."

"That Willow, he needs taken down a tooth or two," said The Boss.

"Maybe the humans will do that," said Rosie, "It'd serve him right."

"I hope not," said Bear, "He might be a bossy young idiot but he's a good scout. He'll grow up eventually." Bear always tried to see the best in all of his pack. Rosie just shook her head; her brother was just a big softy.

The Boss simply sighed in exasperation; she had to get this Ploppy business resolved and get back to the den to feed the wolf puppies, "Come on, let's get on with this, we need to rescue Ploppy before something dreadful happens to him. We'd all better be ready for trouble – and we'd better catch that idiot Willow before he does something silly."

"Oh dear," said the Galloot to himself as the wolves left. "That doesn't sound very good. I hope I haven't upset the balance of nature by having a wolf and a human talk to each other." Then he thought for a bit, "On the other hand, it's been very interesting so far: the Spoonytooth and Ploppy Hairylummox actually got on very well, they've been the most fun and best company I've had since the Cretaceous perio. And anyway, I haven't done any magic for a while, might as well let all of those wolves talk to the humans, and then I might get the whole pack and the humans back here for some nice humming. Wolves can do some pretty good harmonies when they howl."

As it happened, Willow wasn't charging ahead as fast as he could; he was hoping the pack would catch up with him in case he encountered humans or a bear whilst he was on his own and pretty soon, much to his relief, he was running in the middle of the pack after being overtaken.

"Oh dear!" said the brown bear to himself. He had given up on stealing honey and had wandered off to a part of the forest with a lot of oak trees to eat a few acorns and look for truffles. He had been slowly settling into a nice dwam so that his bee stings could heal up, "Oh dear! Oh dear! Here comes a whole pack of wolves. First a human, then a human with a wolf, then more humans with a wolf, then a bunch of stupid wolves, now a whole pack. This forest is no longer even a slightly tranquil part of the primeval landscape! What's the point in living in the primordial idyll of pre-history if you can't get some peace and quiet?" Brown bears really can't be bothered with any bother from bothersome folk but he thought he ought to say something on a point of principal; he liked having the place to himself. The wolves hadn't yet seen him, so as they approached he stood up on his hind legs and roared an extremely loud roar.

"Rowwarrr!" he roared, so ear-splittingly loud that he gave himself a headache, which made him even more grumpy. The wolves all skidded to a halt in a fright and most of the young wolves were for running for their lives, never having heard anything that loud before. But, of course, when they saw that the older wolves had merely got a surprise instead of a terrible fright they simply bunched up a few yards behind Bear and The Boss.

In a commanding and very loud voice, but considerably less loud than his roar because his own ears were still ringing, the bear said, "Just what do you think you are doing in my part of the forest ... again?" The wolves all stared up at the giant bear and the young wolves were quite frightened; they all did their best to hide behind the older wolves.

"Gosh," said Bear to The Boss, "That goes right through you, what a racket!" Wolves have very acute hearing. And then to the bear he said, "No need to shout."

"I said," said the bear, "what do you think you are doing in my part of the forest?"

"What do *you* think *you're* doing in this part of the forest?" challenged Willow, trying to sound brave and authoritative but from the safety of the middle of the pack.

The bear wasn't expecting this sort of reply.

"Oh, well, I was looking for truffles, but ... Now look here!"

"Trouble? If you're looking for trouble," said Willow, "you've come to the right place."

"Not *trouble, truffles,* you idiot! Oh good grief!" said The Boss, "forgive my inexperienced ..."

"...stupid ...," said Rosie.

"...asinine ...," said Bear.

"… young assistant," finished The Boss. "We did not mean to disturb your repose, oh Great Brown One."

"Quite. What is it this time? Hunting humans again?"

"We are on a mission to rescue one of our pack who has been kidnapped by the humans. We're just passing through."

"Passing through eh? Well, on your way back through my forest …"

"Yes, oh Great Brown One?"

"… don't bother to pass through. Pass past, some other way."

"Oh," said The Boss, "very well. We'll see what we can do." This was unusually obliging for The Boss who was used to being in charge and was rather good at it. But to be fair, it *was*, more or less, the bear's part of the forest even if he was being a bit of a grump.

"Oh, and another thing, now that I think of it," said the brown bear, walking up to Bear, standing up again and towering over the second biggest predator in the land, "There's only *one bear* around here." He had begun to work himself up into a grumptizzie, something which bears sometimes do when they get properly woken up by having too much company. He was waving his huge claws in the air in a very aggressive and dangerous-looking manner.

"Indeed," replied Bear, standing his ground. He couldn't be bothered with a grumpy old bully and wasn't afraid of anybody. "I was thinking exactly the same thing myself." He waited for that to sink in, but it didn't, "Well, we'll be off then. Give my regards to the bees. No doubt we'll see you on the way back," and he walked round the bear's huge bulk without giving him a wide berth. Bear the wolf had been around long enough to know that a brown bear would have to be very quick indeed to catch a wolf like him off guard: wolves have the fastest reactions in the animal kingdom. The Boss and Rosie followed with the rest of the pack behind, but giving the bear a slightly wider berth and quite impressed with their leader.

"How cool is Bear?" said one of the youngsters to Hazel.

"Pretty cool," replied Hazel, "but it helps to be big."

The wolves cruised through the forest for a few miles more and soon reached the woodland edge near the village where Rosie and Bear, Hazel and Willow had spied on the Tooths and Ploppy only two days before. Most of the pack didn't need to be told to hang back in the cover of the trees and undergrowth because they were all a bit nervous about the human den. The Boss, Rosie and Bear with Hazel and Willow in tow went forward to look for any signs of Ploppy. They stood silently and secretly invisible for quite a while, but there was no sign of any activity in the village at all. Truth to tell, as we have mentioned before, humans back in those days didn't have to get up as early as we do today because life was well ordered and as long as things were done on time there was no need to rush.

what with it being so early from a historical point of view and very little time having been used up yet. This meant that what passed as first thing in the morning for wolves was much too early for humans and consequently, nobody was up and about in the village.

After quite a while one or two of the younger wolves began to get impatient and started to mess about at the back, being silly and thinking about having a game of tig. Rosie went back to have a word with them and when she returned she said to The Boss, "We're not going to be able to remain here for long without being discovered. Those young wolves have all got too much energy."

"Well, there's no sign of life down there. Perhaps they've gone hunting. Anyway, we brought everybody here for a show of force. We want them to release Ploppy, so as soon as something stirs down there and we catch sight of him I think we rush in and grab him."

"Exactly," interrupted Willow, trying to look brave again, "We all attack them and when they run away we grab Ploppy."

"Oh don't worry Willow. You can lead us into battle," said Bear.

"Battle?" said Willow, "They'll run away when they see us… won't they?"

"I certainly hope so," said Bear, "but if they don't, you can show us how it's done."

Just then there was some movement at the Tooth house which, you'll remember, was closest to the forest. It was Mummy Tooth with her bucket getting ready to try and milk the wildhairy cattle.

"Look," said Hazel, "it's the one that flies."

"Flies?" said The Boss. She, like most of the pack, had never seen a human before and knew next to nothing about them. Everything she did know about them had been got wrong, half-forgotten, half-remembered, made up and embellished by previous generations of wolves.

"Yes, it flew clean over those bushes and landed on the ground." At this Mummy Tooth went through the gate in the hedge into the wildhairy cattle pen. "Let's wait and see if it does it again."

"Yes and we might see one of those white snow monsters."

"This is all very strange," said The Boss and indeed, it was now strange enough for the younger wolves to have stopped messing around and take an interest. Almost all were standing right at the edge of the forest. They were just in time to see Mummy Tooth come flying over the hedge, clear the top of it by several feet, tumble towards the ground and land on her bottom facing in the direction of the forest. She was followed by the bucket which landed on her head.

"I thought you said it could fly," said The Boss. "That didn't look much like flying to me."

"Come on!" said Bear, "it's not a bad effort." Bear was always trying to see the best in people, even human people.

"Let's attack it," said Willow, liking the fact that there was only one human and it was plainly at a fighting disadvantage, what with having a bucket on its head.

"Don't be so idiotic," said Rosie,. "It's Ploppy we want."

While this was going on, Daddy Tooth came round the hedge and lifted the bucket from Mummy Tooth's head. Now that she could see, she was looking directly at the wolves and saw them all lined up at the edge of the forest far away on the other side of the river, "Wolf attack! Wolf attack!" she cried and jumped to her feet and ran around panicking.

"Don't be silly," said Daddy Tooth. "It's only Ploppy."

"No, no nooo! Nooo, look, hundreds and hundreds of ravening wolves at the edge of the forest."

Daddy Tooth looked up at the forest edge and, sure enough, in the distance, over the river at the edge of the forest, were what looked like hundreds of wolves. Of course, it was only the Lummox pack which numbered not much more than a score, but, to be fair, when you've had a fright, you might as well act as if it's double the danger, just to be on the safe side.

"Aaaargh!" he yelled, "Wolf attack! Wolf Attack! Aaaargh!" and he joined in with Mummy Tooth's panicky running around in circles with, "Hundreds of wolves, Aaaargh!"

"Good grief!" said Bear, "Look at that! And what a racket! All the old stories were true, humans do make loud cackly noises."

"I think we've been spotted," said Rosie "and they're calling the rest of their pack."

"They're not very good at howling," said Willow, "… as you'd expect."

Back down at the village, Mrs Hingmy had heard the racket and, delighted to hear the Tooths panicking about wolf attacks, she obligingly ran around the village yelling, "I knew it! I knew it! Now the Tooths are being attacked by hundreds of wolves. The Tooths' wolf has brought thousands of wolves! They'll kill us all!"

Of course, all this racket alerted the whole village, and by the time reports had reached people at the top of the village furthest away from the Tooths' place, there were, apparently, tens of thousands of wolves attacking the village and hundreds of people had already been mauled to death – even though there were only a few dozen people in the whole village and in those days nobody could count past twenty. Even though most people in the village had more than the average number of fingers and toes[63], some had a lot fewer than that. Some of the villagers, whose curiosity had overcome their fear, began cautiously to make their way down to the Tooths' place armed with gardening tools and farming

---

63. Now as we've discussed previously, you've probably got more than the average number of fingers and toes, even if you've only got ten fingers and ten toes. You can work this out for yourself later.

implements. Other people made sure that all the children were locked up in their rooms, which was difficult because locks had yet to be invented and few of the houses had more than one room, so most of the children simply snuck out to see what the commotion was about. Pretty soon, everybody who was brave enough (not many) had grabbed something for a weapon and made their way towards the end of the village nearest the forest and were peering round corners to see if they could see any wolves. It wasn't long before this bunch of frightened, frightened-but-brave, brave, nosey, brave-and-nosey and frightened-but-nosey or simply easily led people had invited themselves into the safety of the Tooths' house where they could safely look out for thousands of marauding wolves. Those for whom there was no room inside hid nervously behind things outdoors. Meanwhile, Mummy and Daddy Tooth were outside doing their best to panic whilst simultaneously looking for "wolf attack" weapons and regretting ever inviting a wolf into their home.

"I knew it!" said Mrs Hingmy, "These Tooths have brought *death and destruction by wolf* down on us all!"

"Has anybody been hurt yet?" asked Farmer Stuckie.

"Where are the wolves anyway?" asked Mr Biglanky. This was a fair question because the wolves had slid back into the shade of the trees to study the behaviour of the humans without being seen themselves. As it happens, this was the first ever case of what is now known by the Ancient Greek[64] word Anthropology[65].

Meanwhile the wolves were as perplexed and worried as the villagers. "There seems to an awful lot of them around that den now," said Hazel, a little worried that their Ploppy rescuing venture wasn't going to be as easy as they had all hoped.

"Let's just watch them for a while," said The Boss. She and Bear had seen a lot of strange things in their time and the best thing to do was always to do what wolves do well: be silent and invisible until you can assess the situation.

Meanwhile, Rosie, who was like her brother and not scared of very many things said, "We don't have to worry about that lot down there yet, I don't see Ploppy anywhere. If he does show up, all we have to do is rush in and grab him while the humans are arguing amongst themselves. In fact, now that I think of it… Willow! Come here for a minute please."

Down in the village, Mrs Hingmy had managed to gather some support for her anti-Ploppy campaign and a few people were nodding in agreement when she repeated her usual complaints about, "Should never have allowed a wolf…" and, "… no place for

---

64. Ancient Greek: of course, our story takes place much longer ago than ancient so in point of fact, in this case, "Ancient Greek" was actually in the future so wasn't ancient at all; technically, it was Future Greek.
65. Anthropology: the study of humans and their behaviour. Anthropologitists use lots of Ancient Greek words to describe humans and their behaviour. However, their most commonly used words and phrases when studying people aren't Greek but are ordinary words and phrases like, "Oh dear, why did he…?" or "For goodness sake!" and, "Oh! I bet that hurt". Anthropologitists quite often put their hands over their eyes and shake their heads when they're studying human behaviour.

dangerous wild animals" and, "I blame the parents" (meaning Spoony's mum and dad).

All of this time, Spoony and Ploppy had been off playing quite far from the village in the opposite direction from the forest and were collecting herbs and vegetables for dinner,[66] so they had no idea what was going on back home. However, such was the commotion that Mrs Hingmy was stirring up that soon the racket began to make itself heard to Ploppy's super-sensitive wolf hearing.

"Ohh!" he said, "I can hear angry voices back at our house."

"Ooohh!" said Spoony, and she listened as hard as she could, "I think you're right Ploppy. Maybe the sheep and wildhairies have got out again and we'll be needed to get them sorted out again. Come on, it sounds like an emergency! We'd better get a move on!" They headed off at a run back to the village feeling important and necessary.

Around about then, the villagers, instead of hiding behind things, eventually plucked up the gumption to set off to defend the village from an attack by millions of vicious, potentially human-eating, marauding wolves. This was something that was slightly easier to muster now that no wolves could actually be seen, and, indeed, since it was only Mr and Mrs Tooth who had actually seen the giant pack of marauding wolves and they were acknowledged by everybody to be completely daft, then an expedition of at least a few yards in the direction of the forest didn't seem too intimidating. And after all, there was a river between them and the forest which ought to provide some defense against wolves, or slow a wolf attack down long enough for everybody to run for cover.

"They're coming this way," said Willow nervously.

"Good!" sneered Rosie, "you won't have so far to go to show us all how brave you are."

"Just wait and see what happens," said Bear, "They don't look very well organised." And of course, they weren't.

No sooner had he said this than Spoony and Ploppy rounded the Tooth yard and appeared in front of the villagers just as they headed nervously off in the direction of the river and the forest.

"There it is!" yelled Mrs Hingmy, "Attack the wolf, drive it from the village!" This didn't seem such a daunting task because only one wolf didn't present as great an apparent danger as the tens of thousands of wolves rumoured to be waiting in the forest to attack the villag. So a few of the villages walked nervously towards the (potentially) ravening wolf who had been living in the village for the last couple of weeks. However, since Ploppy and

---

66. Collecting food: in those days, people knew where to look to get free food from the countryside. It was a bit like going to the supermarket except that the food was fresh and you didn't have stuff on offer that you wouldn't want to eat anyway. Nobody worried about their diet back then because all of the food was good for you – except the poisonous stuff that killed you outright, like certain toadstools. If you ever eat a toadstool, it'll probably be the last thing you ever eat.

Spoony had already established themselves as the best sheep and cattle management team anybody had ever seen, there wasn't a huge amount of enthusiasm for getting rid of him entirely. Nevertheless, Ploppy, who had a well-developed instinct for self-preservation, began to move away from the villagers while Spoony stood with her hands on her hips about to demand an explanation.

"Goodness me!" said Bear, "There's Ploppy – time to go. Come on Great Pack of Lummox. It's time to show your mettle! One of our kind needs to be rescued!" He set off at a gallop with The Boss and Rosie at his side and the rest of the pack following, albeit less enthusiastically. Wolves, as we've discussed, with the possible exception of The Boss, Bear and Rosie, are not any braver than humans when push comes to shove, so the rest of the pack trotted forwards as nervously as the villagers. The villagers were so focused on their easy-to-deal-with wolf danger in the shape of Ploppy that they failed to notice the wolf pack approaching. But Spoony and Ploppy did.

"Oh dear!" said Ploppy, "Look, it's my pack! What are they doing here? Oh dear!" Now he was stuck between the villagers, who seemed to have turned against him, and his former pack who had snuck away from him and which included the odd nasty element like Willow.

He didn't know what to do, but Spoony did, she couldn't be bothered with all this nonsense. She marched between Ploppy and the villagers with her hand up holding her logdolly in a very authoritative manner. "Now hold it right there!" she shouted. It was so unusual for Spoony to be that bossy that everybody held it right there where they were. Then she turned round and marched towards the river just as the wolves reached the other bank. "And you lot," she yelled, "Just you stay where you are! What on earth is going on around here?"

Absolutely nobody on the wolf side yet understood what she had said, but they hadn't expected such a small, skinny little thing to be unafraid of them, and it seemed that there must be more to this human than met the eye. Perhaps it was more dangerous than it looked. And as far as the village was concerned, they were petrified of the wolves but also felt a bit wimpish because plainly Spoony wasn't scared and she had stopped the wolves right in their tracks. Truth to tell, Spoony had only ever met one wolf in her entire life and he was a very nice person so she had no reason to believe that a whole pack wouldn't be equally nice. Of course, as you know, Spoony didn't always work things out before it was too late.

"Right!" she shouted, "I want an explanation!"

"Blimey!" Farmer Stuckie, "What a brave little girl."

"Unruly child!" said Mrs Hingmy, "I blame the parents."

"Funny little thing," said Mr Biglanky.

"Smells a bit smoky," said somebody else.

"Exactly!" said Mrs Hingmy.

"Ha," said Willow, now feeling a bit braver because the skinny little thing on the other side of the river was a fraction of his size. "I'll show those humans and I'll rescue Ploppy." This was a surprise to all of the wolves because they all knew that Willow, like all bullies, wasn't really brave and he certainly didn't like Ploppy enough to want to rescue him. It was just bravado.

"Oh dear, it's Willow," said Ploppy.

"Is that the wolf who was horrible to you?"

"Yes, he's a big bully."

Willow charged towards Spoony and Ploppy while all the villagers watched.

"Oh dear!" said Mummy Tooth, "Run Spoony!" She and Daddy Tooth ran to the rescue, not knowing what they could do against a huge snarling, ravenous wolf.

Willow charged toward Spoony but just like she had done on the top of the Galloot when she first met Ploppy, she simply stayed where she was because her thinkybrain hadn't ever thought of a suitable reaction to this sort of life or death situation. Willow didn't expect this: the skinny little thing was supposed to turn and run and he skidded to a halt, overcome by a sudden lack of bravado. However, he managed to muster a huge snarly growl.

"Graaawwwool!" he said, right in the skinny little thing's face.

Spoony had seen this sort of thing before. She wasn't impressed.

"Graaawwwool, growl, snarl growl!" said Willow.

"What's he saying?" asked Spoony, who could only make out a little of Willow's angry growly speech.

"He said he's going to kill you and eat you." Suddenly it was too much for Ploppy, "Go away Willow and don't you say such nasty things to my Spoony Tooth or I will, I will…"

"You'll do what, you poor excuse for a Lummox? You had better get back to the pack or else."

"Ohhh!" said Ploppy who was still very scared of Willow even though he was now every bit as big as him, "I'll, I'll …"

"Excuse me a minute!" said Spoony, "Don't you speak to my Ploppy like that."

"Ha!" said Willow, "Who are you to talk to me like that you skinny little…"

Whack! Spoony hit Willow right across the nose with her logdolly, quite hard.

"Ow, ow, ow," whined Willow in a very babyish way, "Owwooo, whine!" To be fair, it wasn't all that babyish because a whack on the nose with a stick, sorry, logdolly is actually quite panful.

Just then Mummy and Daddy Tooth arrived on the scene and very bravely got between

Spoony and the giant ravening wolf who was still whining about his nose in a babyish manner.

"Just as well you showed up when you did Mummy and Daddy," said Spoony, "that is a very rude wolf indeed, I don't know what I'd have done."

By now Bear and The Boss had crossed the river and were approaching at a polite and cautious pace having spotted that the situation wasn't all that bad, Willow, having been shown some manners by a strange little creature a quarter of his size.

"Willow," said Bear as he approached, "thank you for introducing yourself to the humans. Would you now mind getting back to the pack and see if you're needed back there." Bear was an excellent manager of staff in the workplace and knew that it didn't help to discipline staff in front of strangers. Willow didn't need much encouragement so he scarpered back across the river with his sore nose.

When he got back to the pack, Rosie said, with uncharacteristic sympathy, "Don't feel too bad Willow. We all mess up sometimes. At least the youngsters will think you're brave. That skinny little human looks like a real handful, quite dangerous in fact."

The two senior wolves were very, very close now, and Mummy and Daddy Tooth were trembling because the wolves were both huge, especially the one who was much bigger even than Plopp.

"Oh… hello Mummy, hello Daddy," said Ploppy. Spoony stared at Ploppy, completely surprised to find that the two in-charge looking wolves could be his real mummy and daddy.

"Hello Ploppy," said The Boss, sniffing him as wolves do when they meet, "how are you?"

"Oh, I'm fine … How are you?" Ploppy was wagging his tail furiously but not sniffing back because you don't sniff your superiors until you've been invited.

"We're fine," said Bear, "We've come to rescue you from the humans."

"Is that your mummy and daddy?" interrupted Spoony getting out from behind her own mummy and daddy where she'd been pushed for safe keeping by her extremely frightened parents.

"Yes," replied Ploppy, "It's my real mummy and daddy, my mummy and daddy are leaders of The Great Pack of Lummox." Ploppy was quite proud of his parents. "Mummy and Daddy, meet Spoony Tooth. Spoony Tooth rescued me already so I don't need rescued actually. But it's nice to see you."

"You don't tell me that that little thing understands what you're saying?" said Bear.

"Oh yes, it's a special type of human called a Spoony Tooth and it's ever so clever."

"Blimey!" said Bear, "When did it learn to talk?"

"Oh, I've always been able to do that," said Spoony, "Oh, Ploppy, isn't it wonderful that your daddy can talk to us?"

And at the same time, after he'd jumped with surprise, Bear said, "Blimey, listen to that Boss! The SpoonyToothhuman creature can actually talk, it can talk proper wolf! Who'd have thought eh? A talking human! It's quite a cute little thing too."

"Oh, I know what it is," said Spoony, "Did you visit the Galloot on your way here?"

"Well, yes we did," replied Bear, still astonished with himself that he was actually talking to a dumb animal like a human. He sneaked the occasional look over his shoulder to see if the pack were laughing at him.

"And did he talk to you?"

"Well, ehhhm," said Bear, "I've heard that galloots are supposed to be magic but, well, it's only a, well, I don't think a hill or a mountain can talk."

"If you can talk to a human," said The Boss, whose ears were still on the top of her head in surprise, "and if a skinny little runt of a thing can knock some sense into that idiot Willow, anything's possible."

Bear whispered in The Boss's ear, "I think you're forgetting that it can understand you, try not to be so blunt. You'll hurt its feelings." Bear was a superb negotiator.

"Oh, I'm not bothered about that," said Spoony, "You haven't met Mrs Hingmy yet, she's really blunt. Anyway, about the Galloot, he's a *magic* Galloot. He fixeded it for me and Ploppy to talk to one another."

The Boss leaned over towards Bear and whispered, "Its grammar's not very good."

"Yes, well, it's probably still learning proper wolf," whispered Bear, as usual seeing the best in everybody, "Not its first language and all, still getting the hang of it I would think." Then to Ploppy he said, "Are these the human pack leaders?"

"Pffff," giggled Spoony, "Oh no, we don't have a leader, that's why we always argue amongst ourselves."

"Take it from me," said The Boss, "having a leader wouldn't change that one bit."

Ploppy, remembering his manners, decided to get everybody properly introduced. Using his mummy and daddy's proper names he said, "The Boss and Bear, this is Spoony Tooth's mummy and daddy. They're called Mummy and Daddy Tooth, Mummy and Daddy Tooth meet The Boss and Bear."

"How … how … do you do, Mister The Boss," said Daddy Tooth bravely coming forward and extending a trembling hand towards the largest of the two wolves, "I'm Daddy Tooth."

"Oh no," said Ploppy, "that's Bear, this is The Boss and he directed Daddy Tooth's shaky hand towards the other, slightly smaller but nevertheless very large wolf who sniffed it in polite wolf manner before Daddy Tooth quickly withdrew it in case it got bitten off.

All in all, Spoony was warming to this new development and decided to get everybody introduced properly. Obviously, her friend the Galloot had decided to make it a bit easier for the Lummox wolves and the Tooths to communicate and it was all turning out so well. Spoony got behind her mummy and pushed her towards Bear where she got sniffed politely around the face by the huge predator. Mummy Tooth, being an excellent diplomat, leant forward and sniffed Bear politely around the face. Both of the wolves could tell by sniffing them that these were the humans who had visited the Galloot and they could also tell that the skinny one was the sweet sooty one whose smell had rubbed onto Willow and Hazel's fur when they first reported that they'd met Ploppy.

Watching from the safe distance where they had all decided to remain, the villagers were completely flabbergasted. They had just seen Spoony Tooth repel a genuine Wolf Attack using that silly stick that she called her dolly and now she and her daft parents were standing there apparently talking to another two giant wolves, one of whom was particularly giant.

"I knew it! I knew it! It's all a plot by the Tooths. Next thing you know there will be wolves all over the village ravening away like mad, eating sheep and cattle and people…"

"Mrs Hingmy," chorused the villagers, "do be quiet for a minute." A few of them were now less afraid than they were intrigued, and Mr Biglanky and Farmer Stuckie wondered out loud whether, now that there seemed to be a glut of wolves nearby, perhaps a wolf or two couldn't be acquired from the Tooths for their own personal sheep rounding up duties.

"I wonder what they're talking about," said Farmer Stuckie, "but it doesn't look like there's going to be any trouble. That giant wolf's wagging his tail like the Plumpylommyhairox does when he's being friendly."

"How can they be talking to wolves? Wolves can't talk," said Mrs Hingmy, as usual looking for an argument and sounding a bit like Willow.

"How do you know?" put in somebody else, "They must be able to talk to one another."

"Rubbish, they're just wild animals, dangerous, ravenous wild animals," Mrs Hingmy wasn't going to give in. "Animals can't talk."

"Well them Tooths talks to the Pommylairyhumplox as if it could understand them," added Mr Biglanky, "and it seems to answer them back."

"Just stupid slobbery growly noises," insisted Mrs Hingmy.

"And young Spoony seems to be able to tell it what to do when it comes to rounding up the sheep and the wildhairies, and it hasn't been dangerous at all yet," said Farmer Stuckie.

"Well, if you think wolves are so safe then why don't you go and ask them what they're doing here?" said Mrs Hingmy. "They could be planning an attack."

"I might just do that … in a minute." said Farmer Stuckie, "And anyway, I thought you just said that they couldn't tal. And I don't think they'd come and tell us if they were planning an attack would they?"

"Ohhhh, ohhh!" spluttered Mrs Hingmy and stormed off in the huff, muttering angry stuff under her breath.

"Tell me, Ploppy," said The Boss, "have you been getting enough to eat?" She had noticed that Ploppy was looking very well, and indeed, had turned into an exceptionally handsome young wolf. Even though she was an Alpha wolf, like all mummiess she could ask embarrassing mummyish questions in front of other people.

"Oh yes," replied Ploppy, "We have soup and stew and occasionally pie and flatandchewybread and all sorts of things."

"Soup and …? So what does a soup look like? Or a schew?" asked The Boss.

"And how do you hunt them?" asked Bear.

"Oh you don't hunt soup," replied Ploppy. "It just turns up in a bowl and you eat it." Ploppy still wasn't sure how Mummy Tooth managed to magic up things like soup; it just seemed to turn up when it was needed.

"It just turns up to get eaten?" said Bear looking at The Boss, "We're missing out on something here, a prey species that just turns up to get eaten?"

Spoony stepped in, "Oh no Mr Bear, my Mummy makes the soup out of stuff, don't you Mummy? She makes soup and pie, and Daddy makes flatandchewybread."

This made no sense to either Bear or The Boss. "Well, as long as you're getting enough to eat Ploppy," said The Boss, "Balanced diet and all."

"Would you like to come and try some?" said Spoony and she turned to her parents, "Can we invite Mr. Bear and Mrs The Boss over for some lunch?"

By now, curiosity had got the better of Rosie. Things seemed to be getting along fine with her brother, The Boss and the humans so she turned to Willow.

"Willow, take charge please," she said.

"Really?" said Willow, glad to have something senior to do. Several of the young wolves groaned, none of them liked Willow much. Rosie and Hazel began to approach the meeting in a calm and polite manner. Pretty soon they were introduced, and Spoony invited them for lunch too.

Mummy Tooth whispered, "I don't know if we've got enough in the larder for the whole pack."

"Well, maybe not the whole pack, but they can have a taste," said Spoony, "Come on everybody, let's all go and try soup." With that, she led Bear and The Boss, Rosie and Hazel, Ploppy and Mummy and Daddy Tooth back toward the house.

"Oh dear!" said Farmer Stuckie, beginning to reverse in the opposite direction, "They're coming this way."

"I think Tooth the Daft has knocked it off this time," said Mr Biglanky, also in reverse, "Maybe he's captured a sheepwolf for everybody!"

"You'll all be eaten!" screamed Mrs Hingmy from quite far away. "The place will be overrun with ravenous wolves!"

"What's that?" asked Rosie, who was still a little bit on her guard.

"Oh it's just another type of human," said Spoony, "One that always says rude things."

"A bit like Willow," said Ploppy.

"Oh dear!" said the wolves.

"Come on everybody," called Spoony to the villagers, "Come and meet Rosie and Hazel and Mrs The Boss and Mr Bear."

"Oh, she hasn't brought a bear as well as wolves, has she?" said Farmer Stuckie.

"Nope, I don't see a bear, I only see wolves."

"Funny child!"

"A bear?! A bear?!" cried Mrs Hingmy who hadn't stormed off all that far because the situation looked like it would provide ample scope for more grumpiness, "Those Tooths haven't seriously acquired a bear as well? We'll all be killed and eaten!"

Chapter 9

Lunch with the Tooths

Spoony ushered the wolves and one or two of the less nervous locals into the Tooth house. Despite Spoony's reassuring enthusiasm, everybody was more than a bit nervous, the people because they were very close to some very big predators that folklore had always informed them were dangerous and ate humans and the wolves were nervous for similar reason. The wolves were all so big that they just about filled the Tooths' small living room and Mrs Tooth had to walk round those that were standing and stepping over those that were lying down which was like stepping over a settee they were so big. Meanwhile, Farmer Stuckie and Mr Biglanky stood in the corner near the door feeling privileged to have been invited and terrified at having accepted. The Tooths were talking away to the wolves and behaving as if they understood what the wolves had to say; it would all have been even more confusing if they hadn't already seen them talking to Ploppy the sheepwolf.

"This is ever such fun!" exclaimed Spoony, "I can't remember the last time we had a party!"

The wolves didn't know what a party was but nodded politely. They wondered how the humans could put up with such cramped conditions when they could simply have lived in the forest. Bear in particular did his best to be small and take up less room but he wasn't

139

very good at being small so he decided to mingle with the humans. He went over to Mr Biglanky, gave him a polite tail wag and sniff then looked up at him with his tail wagging. Mr Biglanky was still very nervous of wolves and didn't know polite wolf protocol, so he gave Bear a big broad toothy smile. Bear wasn't very sure of polite human protocol either, but he decided that Mr Biglanky wasn't snarling and meant to be polite, so he returned the compliment with a show of the biggest set of glittering white teeth that Mr Biglanky had ever seen. They quite scared the willies out of him. "Oh, I'm so glad everybody is getting along so well!" said Spoony and she gave Bear and Mr Biglanky each a big hug. Neither of them got hugged very often so they both went all bashful. Mr Biglanky blushed to the roots of his hair and Bear's ears went a bit floppy, something that the other wolves had never seen before. If you're an Alpha male, you're not meant to be soppy.

The wolves didn't think much of the fire which Daddy Tooth lit to heat the soup on, but Ploppy and Spoony assured them that it was perfectly safe having a fire in the middle of the house. And although there was only a little soup for each of the wolves they all cleaned their plates and wished they could have had more. The Boss asked Mummy Tooth where you could go to hunt the soup, what did a soup look like, were they wild and dangerous and could they run very fast and was it necessary to be able to fly like Mummy Tooth to catch them. Mummy Tooth replied that the whole thing was done in this very room and that caused much furrowing of wolf brows. It also caused Mummy Tooth much perplexity to wonder why they thought she could fly when she couldn't, but she didn't want to be impolite and anyway, it was quite flattering to have others think you could fly, even when you couldn't. Next she brought out some rabbit pie and Ploppy blushed to the roots of his fur when Spoony proudly announced that rabbit pie was quite the rarest of dinners until Ploppy came to stay because he was quite the best rabbit hunter in the world. When they heard this, Bear and Rosie and The Boss all looked at each other in wonder at the transformation that had taken place in Ploppy. Up until now, he'd been quite rubbish at hunting anything other than worms.

After some getting-to-know-each-other talk Bear couldn't help but enquire why the humans kept sheep but ate soup, not that the soup wasn't wonderful. Spoony explained that the sheep provided wool, because humans don't have a lovely thick fur coat like wolves do.

"And why do you keep dangerous wildhairy cattle?" asked The Boss.

"Ehm," said Daddy Tooth when Mummy Tooth wasn't listening, "we're not really sure why, we just do." This was an answer that seemed to satisfy the wolves, because although it seemed daft, dangerous and pointless, there were many things that wolves did that made no sense even to them, like howling, which they just did because they could[67]. Indeed,

---

67. Howling:- wolves howl to communicate over long distances but they also howl for no particular reason; perhaps it's

wolves still howl even today.

After a while, The Boss, who didn't want to overstay her welcome, said, "Oh well, I think we'd better be getting along now – got puppies to feed."

"Yes and we'd better see what that idiot Willow is getting up to," said Rosie.

"Indeed," said The Boss, "Shall we get on home now Ploppy, I expect you've missed everybody in the Great Pack of Lummox. And you haven't met the puppies yet!"

Ploppy hadn't missed many of the pack and Willow not one little bit, and now that he'd found some new friends, especially Spoony, who understood him, he wasn't very sure that he wanted to rejoin the pack.

"Ooh, ooh … good, that's nice." But he didn't sound very enthusiastic.

Bear, who was, as you know by now, very good at managing other wolves and a superb diplomat, could see that Ploppy wasn't looking very happy at the idea of rejoining the pack. Truth to tell, Bear had never been very happy with the idea of "teaching Ploppy a lesson" by sneaking away from him, even though, at that time, Ploppy had been quite useless at being a wolf. And the strange thing was, it was the humans who had helped to transform Ploppy into a very handsome and grown-up wolf indeed. And that young Spoonyhuman didn't look very happy at the idea of him leaving either.

"You know what?" he said to Ploppy. "I'm very impressed indeed at the way you've tamed a whole ravening human pack singlepawdedly and made them all quite docile and manageable."

"Really?" exclaimed Ploppy, who was quite unused to compliments, at least from other wolves, even from his dad.

"Except Mrs Hingmy," said Daddy Tooth unhelpfully, and he got a dirty look from Mummy Tooth.

"Yes," continued Bear, "and I think we ought to acknowledge the good work you've done." Bear looked at Rosie and The Boss for approval. He didn't get any but carried on regardless, having made an executive decision[68], "So I think, to begin with, it's high time we started calling you by your real name now."

"My real name?" said Ploppy, quite surprised; he couldn't remember ever being called anything other than Ploppy, or something unkind or rude.

"Yes, your real name is Silverleaf, after the silver birch trees," said his mummy The

---

simply because they're good at it; it's fun to do things you're good at. Why not give howling a try? Get up in the middle of the night, sneak downstairs and start howling. Try to make it as wolf-like as possible and see if your mummy and daddy come downstairs to join in. They will almost certainly come downstairs anyway. If they've panicked, tell them to calm down.

68. Executive Decision: a decision that you can make without consulting anybody because you're in charge. Executive decisions are rarely the best type of decision, not because they don't involve consultation with others (see 68, Discussed this in detail & Committee Decision overleaf), which they don't, but because most executives are not qualified for the job, having been promoted in order to get them out of the way.

Boss, "We named you that because of the silver fur you had when you were a wolf puppy. You were such a pretty puppy." She was beginning to go a bit gooey as mums often do.

"Oh!" said Spoony, clapping her hands and bouncing on her toes with pleasure, "I always knew you ought to have a name that told how beautiful you are!" She threw her arms around him, "but you'll always be my special Ploppy Hairylummox, the best wolf in the whole wide world … ehm, no offence to the other wolves present."

"None taken," said Rosie, who was staring into the middle distance, like any sergeant major, quite uncomfortable with all this soppy gooeyness.

"And I can see that you have work yet to do in the human taming department," continued Bear, "so I now hereby promote you to the brand new official Lummox post of Human Tamer-in-Chief."

"Ooooh!" was all that Ploppy could manage to say, blushing like anything beneath his fur. He wasn't very sure who had tamed who. Spoony suggested that this new wolf position would go very well with his other title (which she invented on the spot) of Official Village Sheepwolf. And Mr Biglanky and Farmer Stuckie were quite astounded because, not only had they never heard of a wolf having an official title, they had also never heard of a human having one either. It sounded very important and official and they would have doffed their hats to the wolf when it walked by except that they didn't have hats because that was yet another thing that had yet to be invente. So they just gave Ploppy their best effort at a wolf smile, with their tongues hanging out the side of their mouths wolf-fashion.

From outside, where she'd been eavesdropping, Mrs Hingmy could be heard saying, "Official Village Sheepwolf? What's this? Nobody asked me! We should have discussed this[69] in detail!"

"Oh do be quiet!" said all the other villagers who had also been eavesdropping.

"Well, I suppose we'd better be getting along now," said The Boss, "do drop by as soon as you can Plop…, I mean Silverleaf. When you're not too busy sheep-wolfing or whatever it's called."

"Yes," said Bear, "and bring the Spoonyhuman too. I expect it would like to come hunting." Wolves are not put out by talking about somebody in the third person within earshot because they have such sensitive hearing that almost everything is within earshot. Besides, Bear had still to get used to the idea of a human being able to talk, let alone understand wolf language.

"Yes, I expect it can go at some speed on those skinny legs," put in Rosie, trying to be positive although she had some Mrs Hingmy-type misgivings about anything as small and

---

69. Discussed this in detail: when things get discussed in detail by a whole bunch of people, usually called a "Focus Group", it is impossible to come to a sensible conclusion because everybody wants their opinion accommodated. The result is a compromise so wishy-washy that it couldn't work in a million years. This is known as a Committee Decision. This type of decision is dreaded by grown-ups the world over because it is even worse than an Executive Decision.

skinny as Spoony being much use. She added, "And it could take us on a soup hunt. We're definitely missing out on something there," which sounded like a very good idea to those who had enjoyed the soup.

Wolves aren't very comfortable with long goodbyes so the four Lummoxes turned and trotted off towards the forest to rejoin the other Wolves. In a few moments they had crossed the river and disappeared into the forest and the whole pack gathered around Bear, The Boss, Rosie and Hazel, clamouring to find out what had happened.

"Was there a terrible fight?" they asked and, "What's become of Ploppy? Why hasn't he been rescued" and so on.

"No," said Rosie, taking charge as bossy people often do, "Ploppy has singlepawededly tamed the humans."

"Huh!" said Willow sarcastically but he got one of Rosie's looks which shut him up in case the subject of being whacked by a tiny human came up again.

"And there was no need for any conflict. Indeed, he has been promoted to Human Tamer-in-Chief and we have left him there to keep them under control and stop them from ravening all over the place."

"Were they ravening?" asked one of the younger wolves nervously.

"No," said Bear, "Ploppy, I mean Silverleaf, has got them so tame that they no longer go in for any ravening and are quite peaceable. But you just can't be too careful. After all, as some of us witnessed, they can tame wildhairy cattle and other clever stuff … and one of them can fly."

"A bit," said Rosie.

"Yes, and they have tamed the soup so that it just seems to turn up and get eaten – or something like that," said Hazel.

"Blimey!" exclaimed most of the pack.

"Well, this won't get any hunting done or wolf puppies fed. Come on Great Pack of Lummox, back to the den!" ordered The Boss. She turned and bounded off into the deep forest. Very soon the wolves were travelling back to the den at the sort of speed that wouldn't be matched until the invention of motor cars and other very fast things.

"By the way," said Hazel, "did anybody find out how to get soup to turn up?"

"No we didn't," said Rosie, "Bit of an oversight that; might ask Ploppy when he brings the Spoonyhuman to visit."

"The what?" said everybody.

"Oh, I'll explain later. It's all very complicated, but you could ask Willow about the Spoonyhuman if you like."

Ooooo!, thought Willow, dropping back to the tail of the pack to do some blushing, "Watch out for the bear!" he said, changing the subject.

Very soon the pack arrived at that part of the forest where they'd last encountered the brown bear but he was nowhere to be seen so they kept on going. Then, all of a sudden they came across him, sitting with his back resting on the bee tree and totally surrounded by bees. They slowed down to see what was going on.

"Good grief!" said Rosie, "He'll be in trouble, best not to get too close Lummox Pack, in case you get attacked by the bees." But the pack were quite well aware of their being under no obligation to get stung to pieces, and kept a good distance away from the bear and the bees. Strangely, however, the bear didn't seem to be eating honey and he didn't appear to be getting stung so they pressed on through the forest on their way home.

"What a strange day it's turned out to be," said The Boss. "Can't wait to tell Squirrel and Spot."

"You'd better leave most of it out," said Bear, "None of it seems in the least bit plausible even now."

"What a strange day it's turned out to be," said Daddy Tooth, "I'm only glad that half the village was there to witness us inviting some huge ravening wolves home or they'd never believe us." But of course, they would believe it because, as you know, the Tooths had a reputation for doing daft things.

"And nobody got eaten," replied Mummy Tooth. Spoony, of course, had no reason to feel that any of it was strange or that anybody would get eaten because she had, as you know, a very positive outlook. Ploppy, on the other hand, was still quite stunned that it had turned out so well, that he hadn't had to put up with Willow picking on him, (much), that he'd been promoted from useless wolf to Human Tamer in Chief and that he had another name which he didn't know about or had forgotten and which everybody preferred except Spoony, who said that she loved 'Ploppy' because that was a perfect name for such a perfect wolf, and Willow who thought it suited him because he still thought Ploppy was an idiot. It all made his wolfcraftythinkybrain quite sparkly inside. But it was a happysparklybrain.

That evening they sat around the fire having supper, a meal which Ploppy was still getting used to because he could remember a time when he didn't even get one meal a day. "Do you think we should go and visit Mister Galloot tomorrow?" suggested Spoony, "After all we really should report back and tell him what a successful few days we've had."

"Oh yes!" replied Ploppy, who always thought that Spoony's ideas were the best. "And we can tell him that my mummy and daddy and the whole pack came to look for me because I was losted."

"But you're not losted now," said Spoony.

"Amn't I?"

"Oh no, I know exactly where you are," said Spoony in her most assertive tone.

"Really?"

"Yes. You're right here with me." She wrapped her arms around him and gave him a special Spoonyhug.

"Ooooh," said Ploppy, and his ears went all floppy.

They sat around for a minute or so with silly smiles on their faces.

"I've had a brainy idea," said Spoony.

"Oh goody!" said Ploppy, who always thought Spoony was very brainy indeed."

"Let's go and have another adventure! We could go and visit the Great Pack of Lummox and show them how to make soup."

"Ooooh!" said Ploppy, not sure that anybody could ever make enough soup for a pack of hungry wolves, but if Spoony thought it could be done then it probably could, "What kind of soup?"

"Good point," said Spoony and she gave it some thought with her Spoonycraftythinkybrain all furrowed. "Well, we could just make it with stuff we find."

"Yes!" said Ploppy, because he was always eating things that he found lying around, although not much of it would have looked at all appetising to many humans. However, Spoony was the sort of resourceful type that will try anything and as you already know, wasn't averse to trying the odd thing that Ploppy found, like worms. Of course, the land in those days was full of really good things to eat, all you had to know was where to look for it.[70]

Back at the bee tree, the brown bear said, "So let me get this straight, I can have a slap-up honey dinner once a week as long as I don't smash the nest up?"

"Yes," buzzed about a hundred bees in unison, "a limited slap-up, and only in the middle of summer and as long as we've got enough to see us through the winter."

"Well, I'll be hibernating then …," said the bear, "…and I won't get stung?"

"Nope," buzzed the bees in unison, "not if you stick to the rules."

"It's a deal then," said the brown bear.

Not far away, the Galloot was wondering to himself how the bear and bees might be getting along. This business of getting everybody talking to one another was great fun but he needed a report every now and then to see whether it was working and if it was a help.

---

70. Where to look for it: even today, if you know where to look you can find food growing wild in the countryside, everything from berries to mushrooms, you just need to know what to look for and where to look, it's all just waiting to be eaten. Mind you, if you're a lion then humans can be considered as "waiting to be eaten" so it's best to remain aware of your place in the food chain if you're not absolutely at the top.

Back at the Galloot

By now, Mummy and Daddy Tooth were not at all bothered about Spoony setting off on another adventure in the forest because she had Silverleaf, the Human Tamer-in-Chief (also known as Ploppy) a huge, ravening (but not terribly), always nice and friendly wolf to look after her. Indeed, they had met the commanders in chief of the ravening wolves and they seemed to be nice people and not all that ravenous despite what folklore had indicated. So Mummy Tooth made up a packed lunch with some crumblycheese and flatandchewybread so that they could have a picnic on the top of the magic talking mountain.

The two of them set off, Spoony with her logdolly and lunch in her knapsack and her walking (and sometimes standing-there-thinking) stick and Ploppy without anything, having politely decided that a walking stick was not much of a help to a wolf when being carried sideways in his mouth through the forest. He had concluded that a walking stick was like a human having three legs and he already had four, so he didn't really need one. However, something to assist him in standing there thinking would have been a help because he didn't think that thinking was one of his strong points, so any help from modern thinking technology, like a long stick[71], would be appreciated.

It didn't seem to take all that long before they were deep in the forest and were approaching the spot where they'd seen the brown bear being stung to bits by all those angry bees. Indeed, there he was, sitting with his back to the tree completely surrounded by bees and with a little piece of honeycomb perched on the end of one of his giant claws. The strange thing was that although he had bees buzzing round him and sitting on his nose and eyebrows, he wasn't being stung to bits. Spoony and Ploppy stopped for a look. It was quite an unusual sight, made all the more unusual by the bear raising his other paw and waving to them. He didn't say anything but his lips were pursed and he was making strange buzzy noises. Spoony waved back and they went on their way.

"That was lucky," said Ploppy, "We didn't get stung like we did last time."

"No, perhaps the bees have run out of stingmunition from stinging the bear so much. Come on Ploppy, let's run the last bit to the Galloot. I need to get in some running practice if I'm to show Rosie the Lummox how fast I can go when we go hunting." Off they went, Spoony running full speed with her boundy, lollopy way of running and Ploppy admiring her ever so much because he had tried running on two legs and had just about found it impossible. Soon they were climbing up the steep slope of the Galloot from the deep shade of the forest into the morning sun. They sat down on the rock at the top, and said

---

71. Thinking Stick: of course, nowadays people (other than farmers) don't tend to use long standing-there-thinking sticks. For a while, they used to use short ones. They were called pencils and people didn't lean on them, they used to chew the end. Unless it had a rubber, in which case they chewed their fingernails, which is silly. However, both types of thinking stick have been replaced by things called 'devices' which, strangely and sadly, although they're meant to help thinking, have the opposite effect and turn people into zombies with no interpersonal skills.

a polite good morning to the Galloot and waited patiently for an answer. This time they didn't have to wait long because, truth to tell, the Galloot was having a lot of fun with this business of magicking it so that all sorts of forest folk who normally couldn't, would be able to talk to one another. As soon as they had all said a polite "Good morning" to one another, Spoony and Ploppy launched into a full and excited report on all the things that had happened the day before.

"Well, pardon me for interrupting," hummed the Galloot, "I think I have a pretty good grasp on events."

"You do?" said Spoony.

"Oh, yes. You see the Lummox pack stopped here on their way home and The Boss wolf was telling the younger wolves everything that had happened."

"Did you speak to them?" asked Spoony.

"Oh no. By the sound of it they'd had enough new experiences for one day. I think a talkhumming mountain would have scared the willies out of the lot of them. Tell me, did you meet the brown bear on the way here?"

"Well, we sort-of met him but he was completely surrounded by bees and was making buzzy noises with his big lips. But he did wave."

"Oh, I wasn't sure that would work. Was he getting stung?"

"I don't think so. He seemed quite happy." In fact, as you'll remember, although Spoony, Ploppy and the Galloot didn't know it, the brown bear and the bees had struck a deal whereby he could have some honey and not get stung if he agreed not to smash up the bee's nest, steal honey, waste a lot of it and cause a lot of bad feeling.

"Excellent!" said the Galloot, "I'm going to do more of this, getting all the different species to talk to one another." He chuckled mischievously to himself. "I wish I'd done it aeons ago, could have got all of those prehistoric animals to talk to one another – except for the Terrordragon, who'd just have eaten the others before they got a word in."

"What's *prehistoric*?" asked Spoony.

"Oh, it's a timeframe," said the Galloot, "We're actually still in it." This was no help, but he continued, "By the way, what's a soup? Never met one of those. The Lummoxes were talking about a prey species that turns up at the den to get eaten. And another one called pie."

"Oh no," said Spoony, correcting the misunderstanding, "My Mummy *makes* the soup."

"Eh?" said the Galloot.

"Yes, it's not a prey species, it's a type of dinner. My mummy makes it out of leftover stuff and vegetables and herbs and other stuff that she finds."

"Oh, so it doesn't just turn up and get eaten."

"Well, it does, sort of," said Ploppy, who was still quite puzzled by Mummy Tooth's

147

apparently magical ability to conjure up a dinner out of a lot of stuff that was lying around.

"I thought maybe she caught the soup on the wing … when she was flying around."

"N-o-o-o," replied Spoony, and she giggled at the thought of her mummy flying around deliberately when she had only been tossed in the air by a wildhairy cow. "No, she doesn't fly after it, she just makes it from stuff."

"That's odd, the wolves all said that she could fly. They saw her do it."

"Oh no," said Spoony, seeing where the wolves' misunderstanding had come from, "she just gets airborne occasionally when she's dealing with the wildhairy cattle. So does her bucket."

"Hmm," hummed the Galloot, who didn't quite understand, "anyway, I understand that you're going to visit the Lummox den and go hunting with them and do other wolf stuff.

"Oh yes!" said Spoony gleefully, "But how did you know that?"

"Eavesdropping," replied the Galloot. "Those young wolves were so desperate to hear what went on in your den Spoony that The Boss wolf stopped and told them everything. Did you really whack that Willow on the nose with your bit of stick?"

"Yes, and it's not a bit if stick, it's my logdolly. My daddy made it for me."

The Galloot was none the wiser, and, truth to tell, neither was anybody else because Spoony was the only one who thought it looked much like a dolly.

"And I understand that Ploppy here is going to stay with you to make sure that you humans all remain tame and don't go marauding in Lummox territory."

"That's right," said Ploppy, "I'm Human Tamer-in-Chief!"

"And he's Official Village Sheepwolf too!" said Spoony.

"What?" asked the Galloot, somewhat surprised, "Ploppy hunts your sheep and eats them?"

"Oh no, he doesn't eat them. We keep the sheep so that we can make nice warm clothes and things from their wool. But they're very difficult to round up if they don't want to be. Ploppy has invented sheepwolfing to help collect them all in one place."

"Goodness me! Oh well, I can see why you might need somebody to round up sheep, they're all a bit silly," said the Galloot, "but do those humans of yours really need to be tamed Spoony?"

"Well, some of them do, one or two of them do. So Bear made Ploppy Human Tamer-in-Chief of the Great Lummox Wolf Pack."

"Really?" asked the Galloot, "What did he do to earn that illustrious title?"

"Oh, I think it's because he's the first wolf ever to tame humans and definitely not get eaten by them. Something like that."

"But humans have never eaten wolves, in all the time I've been here, which is umpteen million years."

"Yes, but he's the first *definitely* not to get eaten," said Spoony, "Up until Ploppy, there had been no proof. So he's been promoted."

"This is all very confusing," said the Galloot, "You've tamed the humans and have been promoted to Human Tamer-in-Chief because they didn't eat you even though they wouldn't have eaten you in the first place."

"Yes," said Ploppy, "that's right. It's really good isn't it?" He was quite proud of being promoted. "But I need to make friends with Mrs Hingmy. She thinks I should be banished."

"Well, I suppose you'd both better run along and deal with Mrs Hingmy, whoever she is," said the Galloot, who was on the verge of getting in a brainfankle, "and round up sheep and wildhairy cattle. You know Spoony, it's been jolly nice having you and Ploppy around." The Galloot couldn't remember having so much fun since the cretaceous period. "Do come back soon when you're off on another adventure, both of you."

"Oh we will, we will," replied Spoony and she lay down on the rocky outcrop and gave the Galloot a huge cuddle. Ploppy did his best to do the same.

"Oh, that's nice," hummed the Galloot, who didn't get cuddled much,[72] "Now run along both of you, it's probably suppertime, whatever that is."

"Thank you Mister Galloot for helping Ploppy and me talk to one another. It has been a wonderful, sorry, wondleyful adventure," said Spoony.

"It was no trouble at all," hummed the Galloot, "Think nothing of it, I hope you have lots of adventures together. Now run along, the two of you, I need to have a snooze."

"Ooooh," ooooohed Ploppy, "Have we really been having an adventure?"

"Oh, yes," replied Spoony in a very emphatic Spoonyish way, "Look at all the adventuresome things we've done!" Then she reminded Ploppy of the really exciting, not to mention thrilling things that had happened, from meeting one another on the Galloot, to Ploppy having a full tummy for the first time in ever such a long time, which was one of his favourite adventures.

"Yes, I did have a full tummy, thanks to my special Spoonytooth."

"And I found somebody else to be a bit odd with...," added Spoony, "including a Magic Galloot."

"Yes, and we invented getting banished," said Ploppy, who was still somewhat under the impression that that counted as an achievement, at least compared with being snuck

---

72. Getting cuddled much: of course, we must remember that the Galloot, like most other small mountains of his species, was born during the Carboniferous period. There weren't many animals around on land back then and when land animals eventually *did* arrive that was a gazillion years before they evolved from fishy-looking things into anything with arms so giving cuddles was pretty difficult for them, even if they'd been the cuddly kind. Eventually, they evolved arms but as you know, dinosaurs were either vicious (Terrordragons) or aloof (Dopylopycuses) so being seen cuddling would have been considered totally uncool.

away from by his pack.

"And we had some deadbrainy ideas, like inventing sheepwolfing Ploppy, and humantaming," said Spoony.

"Except for Mrs Hingmy," said Ploppy, "but you invented wolftaming."

"Except for grumpy Willow," said Spoony.

"Ooooh, I think you tamed him ever so good and proper," said Ploppy, "I bet he's still got a sore nose. Adventures are jolly good things to have."

"Yes, I think we should have a lot more adventures," said Spoony. Then she gave the Galloot's rocky outcrop another cuddle. "Well, goodbye Mister Galloot," she said, "thank you for everything." But the Galloot didn't reply. He just made hummy snorey noises and had plainly fallen asleep, he'd had a very busy few days.

So Spoony Tooth and Ploppy the Hairy Lummox set off for the village, skipping and lolloping and bounding and running and jumping, both of them as happy as a little girl and a young wolf had ever been in the brief history of the world so far.

The End

Thank you for reading

Spoony Tooth, the Hairy Lummox and the Big Galloot.

I do hope that you have enjoyed this story and if you did, I would love it if you could share your thoughts with others so that they might enjoy it too.

It will also help me to roll out the next of Spoony and Ploppy's adventures: "Spoony Tooth, The Hairy Lummox and the Giant Jawclanging Terrordragon."

Leaving a nice review on Amazon is one way to tell other people that they might enjoy this story too and I'd appreciate it very much if you did.

Love and best wishes,

David

About The Author

David Allen Rice lives on the cold, windswept, bug-infested swamps of the Lang Whang, that long, bootstrap of a road that tears as fast as it can past the lonely Pentland Hills of southern Scotland between Edinburgh and Lanark. When he's not hiding behind a windbreak with his wife Fiona, he writes things down and then tears them up. Sometimes he paints and draws things and then tears *them* up. Very occasionally he finishes something.

About The Illustrator

Gabby Grant always wanted to be an illustrator, so why she ended up in admin and direct marketing will forever remain a mystery, particularly to Gabby. One day she ran away to Westminster University to study Illustration, and since then, has been much happier illustrating children's books and-making theatre props. Gabby loves working on her computer but pencil, pen and ink are still the foundation of everything she does. She lives in London with her husband and children.